Short-Story.Me!
Best Genre Short Stories
Anthology #2

Edited by Larry Crain & Dixon Palmer

To Christine + PASCO,
Thanks for all your support. I love you guys.

Copyright©2010 Short-Story.Me! Genre Fiction
Individual short stories are Copyright their individual authors.
All Rights Reserved. No part of this book may be reproduced
or transmitted in any form without the express written
permission of the Publisher.

Will [signature]

≈▶ Also read Anthology #1 ◀≈
Available in electronic and print form in the same bookstores
where you purchased this volume - Anthology #2

Printed in the U.S.A.
Short-Story.Me! Publishing Company

Short-Story.Me! - Best Genre Short Stories #2

Edited by Larry Crain & Dixon Palmer

Table of Contents   Page

1. **Wednesday's Seagulls** by Michael W. Lucas   3
2. **Corner of River and Rain** by Gary Cahill   10
3. **My War Against the Invisibles**   22
   by Jeffery Scott Sims
4. **Pack-Brothers: The Ambush** by Will Frankenhoff 33
5. **Man Tracker** by Kevin M. White   51
6. **River Road** by Cary R. Ralin   55
7. **The Taller and Tumult** by Augustus Peake   58
8. **Clawbinder** by Marlena Frank   60
9. **What Philip Did in Tulsa** by Steve Lowe   66
10. **Funeral Flowers** by Edoardo Albert   70
11. **The Cromera** by Lydia Kurnia   77
12. **Bootleggers** by Dale Phillips   83
13. **The Brokenhearted Leper** by William Knight   96
14. **Eye Quest** by Jeffrey Freedman   106
15. **Blood of the Father** by Philip Roberts   119
16. **The Taco Bell Heist** by Robb White   129
17. **No Alarms and No Surprises** by Brian Lyons   145
18. **The Nine Lives of Chairman Mao**   161
    by Craig Gehring
19. **The Bull Riding Witch** by Jamie Marchant   173
20. **Silent Partner** by Henry Gaudet   186
21. **Favours** by Richard Keane   194
22. **Zombies Have No Respect for Plumbing**   215
    by Tony Southcotte
23. **Throw Him Away and Get a New One**   216
    by Patrick Whittaker
24. **Damaged Goods** by Dinesh Pulandram   235

Wednesday's Seagulls
by Michael W. Lucas

I'd dry-swallowed the last instant coffee days ago, but the thought "Oversleep and he'll eat your brain" gutkicks you awake. No matter how tired you are. Two or three nights with only a couple of hours sleep puts sand in your brain and smothers your joy in life. Six nights like that, and your brain glues shut and your energy dwindles into bovine endurance just this side of death.

I spasmed awake at the first flicker of dawn. When I saw that enough tide remained to leave a ribbon of saltwater between Wednesday and myself, I released my breath and massaged crud from my eyes. Nothing had changed. A hundred-foot rock in the middle of the South Pacific. The shattered plane I slept in. And the dead man, Wednesday.

Wednesday stood so still the island danced in comparison. Sunlight glinted off the golden hoop dangling from the desiccated stub of his left ear. His right leg ended in twin spears of worm-eaten brown bone. Salty air coursed through the crack in his skull and out his broken teeth, whistling loudly enough to penetrate the crash of the ocean's fierce churn around us, and the corrugated tear across his gut displayed mummified bowels and stumps of rib. I couldn't imagine how long he'd been on this rock – years? Centuries? How long did it take to turn a human being into jerky, and how long could human jerky last? Six bullets had lodged harmlessly somewhere inside him, and the flare gun hadn't singed his petrified invulnerability.

Only paces behind Wednesday, the island's west end rose in a flattened dome of broken rock. Hundreds of seagulls wheeled overhead, and the rising sun flickered on the waves, but nothing else moved. The sky mirrored the ocean, diffusing the horizon. Traditionally a castaway gets a single coconut tree, but I'd been shorted even that. Robinson Crusoe even got a native to help him live like a civilized man. I'd called mine Man Wednesday, as he was obviously a couple days short of a Man Friday. It had seemed funny, the first day. Everything had seemed funny that first impossible day, but the endless days bludgeoned surrealism into blunt reality.

If I could survive long enough to be rescued, it would be on seagulls and plane wreckage alone.

I forced myself to relax, leaning against a spire of rock and cradling the strut I'd finally pried out of the wreckage. The strut had felt solid and invincible when I'd been pounding and prying and scraping at the bolts holding it to the wing over the past few days. Now it felt too frail to support the hope I had for it. I'd had a much better shaft the first day, solid steel an inch thick and two feet long. I'd tried to crack Wednesday's skull the rest of the way open. He'd raised an arm to block it, and the impact of the bar against his exposed bone was like hitting a light post. The shock had stunned my grip open and I let the shaft bounce deep into the churning water. That was when I realized that if Wednesday came close enough to grab me, I was dead.

The cuts and tears lining my palms and fingers weren't painful compared to how the rest of me felt.

The receding tide had almost erased the moat when a seagull landed on Wednesday's shoulder and tentatively pecked at a tangle of human jerky. Wednesday resisted as much as any other piece of garbage, so the bird sank his beak into a tricep and flapped to tear it free. Rattlesnake-quick, faster than I could follow, a skeletal hand lashed up and seized a wing. The bird screeched and thrashed, but in moments Wednesday had gnawed open its skull and scraped out the runny gray insides with his ragged tongue. I had thought brain-eating zombies were just in the movies, but once again he dropped the hollowheaded carcass at his feet.

When Wednesday finished eating, the tide had fallen enough that he could totter towards me without getting wet, the bones in his right leg skewing around each other with every step. I staggered a wide circle around him, skirting the north edge of the island, then slowed so he could trail only a few yards behind.

The island's west end jaggedly plateaued ten feet or so above the low-tide line, cracked by exposure into a three-dimensional jigsaw with countless handholds and ledges. Kids would love climbing that slope, but six nights of scattered sleep weakened my grip and scratched my vision. Each step was an act of will. The strut clenched in my armpit made me a little more clumsy, but I'd circled this rock every fifteen minutes, eighteen hours a day, for days now, and my hands and feet knew the best route without troubling my exhausted brain. I clambered a few yards across the rock until I hit the spot where two small stone shelves cradled my heels a foot above the crashing water and I could rest my buttocks on the slope.

Wednesday's sunken eyes studied me, then he stumbled into pursuit just as he had every other time. Stump leg flapping uselessly, he dragged himself across the slope with his hands and used the remaining leg as a brace. His fingernails, brown as gnawed tombstones, did not break no matter how fiercely he clawed the stone. He needed almost two minutes to haul himself to within five feet of me. The first day I'd learned that if I got more than twenty feet ahead he circled around the other way, which made his stumpy leg almost useful. If I let him come too close, he'd use those cadaverous teeth on my head.

He never stopped following. *Never*. No matter how I begged, or screamed, or prayed. Without the twice-daily high tide to put six feet of uncrossable water between us for a couple precious hours of sleep twice a day, I would have been dead a week ago. I'd tried bashing in his head with a steel bar. I'd tried a lasso, and a tripline. I'd rigged the plane's battery and salvaged wire into an electrical trap that would have knocked me out. He couldn't be crushed, he couldn't be tied up, and electric shock hadn't even raised the few ghastly strands of hair left on his head. I was down to sticks and stones – and on this rock, I had to provide my own stick.

Halfway around the island, instead of resting, I threw the strut on top of the rock and pulled myself up after it. Usually I'd follow the easier route near the water, but this turgid chase would end today. It had to end today. I didn't have the strength to try anything else.

#

Fractures and crevices covered the summit, and I quickly wedged my strut into the crack I'd selected days ago. With Wednesday out of sight I only wanted to rest, but I leaned into the lever instead. Cadaverous hands clenched the edge as I felt the crevice groan, and a rock about my size might have shifted underfoot. I caught two deep desperate breaths before Wednesday's head appeared. Once he started hauling himself up, I dropped down the other side.

I veered from the loop to snatch the decapitated seagull. If I didn't have a zombie after me I could catch my own seagulls, but until then I'd live on Wednesday's leavings. For the last three days, I'd used these most of these precious minutes to pound and scrape at the bolts holding the strut in place; a few moments to simply breathe felt almost like a vacation. My hands plucked as I waited, spiny feathers inflaming my savaged hands.

When Wednesday shambled into view around the rock I took a deep breath, waiting for him to come close enough that I could trot around him and make him scuttle all the way back to the rock, treasuring every minute I could to try to rest.

First trip of the day, finished. Dozens more to go.

On the sixth circuit I finished plucking and used my pocketknife's last remaining blade to scrape out the bowels, then spread the carcass on the wreck's south wing for what cooking the sun provided. My mouth tightened at the thought of an evening spent perched on the wrecked plane devouring that juicy pink flesh, only faintly grilled by the sun-heated wing, watching Wednesday shuffle back and forth, frustrated by six feet of thigh-deep salt water. Seagull and a couple pints of collected rain water would hold me together for another day.

Then I went back to heaving at the rock. My head spun and my guts burned, but I pushed for a panicked few moments every time we circled the rock. My twelfth session, the rock creaked and left a finger-wide gap behind it. I left the remaining skin from my right knee behind in payment, stumbling and swearing until the sting stopped.

A brief rain shower interrupted me on my twenty-second trip around the rock. Wednesday kept after me, but with the slope too slippery to ascend I contented myself with following the easier path around the shoreline, soaking up water in my shirt and licking it from crevices in the rock. I lost track of how many times we went around before the rain stopped, the sun dried the rocks, and I could climb back up again.

During my twenty-ninth stint at the prybar, the rock shifted far enough that I could thrust a fist into the gap. Finally, on the thirty-first circuit, the boulder groaned and lurched free, shifting a vital few degrees towards the edge. I held my breath, afraid a scream of hope and frustration and would drive the rock over the edge and into the water. When the rock balanced and held still, my laugh sounded more like a harsh croak. For once, I felt like telling Wednesday to hurry up.

The next pass around I took the lower, easier path rather than climbing to the summit. That route had the best resting spot, a smooth patch some three feet wide with a gentle pitch towards the ocean. My boulder now loomed over it. I jammed my abused hands flat against my legs to force my fingers straight, grimacing, waiting.

Wednesday dragged along my trail, the stump of his right leg flailing uselessly over the water. His hip scraped with each lurch. Five feet away, the grind of dead flesh against rock drowned out the ocean's constant splash, and I smothered an urge to bolt. I'd never let Wednesday come this close before, but I needed his feet on the very spot I stood. A bright slice of blue ocean shone through his cracked skull and out his mouth.

One bony hand gripped an outcropping a foot from my head and I leaped, seizing a ledge beside the loosened boulder and blowing out air as I dragged myself up. I imagined those withered claws snatching my legs, and I kicked frantically as I clawed and jackknifed my weight, not even slowing as my fingernails ripped from their beds. Wednesday's hands scuttled below as I knelt beside my teetering rock, only a few feet above him. In less than a minute he'd find a way up, or decide to go around. I wedged the strut tightly against the rock and heaved.

The boulder groaned against its parent rock, immobile. I suddenly thought that I'd been wrong, that this chunk of rock was actually the tip of a spire rooted deep below, it wasn't actually detached and I was trying to split raw stone with my puny lever. I pulled even harder. Wednesday shuffled back and forth underneath, almost ready to circle around to an easier slope.

The boulder shifted a foot, and the strut screeched into a curve. I threw my feet against the freshly-exposed stone, braced my back against another rock, and straightened my legs. The boulder lurched away from the plateau and balanced, wobbling, as if considering falling back towards me. With a wordless snarl I shoved harder. I tasted thick blood, pain fluorescing in my back and panic in my brain, then gravity snatched the boulder and yanked it down. The thunderous crash wasn't as harsh as its echo through the rock.

I lay motionless, trying to make my lungs stop heaving and my empty bowels unclench. Even the thought that I'd missed, that Wednesday was climbing after me, didn't give me strength to move for another dozen breaths. I finally dragged my legs under me and shuffled painfully to peer down.

The boulder had nailed Wednesday, pinning his legs and lower torso. He'd stopped sliding short of the tide line, but the way his arms flailed at the boulder proved he couldn't get enough leverage to move.

My head drooped over the outcropping, eyes glazing, then I rolled onto my back and painfully sucked air for a few minutes before allowing myself a bloody-toothed smile. I idly wondered if I'd mention Wednesday to whomever found me.

#

I awoke in that spot at sunrise with fresh seagull shit on my chest, a new layer of sunburn, and my brain where I'd left it. Every joint felt full of ground glass, and my nose and mouth burned. I'd never been happier. Below me, Wednesday still flailed at the boulder, possibly just a little less quickly. Seagulls had soiled my dinner, so I chucked the carcass into the ocean and promised myself fresh poultry that evening.

Weakness had replaced hunger, so I worked slowly and cautiously. Favoring my sprained back and endless contusions I assembled scraps of twisted metal and fabric into a dark SOS against the shiny fuselage. By noon, a plastic bag became a funnel to guide more rainwater down the wings into a makeshift bucket, and I found nine salt-damp gumdrops between the seat cushions. My white shirt became a distress flag. A soapless saltwater bath in a still tidal pool deliciously scoured days of sweat and filth from my skin. When the rain came I lay on my back and laughed as fresh water burned my sunburn and gnawed lips.

Seagulls whirled overhead. I hurled a fist-sized rock at one. I missed.

#

Seagulls were harder to catch than I had thought. They dodged thrown rocks, not that I had many to throw. A sharp twist of fuselage became a spear, but they fluttered away before I came close enough to stab. If I stood still they approached, but never close enough to seize. The screaming rush with outstretched hands didn't work at all.

My checks on Wednesday assumed new intensity. If he grew resigned and stopped thrashing, gulls would approach him. Surely I could spear a *decapitated* seagull from beyond his reach! His movements slowed, but grew no less constant. Surrounded by blue water mirroring the sky, with no horizon between the two, I felt suspended in an endless waste. Weak swallows of precious rainwater couldn't drown the tastes of rancid gumdrop or seat padding. I began wondering if I could slice chunks off Wednesday, or was his flesh too pickled by age and salt to chew? Forget cannibalism; was "dead man walking" contagious?

I tried fishing, standing in the ocean two feet from the shore but up to my waist, sheltered from the ocean current by the rock itself. My line was thread from the seat, the hook a twist of wire. Fish don't bite on seat cushion. I managed to seize a few of the tiny minnows in the tidal pool, but the starfish I chewed up had me doubled around my gut in pain for an afternoon.

#

Days passed. Maybe a week. My body felt as if it belonged to someone else and I just sat behind the eyes occasionally pulling levers. Sweet, luscious gull meat filled my dreams. I heaved chunks of broken engine at the sky and fashioned baitless traps from wreckage. Succulent seagull taunted me from just out of reach. Soon, I would be just as sun-dried as Wednesday. Unable to escape or eat, Wednesday would eventually lie still in real death.

Too little sleep is better than the long sleep. I had spent an agonizing day trapping Wednesday, but pushing that rock off him and into the ocean only took three minutes.

∞∞∞

Corner of River and Rain
by Gary Cahill

From the birdseye view, above the old tenement rooftops down to what's left of Hell's Kitchen, through the spinning rain that flipped between covering like cream and icy bite, our lonesome parade looked like two campesinos droving two wayward burros to water. Switch out the Mexican peasants for me and Willy, the watering hole for the Hudson, and the doleful donkeys for a pair of booze sweating, bleeding, braying jackasses, and you've got it.

A little earlier, I'd seen this coming. Things were going to go badly if these guys didn't shut the hell up.

#

On the way to meet him, I'd answered a call from Willy on a cell I answered only when it was him.

"G...G... where the hell are you? I'm waitin' here." Here being the old bar on the edge of Manhattan's West Side where we met socially and professionally. Professionally being if we needed to collect money -- owed on outstanding loans with exorbitant interest rates, or illegal gambling losses, or to insure a string of broken windows and fires of unknown origin would not interfere with someone's fledgling business becoming a success. Like that. All the stuff that invigorates our underground economy.

Not that me and Will are on equal footing in this endeavor. He does most of the heavy lifting; I kinda sweep up after the dust settles. Or mop up if it gets messy.

He sounded edgy, not like him, and I said, "On the way big man, I'm right down the street. What's the matter?"

"Just get here. These dopey bastards are killin' me." He's definitely itchy around the collar, and certainly considering turning around that phrase about dopey bastards and killing. I hopped to it and jogged the last block. Every second counts with Willy.

Through the glass front doors -- tables and booths on the left, the worn wooden long bar on the right, and behind the beer sticks, blessedly, Stella, our friend and sensible respite from all that "Hi! How're *you* doin'?" "You bet!" "Oh, sure!" barkeep word slop that's the ruination of decent tavern talk almost everywhere.

And Willy, thick fingers grasping a tumbler way too hard, a couple empties in front of him, glistening with the strain of controlling himself. He turned and looked at me with an odd combo of rage and relief.

"These guys are wearin' me out."

"I can see that." I took a look around. "What guys?"

"Freakin' Frick and Frack in the back here."

I'd seen, and heard, them here before -- a pair of business grads who'd stumbled into the goldmine that was flipping, redeveloping and building on properties where landlords stopped at nothing driving tenants out and local governments worshipped at the throne of Eminent Domain, simply taking people's private property and giving it to a big-money-someone-else. You'd think a crappy economy would slow them down, but that puts the brakes on building, not buying. So these guys were rolling today; drunk and stupid, wallowing in both, even more offensive than they tried to be. And they would not be ignored.

Beany and Cecil. Beany the Fawning Younger wearing very blue jeans, bluer pullover, knocking down two or twenty beers, no way to tell 'cause he's loaded after one, sniffing at a whiskey. And nothing against knit caps or Calvin Klein, but a Calvin Klein knit cap? With Cecil the Honored Elder sporting a "Trump Int'l Hotel and Tower" t-shirt and donning sunglasses to poke at buttons on his BlackBerry.

"Jesus, it's easy. Just run 'em out and roll it over. It's not like Gramps and Gramma don't have places to go, right? Hit up the family, or use up whatever they've got socked away for, what's that called, assisted living or an old age home or whatever. You see that deal in Connecticut?"

Beany had. "Oh, yeah, government just took that shoreline and handed it off. I don't know, people just move on and go live somewhere else, right? Homeless corpses aren't piling up by Long Island Sound."

That got the veteran to laugh, and the newbie was happy he'd sucked up appropriately.

It was erotic. They tongued it. You could smell it on them. See it behind their alky glazed eyes.

"And the Jersey Shore," said Cecil, lips smacking. "Long Branch to Wildwood and Cape May, just one after another. Piles of money for nothing."

Cecil was right about that. Buy 'em out, kick 'em out, throw money at motels and knock 'em down, spackle and strap together cardboard boxes and call them condos, and every dope from Maryland to Philly to NYC sucks them up. Selling sunshine. And when they can't pay off, you sell them again. Just take it back and milk it dry. Christ.

"And plenty left in the city, right boss? Chinatown, Little Italy, places still right around here? Down and out it goes." Was Beany the butt wipe talking about downtown and "right around here" in this place? Have another, pal. Here's to your health.

Cecil the boss raised a glass. "And down and out *they* go. All of 'em," toasting and cheering themselves, not smelling the smoke rising from a smoldering Willy.

"What the hell, Will?" I went easy. "We've heard this crap before. It's business. It's America. It sucks, but it's business." I was tempted to add "... not personal." I was glad, maybe lucky, I didn't.

I knew guys who'd saw your head off for practice, and Will isn't one of those, but we were all slipping into darkness.

Hands on his glass, elbows on the bar, feet on the rail, Willy raised his head, turned right to see me square, started with, "My mom," quivered, and stopped.

Oh, my, Guilliermo Casella's mama, one of the Little Italy ladies in perpetual mourning. She'd worn nothing but black since her husband bought it long ago in Jersey over some street monies not getting where they were supposed to go. Of course the official version called it an accident, gas pedal instead of the brakes, you can't imagine our sorrow, we'll look out for you and the boy, and after Willy's stint in the army to avoid jail time and learn to kill, a watchful "uncle" turned him out into the world he inhabited now.

Mama was moved into a walk-up around the corner from where Hollywood had located Vito Corleone's olive oil business, and she'd never been in need. It may well have been her, years ago, pointing out a much younger me one sunny afternoon, stranger in a strange land, circling the block once too often looking for a cold beer. A classic trio of sleeveless t-shirt, turtleneck with open jacket, and three-quarter trench coat in dead of summer appeared out of nowhere to size me up, deliver a message, and their presence hipped me to the eyes in the sky, watching over from the windows and the fire escapes, all rosary beads and veils, and shoes that could crack a shin.

And now Mama Casella's home was in the crosshairs of the real estate boom.

#

My career of evil at Willy's side is a sprinkle on a cloudy day. Just two drops on the

pavement; one dead (totally self defense, I swear), one now a mangled gimp (boy, did he have it coming). A couple wet spots on the sidewalk.

Where Willy's career is, oh, more like a river.

So it was not good for Rich and Richer to slip up and butt in, not good when Will finally spoke again, responding to some half-heard idio-comic remark about "... breast reduction..." with "Why don't you get your ass reducted, change your hat size?"

I couldn't let that go. "Reducted, Will? Wow, you've broken new linguistic ground wi... "

"G? Stop. Get the hell away. Or sit the hell down. Just..." I chose the former, and slid down the bar toward Stella.

Dependent on moon phases or something, there are times when it's hard to pay for a drink with Stella around. Not that I don't have the money. She just won't take it.

I opined. "You and me, we're going to drive this place under."

"Listen…"

"No, you listen. You know what it is between me and you? You're coastal. Me too. The closer we are to open salt water the better. I'm from here, Mid-Atlantic. You're New England. And you know what I remember's the best thing about New England girls? The ocean's warm enough down the shore here in summer, they think it's the Caribbean. Relatively speaking."

"Except for…"

No need for her to go on.

"… all that *Jersey*…"

I raised my hands in resignation. Yes, all that *Jersey*.

"You know," she said, leaning forward in all fluttering faux sincerity, "you're *so*

interesting."

"It only seems that way because of all the interesting things I do and say."

Which earned me the half-upper-lip-curl-and-nostril-flex, extra toothy. It's so charming on anyone over twenty-five.

Well, her.

"Hey, looks like Big Willy's on the outs!" And after a break for sotted chuckling and gurgling, "Yeh-aah, Will, looks like a *barmaid's* beatin' your time with G." Beating would be only the beginning if these guys didn't let up. Then, of all things, grade school, just mindless, "Willy and G, sittin' in a tr…"

Now it was too late for these guys with Willy. A little quick on the draw, I thought.

And then the wave of bar noise troughed and the lull allowed the word "… sugarbitch…" to reach Stel and me and I'm up, one stride to reach Willy's stool and one stride past him before he got me by the collar with a sweaty lefty grip and Moe or Larry or whichever stooge it was had his hands in the air yelling, pleading, "I meant you not her I meant you not her!"

Oh, well that's better.

"Think about that long and hard, asshead. I'm sure you both dream about it being long and hard, you and Jocko over there."

And now it was too late with me. Both of us a little quick on the draw.

Willy cut in to wise off. "Jeez, take it easy, G. We've heard this crap before, right?" I managed not to gape at him, and somehow not to laugh. I stared at the floor, said "Quite an echo in here," kept biting my tongue, and took off for the men's room to let it out and throw some water on my face, to calm and cool off.

I found four working guys, construction, iron, electric, the manly crafts, among the two stalls and one seat. They got quiet. Except for one with, "I'm too old to go over a wall, bro..." And another with, "We gotta do it." Now what was this? Something's going to have a new home -- somebody's tools, somebody's jewels, somebody's daughter? In two quick shifts they left, so I just got out in case they wanted to reconvene. What a world.

Stan and Ollie piped up.

"Listen, we're just celebrating our... good fortune's all we're doing. It's just workin' out for us real well. Oh, yeah, real well." Guffaws, clinking glasses, making a pass at the whiskey and looking like it was about to come back up onto their shoes, and then this.

"Look you guys, we know, you been around here quite a while, like, everybody knows, and we're thinking about keeping the party going, you know, maybe a little lift?"

And the other went one step beyond. "Yeah, a little somethin' somethin', pick things up, right?" And then low, conspiring. "Willy, you know any stuff around, any place to go around here?"

Willy's head, almost disembodied, turned left to face them, and in a ragged half-whisper he said, "Sure, sure, a few blocks up and then over toward the river, what's left of the old neighborhood. What's that place, G, the good one? The Smilin' Shamrock, or was it The Gilded Harp?"

"Oh, The Shamrock, definitely," I said. "Always been good for adding a boost to the day. Will, I'm not quite sure -- you can direct these guys, right?"

"Yup," Willy said, "I'll get these guys on their way, and maybe we can catch up in a few minutes after we finish up some stuff here. Better to not show up together anyway. OK with you two? We can straighten this whole thing out, set it right. Cool?"

Bud and Lou were thrilled as Willy walked them to the side door and sent them on their way into the swirling rain and the blue-black evening chill. And when he came back to the bar, working his jaw, he was uninterested in his glass, brimming with another round.

"Please... The Smilin' Shamrock? The Gilded Harp? You tell them that's where they filmed "My Heart Belongs to Mickey" and "Bloody Revenge of the Little People"? Let me handle the Irish lies, you stick with the red sauce, goombah." He heard me, but was busy dressing for the outdoors. "Can I assume you don't want to leave those two boys alone deep in the Wild West Side on a night like this?"

"Let's go. Stella," he called, "be back in a bit, OK?" Her shift was over, but she'd had a look at what'd gone down. Whatever else, she'd figure a way to still be here when we got back. In deference, we turned our backs to her at the door to put our work gloves on -- not much help in winter, but thin, supple, good grip. I stuffed my hands in my pockets and turned around, but she'd been sure to have her head down, washing glasses, didn't even peek, and we stepped outside.

#

Monday, November, lots of restaurants closed, lots of theaters too, bad night, not pouring rain, but coming from every direction, a soaking fog, like it's being whisked up into foam. There's almost no traffic this far over, everything's muted, all sound a soft whoosh, sight like through those

soft lenses they use to polish up aging actresses. Red and green cutting through, but everything washed in a broadbrush-yellow jaundiced street light, with due caution tossed aside by two silhouetted stick figures up ahead, slendered by their lack of soul. We were bird dogging them, a few blocks up, then over toward the river, and the old neighborhood was back in its prime. We caught up.

Ike and Mike were stumbling, laughing, drooling, way gone, but starting to wonder if Willy'd been tripping, or just wrong, when he conjured a bar that didn't exist.

Ike, or whoever, spoke up, words wetted down, and asked, "You guys sure about this... uh, place? No signs. It's pretty...urrm... dark the next block down and, uh…"

"It can be pretty dark wherever you are," I said, and saw Willy snap his eyes toward me and take one big stride forward, and we each grabbed one by the coat and yanked right and bashed them both noses first into a hundred year old building they'd failed to tear down, did it again, then sanded the brick and stone with their faces as we brought them down to the sidewalk. Standard procedure is a tap with the spring loaded sap, just keeping them groggy, then Willy pulled out the leather straps and I mirrored and we cuffed them behind their backs. On their feet, we started herding them west. And at the corner, you know that salty shellfish beach smell, you can taste it, comes off the harbor and the brackish river mouth when the weather's right? Pulled me right into summer. It was wild.

Nothing much intelligible from the Bobseys, not that it would have mattered.

But I was not on solid ground with this. "Will, really, what are we doing here? I mean, I'm not so sure these gu..."

"You're in or you're out, you're in on everything else, you're in on this, or just get *all* the hell out, it's..."

"OK, ok, in, in." Both of us a little frantic.

Rain, wind, diffused vision had us under cover. We crossed the street behind a lone taxi, occupied, busting downtown, and then I caught movement over my right shoulder and looked up the block from the corner. Stuffed back into a doorway, somebody short, round, hobbling, did I know him?, bent over, hurting for something strong and moaning "wha'd' I have to do?, wha'd' I have to do?" and standing next to him a human praying mantis named Juan Cordova -- a long, lean local boy, involved with the substances, a hustler, an obsession with all things Batman earning him the tag Juano Guano.

We know each other, and Guano knows the score. Hands up, palms forward, classic surrender pose, he lowered his arms to shoulder height and held them to his sides, like he was hammered up by Roman guards, floppy cap and fish hooks in for the crown of thorns.

But Juano Guano was sacrificing nothing for anyone.

And some people die for their own sins.

Willy and I traded smiles. I thought it unlikely anyone would say anything. In the Kitchen, a tale told out of school about me and Will wouldn't travel far. Like a train reaching the end of the line, it would take a final turn, screech and slow and slide into the last station, and stop dead. Juan would be no trouble. We left him in the mist.

#

The begging from Rod and Todd, barely understandable as English yet clear as a bell, had come and gone, smacked back into silence, and now the river showed black at the pavement's end. Out of nowhere, Willy started talking -- to me, to the wind? I couldn't pick it up.

So I started myself, opened the door. "Man, some rain, Will. And water all around

tonight."

We were mighty far along on this trip -- but maybe not too far.

Willy, looking down at the luggage, gathered himself, wiped his eyes. Reaching. "What's that old thing about water... cleansing? And not the street, moron." He was struggling, looking for an out. "The water... it's a symbol, a sign, what's that old crap they say," and trying to stay tough, "it's cleansing, but bigger. A deeper way." And you know, right then, the air went out of the balloon.

What did he mean? Like, oh, happy day, when Jesus washed my sins away?

I guess. "Well, yeah, I suppose every place, people everywhere, that's the deal. Water does it. The sea, the rain. Gives you hope. Start again. All that." Myself, I was hoping the water had washed the blood off the wall, and hoping these now very lucky bastards would appreciate discretion, holding thy tongue, clamming up, understanding silence is golden.

We each took deep breaths, Willy a few more. I rolled my head, shimmied, shaking it off.

Will had gone to pleading, looking down, trying to shed this. "G, you think even here -- now? With them?" Still looking down.

I gave him an out.

"Man, I hope so."

#

We'd turned around. There'd been one last buck of wind and water that swept up off the street and bounced right back down, left us drenched. We slumped toward home, trading cross corner waves with Juano Guano, looking forward to a civilized gentlemen's drink and Stella waiting to hear what happened.

Which was we'd run these two guys to the river, a classic journey around here, paused to reflect on an alternate to the journey's classic end, and took our eyes off Pancho and Lefty, who panicked, used the eyes they had left between them to signal a last ditch charge, and heads down they bull rushed us. I ol`e'd Pancho past me and he banged face first to the street but Lefty plowed Willy right down the middle and knocked him on his ass into the rain puddled gutter, so we dragged them to the edge, and stopped, just so. Enough. Fear had melted them into themselves, they hadn't heard the word of Willy's epiphany, and had done only what comes naturally when facing a deep-six demise. Choosing not to hold a grudge for once, Will figured they were no more likely than Guano to feel the need to discuss this with anyone, so he delivered an appropriate sermon, real finger-wagging wages of sin stuff, uncuffed them, collected leather straps and gloves and ruined clothing, sent Bob and Ray on their silent way, and foot shoved the mess into the drink, kicking and kicking Pancho's goddamn jacket loose from the edge to finally drop it, the end.

I found out later it was a new moon tide that yanked it all into the down river current, and I watched everything get sucked away.

And for the first time, not good for someone in his line of work, I watched Willy crack, looking out onto the water, eyes wet again, shoulders sagging under the weight of what was in his head.

"Jesus. G. G... I didn't even know their nam... "

Can't have this, real hard, right away, I said "Will" and stopped him, grabbed each shoulder tight and turned him to his right to face me and said, strong again, into his eyes, "Willy."

I took one breath. I spit it out with "It doesn't matter. They're all the same."

I believed it when I said it, and I believe it now.

Willy was flat, done, crying. "Those guys. They didn't kill her."

Didn't kill her? Kill who?

Now I got it.

"No. But they would have."

#

On the way back we talked about what needed to be done -- getting Willy's stuff out of Mom's apartment, getting Mom's stuff out of Mom's apartment, letting the landlord know the place was available for rent or sale. How we'd lay her out and wake her in one of the old Village parlours and, of course, bury her out of St. Anthony's on Sullivan, no question there, and think about whether or not to put her in Jersey next to the old man.

I can't imagine why that matters.

We did not talk about loss, grief, suffering, guilt, or madness. Not yet.

And with a messy day behind us I reflected, realizing that since hooking up in business with Willy my personal tally sheet reads one dead, three bludgeoned... none of them in the line of duty.

If I was a cop they'd take away my badge.

∞∞∞∞

My War Against the Invisibles
by Jeffery Scott Sims

The invaders came like thieves in the night. No one ever saw them, no one ever knew of them apart from their effects. They showed up the morning following the night of the meteorites, which can't be a coincidence. They came in something. Things fell to earth around there in the wee hours, and from those something alien hatched. I didn't actually know it at the time-- I learned most of the sparse details later-- for I was up in the hills on holiday from the big city, enjoying two weeks of fishing and other lazy recreation. I sojourned in the little cabin deep in the woods by the stream up from the mouth of Munds Canyon, I and a couple of friends, Mark and Buddy. A good time was had by all, and then that morning they went into Page Springs for supplies. That was the wrong thing to do, because I never saw them again.

By that evening I was really worried about them, but there wasn't anything I could do then since they took the jeep. The next morning I fried myself some fish, ate a big biscuit, and set off on foot down the rocky four wheel drive road to town. All that day I saw no one, which wasn't totally strange, but I'd expected to run across other outdoorsmen, if not my friends. By following Oak Creek I reached the edge of the forest, where it gave over to farmland, before I sacked out again, very tired, confused, and remarkably low in spirits (I say that because I didn't know anything yet of what was coming). So it was one more morning before I hit the winding paved road of the lowlands and made it to Page Springs.

Here began the heavy-duty weirdness. It looked like they were demolishing the town. As far as I could see, the entire population of able-bodied men, a lot of women, even older children, were engaged in taking apart every structure in sight, right down to the outhouse. By observing a bit more I realized they were building something new, one big, long, rectangular structure, like a warehouse or factory building. They swarmed like perspiring ants over the shell of that edifice, which grew as I watched. Already others were working inside. My view of them was cut off as the walls went up.

I saw more. There were dead bodies in the streets, a few, being haphazardly collected at intervals. Most of the bodies were little children and old folks, and they looked messy. The scene was so freakish that I didn't think, but blundered way into it before I decided to feel afraid. Then I crouched against a smashed brick wall, my heart hammering, wondering what had happened, what was happening.

I backed out to the edge of town, hiding in the ruins of a torn-down house, until a solitary figure trudged up the road toward me. He was a lean, weather-beaten old fellow who walked erratically, as if in distress, clutching one arm to his chest. I hailed him, he turned, made hesitantly for me. "What gives?" I cried. "Has the world gone nuts?" "Guess so," he replied. His hand, held tightly to his chest, looked funny, like he was wearing a furry mitten. I begged him to tell me what was going on. He told me, between gasps and groans of pain.

The invaders had come, invisible ones that dropped out of the sky into men's minds, occupied a corner of their brains, dictated orders. They wanted something done, commanded it done, saw to it that it was done. Those who wouldn't or couldn't work died in odd and unpleasant fashions. The surviving folks were being forced to build something, out of the available materials, a kind of manufacturing plant. He didn't tell me what it was for. Shortly he couldn't tell me much at all. His hand squirmed, and I saw that it wasn't covered by a mitten; his hand was a furry thing, an eyeless animal attached to his wrist with a nasty toothy mouth, and it was eating into him. He told me weakly that, unlike most, he'd resisted the sinister spell, so the Invisibles-- that was his word-- willed this creature to his hand, just made it happen like magic. Then the mouth gnawed into a vital spot, blood spurted, the man collapsed. That's how he met his end.

I believed every word of his story, without reservation. Good Lord, after what I'd seen, why shouldn't I? Without missing a beat I took off at a trot down the highway to Cornville, intending to flag a car and escape to civilization, if there still was one. I began to have doubts, because an hour passed, yet I never saw a vehicle on the road. That is, I didn't until I reached a certain point up on those open, wind-swept ridges, where I hiked up a slope and came across half a dozen wrecked cars and pickups all jumbled together. There was human debris mixed among the tangle of steel and fiberglass. I found out why. There was more invisible trickery going on, an unseen barrier laid across the road through which I could not pass. Nor, I gathered, could anything tangible. It affected vision, too, for the view beyond was blurred, misty, meaningless, the sort of distorted view one gets in a fun house mirror. I walked far off the road, still met the barrier. That gave me the shakes. I was five miles out of Page Springs; how far did this murky wall extend?

I hiked it, kept going after the sun went down, just to be sure, and yes, it ran all the way around, a circumference of, I guess, about fifteen or sixteen miles. I was exhausted then, and tired, and hungry. I ate the last of the biscuit, washed down with my canteen. I pondered long before sleep overwhelmed me. As horrible as the situation appeared, one note of feeble hope occurred to me. Whatever had happened here hadn't happened to the whole world. That couldn't be, otherwise the aliens wouldn't require a barrier protecting their lodgment in Page Springs. It might not do me any good, but the real world was still out there.

This meant that, as it was likely to matter to me, the sole enemy was here inside, with me. Whatever must be done would be done here. I determined to do it, or to die trying. Having resolved, I slept, and in the morning walked back to town.

Why had I not been affected by the mind control? I could only take a stab at an explanation, but I figured my saving grace was my previous isolation. Having landed, the Invisibles had gone after everybody they found, and they simply didn't find me. Mark and Buddy picked a bad time to intrude, right when things were hot, so I presumed they'd been sucked in. Maybe I could blend in, pass for one of the mental slaves, learn a thing or two, find a means of making a difference. It was a slender reed, but better than nothing. I tried it.

I strolled into Page Springs, casually dodged the construction teams, sauntered straight into the giant building and got to work. It was a factory of some kind, containing a series of assembly lines, extremely long wooden tables down which mysterious gizmos were being pushed, and added to as they progressed. I haven't the foggiest where that stuff came from; it didn't look cobbled together from local spare parts the way the building did, but rather like material provided from a technologically advanced source. The finished devices, collected at the ends of the tables by teams who carried them away for stacking at the end of the hall, were small machines that could be held in the hand, complicated instruments of convoluted metal casings with wires running all through them. I didn't know what they were, couldn't guess anything from their appearance. I would have bet they were weapons. The Invisibles were constructing these, preparing for the day went they sent their slave army out of the barrier.

To be precisely clear, the Invisibles weren't making anything; their human captives did the work. There were three hundred people in that vast, low-ceilinged room, each doing his minute part, utilizing a mess of common hardware tools to piece these objects together. Those people all looked dirty and weary; some looked sullen, even angry, but they all worked. I joined in, squeezing into line, staking out a space, began to fuss with the gadgets. There must have been a rule I was expected to know and obey, but I didn't know it and didn't care to obey, so I did anything that came to mind, sticking a wire here or there as pleased me. I'd be surprised if any of my productions operated properly.

At midday we were fed by human servants pushing trolleys laden with various-sized bowls of wheat porridge. It was wretched goop, but it filled the belly, as far as it went. Then back to work until dusk, when everybody at once, surely in obedience to a silent command, marched out of the factory and dispersed to the rubble of their homes, where they bedded down among the refuse of their lives. I went along with the bunch I'd labored by, which seemed to be the remains of a family and their immediate neighbors. We crouched or sprawled in the dark, with just a half moon to illuminate the pathetic scene.

"You don't belong here," said a youngish, sandy-haired fellow. I replied, "Nor do you. Why do you do it?" He said, "I have to obey them." "Who, the Invisibles?" "Yeah, yeah, that's right, the Invisibles." He groaned. "I can't see them, but they're there, always talking to me, telling me things. I hate it, but it has to be."

"And a good thing, too," cried another, an older guy with a scraggly, graying beard. "It's right to do what we're told. I'm happy about it." They had him lock, stock, and barrel. Curiously enough, despite his happiness he appeared in worse shape than anybody else present. At the time that didn't mean anything to me.

I turned to the girl beside me, a little bedraggled, but still a pretty girl. "Who do you agree with?" I asked. "It doesn't matter," she said hopelessly. "The monsters have got us. There's nothing we can do about it." "That remains to be seen," I said.

I slept, then woke at dawn, half expecting to wake up hypnotized, but I was my normal self. That was great. I woke because those around me were rising in unison, again obeying the silent command. They marched toward the factory, I tagging along. I was desperately hungry, but we received nothing but a swallow of water apiece. Then back to work we went.

Two bizarre deaths taught me a lesson. There was a frowzy woman at the next table over who worked more diligently than most, even humming to herself. An hour before our crummy lunch was served she broke down. It was as if she were all used up, had burnt herself out. She fumbled her application of wiring to machine, then staggered, then shrieked, "No, it isn't fair, why should it happen to me?" And then she literally fell apart. Bits of her started to come off, until she suddenly unraveled and disintegrated into tiny dusty chunks. She didn't bleed, she crumbled. So she was dead. There were plenty of sad comments, but everybody kept working. After lunch it happened again, this time to the older man who'd bragged the last night of his happiness. He screamed, begged for mercy, ran around shedding himself until he wasn't there anymore. This told me that, whatever the consequences of disobeying might be, too cheerful obedience was a lot worse, the effects more immediate. I debated how this knowledge might serve the cause.

That night I had a long talk with sandy-haired Charles ("Call me Chuck") and his pretty sister Marjorie. I 'd discovered that they were still real people in a sense-- with their personalities and ideas intact-- with the dominance of the Invisibles laid over to a greater or lesser extent. This meant we could converse pretty much as normal. I made use of that fact to get the goods on the situation. "What's it all about, Chuck? What are they up to?" "They want the Earth for themselves," he said slowly, like a thoughtful man puzzling out a tricky point. "They don't have bodies like we do, so they need us for all the grunt work. They jump from planet to planet, making the folks there build what they need, then move on to the next. Now they're here, and they're going to do the same to us. They'll always be hiding, but they'll be running the show, once they control all of us." "If that's the plan," I mused, "I wonder why they start off hiding in Page Springs." "Because," Marjorie cut in eagerly, "there aren't enough of them to control the world with their brains. They aren't that strong. They need the machines we're building for that." "Isn't that a joke," said Chuck. "I'm working all day, no wages, no benefits, to destroy the human race. It's shameful." "Now I get it," I said. "When they have enough machines, down comes the barrier, and their mind control reaches from one end of the globe to the other. After that there won't be any dealing with them."

"Isn't now," Chuck growled. "It stinks, but we have to work."

"I sure don't want to," said Marjorie, "but that's how it is. I know it's ridiculous. I hate them. They killed our little sister Tammy, just because she wasn't old enough to work. They made something awful grow on her. That's how life is, though."

Very earnestly I said to them, "Tomorrow I want both of you to do me a big favor. Each of you, when you're on the assembly line, do this for me: just once, screw up the job. If you're told to put wire A in hole B, do it another way, or break the wiring, or stick a pebble inside a case. Do some little thing just for yourselves, because you want to, because you can."

"I don't know." "I'd feel funny about it." "Somebody might mind." They gave me all kinds of answers, derived straight from their control, but their emotions fought for me. Both agreed to think about it.

I got results. I took a place across from them on the line, made regular eye contact, dropped suggestions. They would smile, glance at each other, do something wrong like naughty kids. They didn't exactly break the control, but they played with it, amused themselves, and in so doing accomplished a few acts of vital sabotage.

That night I praised them, joked with them, encouraged them without pushing too far. I was afraid they'd rebel against me if I drove them. Marjorie seemed-- I really believed this-- to take a shine to me. I didn't mind. I'd done a lot worse in my time. I advised them to spread the word of my cute idea, just for a laugh, if they didn't mind. Chuck was dubious about the enterprise, but Marjorie found it appealing "as long as it didn't make for trouble."

The next day the other shoe dropped. It had to happen sooner or later. I'd been dreading something like this. How long could I wander about without drawing the attention of the invaders? In mid-afternoon I heard the buzzing in my ears, or in my head, a low, insistent drone which rose to a grating whine. I knew right then it was the mental power of the Invisibles. I also noticed, quickly, that everybody in sight sensed it. So it wasn't me in particular they were after; they were hitting the lot of us. Now why would they do that? I thought of a possibility. It was reinforcement, administered like medicine, bad medicine in this case. If you're sick the doctor gives a big shot, then recommends a prescription of small doses to keep the first one going strong. That's what the Invisibles were doing, I concluded, or figured out as the process went on. It might be all the poor folks of Page Springs needed, but would it capture me?

I fought it in my mind, trying to beat it back without being too obvious about it. That sounds strange, but for all I knew the Invisibles could read minds, and I didn't want to think too loudly, if that's understandable. I waged the battle of the brain, guerrilla-style. The force was amazingly transparent, only subtle, insidious, doing its best to become a part of me, to rearrange my views in order to corral them and bring them into line. There was nothing harsh or painful about it. It was as if I was considering another set of values, like a friendly conversation on politics or religion. Oh, I see your point--

yes, you've got something there-- say, that might be worth a try-- I'll give anything reasonable a fair shake. Such thoughts swam within me, and they didn't sound evil or craven. An unprepared victim-- like hundreds of Page Springs folks who awoke to the attack that first morning-- could have fallen for it in a minute. The weak-minded would suck it up and feel righteous about themselves.

I remembered my missing friends. Mark and Buddy were tough, not likely to surrender readily, but they'd walked into the thick of the attack, when the aliens were pouring it on. I'm sure they were killed because they struggled too hard, fought too heroically for their souls. I waged war quietly. I didn't shout, didn't argue, didn't threaten, I simply shrugged and kept moving my hands like a willing worker. I even fitted a few devices properly, proving what a good boy I was. The whine turned into muted but comprehensible whispering, a reptilian voice hissing commands. I kept moving like a non-union employee, eager to get a good job done well.

The voice ceased, the whine returned, gave way to the buzzing, which stopped. I examined all the caves of my brain. So far as I could tell, I was unaffected. My mind was still my own, my purpose unchanged.

The Invisibles weren't so smart! In fact, they were pretty dumb, so smug and sure of themselves that they didn't investigate their results. Maybe they couldn't -- maybe they had to sneak up on their victims to make it work (at least without the machines we were building, a scary thought if the Invisibles ever got loose in the world) -- but whatever the reason, they'd screwed up badly. I was still the spy in their camp, designing schemes for undermining them.

I lost ground with my fellow conspirators, however. That night I found them dangerously obstinate, and guessed I had to just about start over again. I did so, only this time I knew what I was doing.

Here's the following couple of days in a nutshell. We went about our business, as the Invisibles wished it, trooping to work at dawn in our grimy, stinking clothes, the same we'd worn throughout, unwashed, crusted with perspiration. Water, for drinking only, was carried by slaves from Oak Creek, and little of that. Food dwindled rapidly. Either the Invisibles didn't care if we starved, or their plans were reaching maturity. Now and then the best and most pitiful workers blew up or fell apart, a taste of human destiny if the Invisibles got their way. We cranked out a ton of those machines, equipment for a small army, as if the aliens counted on swarms of new slaves soon. I brought Chuck and Marjorie around again, added everybody in our sleeping group, set them to passing the word at every opportunity. Each one of us talked to several-- just throwing out ideas, you know, take them for what they're worth-- and everybody we talked to were encouraged to pass along the message. I relied on the power of mathematics to spread the word: two, four, eight, sixteen, on and on, until everybody heard. Surely it didn't take with some. I heard arguments, nasty comments, threats to "tell". I also saw many quiet nods and secretive grins. Rather than making waves, I set in motion ripples that could pile up into a tidal wave when the time was right. In the end the request was always the same: keep playing along, agree to every mental command, don't fight it or talk back, but disobey it, be subversively creative with the machinery. The Invisibles were clearly counting on that stuff. We must see to it that it let them down.

During those days there were dim flashes of light in the sky, like sheet lightning, and muffled booms from all directions. That had to be the fine warriors of the human race, God bless them, battling to break in to us. Nothing came of it, though. No one came. The alien barrier held firm. We were on our own.

On that last afternoon we received another dose of mental reinforcement. It didn't affect me at all-- I'd figured it right-- but what really mattered was how it impacted the rest. There were some waverers, more than a few I admit, but with lots of them the relapse wasn't severe, and didn't last long. It didn't take with Marjorie one minute. She stuck to me, collared her brother and straightened him out, and what with one thing or another by that evening we were solidly on course, as if the Invisibles hadn't tried their dirty tricks again.

I set Zero Hour at nine o'clock in the morning. Everybody who was ever going to matter got the message. I felt a curious, breathless sensation in my head, rather than my chest, an oppressive feeling which told me that our enemies were already on the move, perhaps suspecting something. That couldn't be helped. Came the moment, and I leaped onto the work table, at the top of my voice declaring a strike. "Stop working," I thundered. "All of mankind are counting on us. No more fooling. Spit out the Invisibles! Smash the machines!" Every device within reach I stomped or kicked to the floor. Marjorie jumped up with me, grasped my hand, added her voice and her feet to mine. "Death to the Invisibles!" she cried. Chuck echoed that call to battle, his strong voice rolling across the factory floor.

Hesitation, a frightening beat of ghastly silence, then hubbub and frantic commotion as scores of mental slaves threw off the weakened chains of their minds and got into the act. They shouted, bellowed, destroyed. Hammers, screwdrivers, monkey wrenches crashed down upon the horrible machines. Wires snapped, casings split, guts of metal tumbled out. Inside of a minute the entire production system was completely wrecked. The place was a shambles of ruined, bent, crushed metal fragments. The far corner of the factory caught fire, set ablaze by a patriotic arsonist.

The Invisibles struck back. Oh God, it was bad, worse than anything I'd felt yet. They came after our brains with red hot needles of unseen energy. That, I'll bet, was how it was that first day in Page Springs, and happy I am I wasn't there then, only had to experience it once. They hit back with fury, a genuine sense of blood-red anger knifing into my mind. Within seconds we learned that our would-be masters were playing for keeps, willing to kill those they couldn't dominate, maybe lusting to kill. They just about bowled us over with their counter-attack. Strong men fell to the floor crying, I staggered, Marjorie screamed in agony, the real thing-- because it really hurt-- and for a second we were checked. We were also aware, understanding as much as we could, united and fighting mad. We beat back the psychic shock wave.

Then came round two, when it seemed the Invisibles tried to murder as many of us as they could, probably to cow resistance. Here, there, at random, hideous growths sprouted on certain unfortunates, things like parasitic animals that attacked their human hosts. Maybe a dozen went down screaming or moaning. Chuck, to my horror and disgust, was one of these. I'd thought him tougher than that, but I can't make big statements. I don't know that it made any difference. It could have been luck of the draw. I don't think our opponents accepted defeat yet, but I'll never know that; either they were making examples of a few, or they couldn't handle us all at the same time. Anyway, a lizard thing grew out of the side of his face, bit into his neck, and that was the sad end of him. Marjorie gushed tears, hot, furious ones. "Death to the Invisibles!" she shrieked, and countless voices maintained the chant. Boots ground on metal parts. Debris was knocked off the tables. Gray smoke clouded the rancid air.

The vast majority of us still lived, healthy, sane, and uncontrolled. Whatever happened to us, victory was almost ours. The Invisibles played their last hand. This is the especially tragic part. There were those among us who had failed to break the control, or who were so eaten up by its power that they hadn't tried. They didn't have the numbers to fight us, but they could still serve their masters with their bodies. Now they seized the remaining intact alien devices from the completed stack, held them before them like the monstrous weapons they were, and prepared, as must be the case, to use them to re-enslave their freed fellows. Of course we couldn't stand up to that, of course we couldn't reason with the deluded ones-- they were too far gone-- so we did the only thing we could. I was neither the first to realize the dilemma nor to advocate the solution, but I was right in there, bawling soon enough at the top of my lungs for necessary action. "Kill them!" We did it, and I'm sorry, but I don't know what else we could have done. I pray we didn't kill anybody on our side by mistake. To pick up a machine, for any reason, was to invite an immediate death sentence. We slaughtered them all; every man or woman who snatched up one of those objects perished, and went fast. It was a messy, bloody brawl, which didn't stop until the final slave hit the dirt, pummeled and broken.

And with that the battle concluded. I didn't know it was over yet, though I sensed a sudden lessening of tension in my mind, a lightening of spirits which had been furtively depressed. Looking back on my feelings throughout those days, I believe the energy emanations of the aliens had been affecting me since I'd approached Page Springs, and I'd grown unconsciously accustomed to them. Now I felt joyous, light of heart, springy of mind. Marjorie came to me from the scene of her last fight and wrapped her arms around me.

I held her. All over the wrecked complex our people were acting as if they were finally able to take a breath and relax from the nightmare.

Our instincts proved true. We had won. The Invisibles were gone, departed from our minds, vanished from the Earth, as we shortly learned. In another hour an avalanche of military vehicles and troops would charge into Page Springs, so we found out before being told that the barrier was down. Indeed, save for the trampled remnants of alien technology, there was no evidence left, nor ever found, that the invaders had even existed. I supposed it would be that way. It's fairly certain they didn't have bodies of their own, so once flung out of ours they had no place to go except Hell. I guess we did that for them.

We were safe, we citizen soldiers, and the world was safe. That's all. I don't know any more about those grim days than anybody else, don't know as I ever will. That's the whole story of my war against the Invisibles.

∞∞∞

Pack-Brothers: The Ambush
by Will Frankenhoff

Dusk settled into the remote mountain pass. A chill breeze arrived, whispering among the stunted birch trees and silver-barked alders clinging to life amid the hard brown soil. An arctic fox, her coat already white in preparation for winter, paused to sniff the air. High above, a pair of red-tailed wyverns spiraled across the sky in an elaborate mating dance. The sole sign of civilization was an old road, its cracked paving stones overgrown with chokeberry bushes and knee-high spikegrass. Climbing out of a small wooded hollow to the west, it ran along the northern edge of the pass before turning southeast to head deeper into the mountains.

Blade-Lieutenant Eldan Swayne crouched behind a lichen-covered boulder thirty feet back from the road, a small hand-held crossbow resting in one gloved hand. Clad in the grey-green buckskin leathers of the Republic of Almaren's Border Watch, including a hood that left only a slit for the eyes, Eldan's motionless form blended into the rock; one shadow among many in the deepening twilight.

He was not alone. Eight other members of his small company lay concealed nearby. Most were armed with powerful recurve short bows; some cradled heavy crossbows. All carried regulation-issue longswords in blackened scabbards across their backs and broad-bladed daggers sheathed at their waists.

A voice whispered in Eldan's mind, *"Chief?"*

The lieutenant breathed a sigh of relief. The "voice" belonged to Canus, Eldan's pack-brother and the final member of the company. Eldan had sent him out to confirm the location of the Ssylarian slavers they'd been tracking the past two days.

"Yes, Canus?"

"I've found them. Three wagons. About a mile to the west, just past Laughing Falls. They'll reach you in twenty minutes or so."

"Good. There should still be enough light. Numbers?"

"A dozen, not including their…cargo." The last thought carried a strong flavor of distaste. The slavers had hit an isolated farming hamlet the day before the company picked up their trail. According to the survivors, eleven people were missing. Anticipating the next question, Canus continued, *"First two are typical slave wagons. One drover, four guards each. Third looks more like some kind of fancy carriage. Has a coachman and—"* A feeling of alarm flowed through the link.

"What is it, Canus?"

"There's a Sand-Dancer with them."

"A blood mage? Are you sure?"

"In the carriage. Would've caught his scent earlier but the wind was against me. If it's any consolation, he doesn't seem to be expecting trouble. I can't sense any active wards or detection spells." Canus paused for a moment. *"I'm a little hazy on the niceties of*

Ssylarian culture, but isn't it unusual for a Sand-Dancer to be travelling with slavers?"

It's more than unusual, Eldan thought to himself. The lizardmen of the Ssylarian Khanate were products of a rigid, caste-based society. Blood mages were drawn from the upper ranks of Ssylarian aristocracy, answerable only to the head of their Order and the Khan himself. Slavers were lower-caste hatchlings viewed as little better than the slaves who harvested *letumol*, the sword-leafed plants whose tiny golden berries once pressed and magically distilled into potions, allowed the cold-blooded Ssylarians to survive outside their desert home. To see a blood mage travelling with slavers was as akin to a senior member of the Almareni Senate sharing an afternoon carriage ride with a pack of lepers.

"Chief?"

"Sorry. You're right, Canus. *It's strange and I don't like strange, especially when we've gone to all this trouble arranging such a pleasant little ambush.*" Eldan didn't need to mention that ambushing a party of Ssylarian slavers was one thing; attacking slavers accompanied by a blood mage was another thing entirely. Even if the ambush succeeded, the death of a high-caste Ssylarian was sure to have diplomatic consequences. The fact Eldan was acting well within Almareni law—slavery had been outlawed in the Republic for over a millennia, a crime punishable by death—wouldn't matter to the politicians who wanted to avoid yet another war between the Republic and the Khanate. He understood their thinking, even respected it, but Eldan wasn't a politician. He was a Swayne of Mosscreek and honor demanded he act.

Eldan turned and signaled to where Blade-Sergeant Falla lay hidden behind the weed-choked remains of a fallen birch tree. She rose gracefully, brushed off a handful of splinters clinging to her dark leathers, and made her way over to his position.

Speaking quickly and quietly, Eldan relayed the information provided by Canus, including the unexpected presence of the blood mage. Falla listened in silence, her long fingers caressing the silver-filigreed pommel of the honor dirk hanging from her belt.

"Well, Sergeant, what do you think?"

Falla replied promptly, her voice harsh, "Our main priority has to be the Sand-Dancer. The rest sound like regular slaver scum—they're tough against unarmed civilians but no match for trained troops, let alone our boys and girls."

The blade-sergeant cocked her head, considering. "Give me Raines and Crumb," she named the two best shots in the company, "and I'll personally guarantee the Snake doesn't get off a spell."

Eldan started to speak but quickly shut his mouth. He was uncomfortable with Falla referring to the Ssylarians as Snakes, but he realized the hard-bitten sergeant wouldn't appreciate a lecture on the use of derogatory language, especially when it concerned the lizardmen of the Khanate.

Unlike Eldan, the blade-sergeant hadn't grown up in Meridon, the cosmopolitan capital of the Almaren Republic where all manner of races lived together in relative peace. Nor was she a Swayne of Mosscreek, a member of the wealthy patrician family that traced its roots back to the founding of the Republic some fifteen centuries past. Falla was of yeoman stock, raised to a different set of standards. She also had more reason than most to dislike the Ssylarians. Her great-great-grandparents were refugees from Triesa, one of the first independent city-states to fall to the lizardmen when they came boiling out of the Smoldering Wastes nearly three hundred years earlier. Eldan hoped her desire for revenge wouldn't lead her to do anything rash.

He quelled the troubling thought. "Raines and Crumb? Very well, they're yours. Hold your fire until the carriage reaches that point." Eldan indicated a lightening scarred tree stump some fifty feet up the trail. "We'll wait on your signal. The rest of the company will attack as planned, concentrating on the slave wagons. One volley, then close with steel. We want to avoid casualties among the captives if possible."

"Understood." Falla's eyes glittered like chips of obsidian ice and Eldan sensed the grim smile beneath her hood. She saluted and turned to go.

"One more thing, Sergeant."

She turned back. "Sir?"

"Try not to miss. Getting killed by some Ssylarian mageling would ruin my heroic self-image. It would also wreak havoc on my dinner plans with Lady Dorriane."

Falla gave an amused snort. The lieutenant's amorous adventures were a constant source of entertainment to the other members of the company. Eldan wasn't handsome in the classical sense but he had an open, engaging manner and an infectious smile, both of which proved irresistible to women. The company had an ongoing wager—now up to 240 silver talents—on when one of his dalliances would last more than a week. It had been close to two years since Eldan had taken command of the company. Nobody had won the bet.

She said, "Don't worry, Lieutenant. We'll get the job done. We can't have you missing your dinner date, can we?"

Glad to have lightened her mood, Eldan dismissed Falla with a casual wave. He reached out to Canus with his mind. *"Anything new?"*

"In the last two minutes? No. Would you like there to be?"

"You know, sarcasm doesn't become you."

"Hah. I think it fits quite nicely."

"Wise-ass." Eldan's reply was tinged with a mixture of fondness and exasperation. *"Seriously though, good job. Now, get your furry hide back here."*

"Thanks, chief. I'm on my way," came the whispered reply.

Eldan paused. Something had been nagging at him throughout the conversation. He realized what it was.

"Uh, Canus?"

"Yes?"

"Didn't you tell me only pack-brothers can mindspeak?"

"Yes."

"And then only over short distances?"

"That's right."

"And we're the only pack-brothers currently outside Mistleaf Forest?"

"As far as I know."

"Which means nobody is likely to overhear us."

"I believe that's a safe assumption."

"Then why in the Names of the Ancients were you whispering?"

"Because I thought it was funny. Didn't you?"

Eldan sighed. He should have expected the response. After all, he had known Canus for the better part of his life. In many ways he was closer to his pack-brother than to his own family, but there were moments when Canus' peculiar sense of humor still surprised him. Eldan winced as he recalled the time he'd informed his new "brother" he wanted to grow up to be a pirate chief. Canus had found the idea vastly amusing. Eight years later, he continued to refer to Eldan as *chief,* much to the young lieutenant's embarrassment. *"Forget I asked. Let me know when you're approaching the ambush point. I wouldn't want to explain to pack-dame Argentia that your motley hide was damaged due to a case of mistaken identity."*

"Hah. My mother dotes on you. She'd probably skin me herself if she thought you needed a new cloak. You're right about one thing: My pelt is too handsome to risk at the hands of some near-sighted humans. I'll contact you when I'm close."

Eldan didn't have to wait long. Scarcely five minutes passed before he felt the feathery touch of his pack-brother's mind. *"Coming in now, chief. Tell those misfits of yours to keep calm. Not that I'm too worried. On a good day, they might be able to hit the broad side of a barn."*

A moment later, Canus came into view, running with a smooth, loping stride that propelled him over the rough terrain at a pace no man could match. He drew nearer and someone gave a low whistle of admiration. Without looking, Eldan knew the whistle came from Blade-Corporal Aleena, the newest member of the company. Aleena had joined the company just a week earlier, transferring in from the Freehold Legion. This was the first time she'd seen Canus in his natural form.

Canus quickly reached Eldan's position. Snapping to attention, he fired off a jaunty salute. *"Reporting as ordered, sir!"*

Eldan eyed him suspiciously, wary of his pack-brother's sudden enthusiasm for military courtesy. Still, he had to admit Canus cut a martial figure.

Standing nearly seven-feet tall on back-cantered legs, Eldan's pack-brother had broad shoulders and a thick, powerful chest that tapered down to an impossibly narrow waist, all of which were covered by a silken pelt of the purest black. His sharp features boasted a pair of blazing golden eyes set above a long muzzle displaying a formidable array of fangs. Clad only in a bejeweled leather harness, a iron-capped ebony quarterstaff held loosely in one clawed hand, Canus looked like the living incarnation of some primordial war god, come to reap a bloody harvest.

Canus was a Forest Lord, a member of the reclusive race of lupine beings who dwelt deep in the heart of Mistleaf Forest, the vast and ancient woodland that ran along the northern border of the Almaren Republic. More commonly known as "wolflings", the Forest Lords were followers of Istenna, Lady of the Woods, and Vadassa, Mistress of the Hunt. Dedicated wardens of nature, wolflings sought to avoid conflict but were formidable foes when roused to anger. They also never forgot a debt. Centuries past, Almareni legions had marched to their assistance during the Shadeskill Wars, saving the outnumbered wolflings from certain destruction. The Forest Lords had been staunch allies of the Republic ever since

Eldan motioned for Canus to join him. As his pack-brother sank down in a loose-limbed crouch beside him, Eldan caught a flicker of movement out of the corner of his eye. Turning, he saw Blade-Corporal Aleena had partially risen from her concealed position and was staring in fascination at the Forest Lord.

Eldan grunted. *"It seems you have an admirer."*

Canus turned to follow Eldan's gaze. Catching the corporal's eye, he favored her with a brilliant, toothy smile. The young woman dropped back out of sight. He sighed. *"Poor lass. She's obviously overwhelmed by my magnificence."*

"Oh, she's certainly overwhelmed by something." Eldan's grey eyes danced with suppressed mirth, then turned serious. *"I can't afford to have the blade-corporal distracted right now."* He paused, the flavor of his thought turning apologetic. *"Also, there will be woman and children among the captives, simple farmer folk. Your appearance might... startle them. Perhaps it's time for you to shift."*

Canus acknowledged the suggestion with the flick of a tufted ear. He settled himself on the ground, legs crossed beneath him, the iron-ferruled quarterstaff placed on the ground beside him. Bowing his head, Canus closed his eyes, took a few deep breaths, and *changed*.

No matter how many times Eldan had seen his pack-brother shift, it still amazed him. Between one second and the next, Canus' lupine form disappeared, replaced by a different but equally recognizable figure wearing the distinctive black kilt, plain black blouse and steel vambraces of Vadassan warrior-monk.

The tall, black-skinned man opened his eyes and rose to his feet in one quick, fluid motion. Reaching down, he picked up the heavy quarterstaff. He spun it in dramatic fashion, weaving through a series of sweeping figure-eights and complex parry-lunge routines. Finishing with a flurry, he struck a heroic poise. *"How do I look, chief?"*

Eldan studied the man's features with a critical eye. The face was as he remembered: long and lean, dominated by a great beak of a nose and pair of dark, gold-flecked eyes peering out from beneath shaggy salt and pepper brows. Strong white teeth flashed from the midst of a thick, well-groomed beard. *"You're as handsome as ever, Canus."*

Contrary to popular belief, wolflings weren't born shapeshifters. Their ability to shift was a gift from the goddess Istenna, a response to the fear and prejudice the Forest Lords frequently faced due to their ferocious appearance. When a wolfling reached his time of Ascension—generally around the tender age of eighty—he was able to choose a single, alternate form to assume at will. This form was known as *Hamis-arca* in the wolfling tongue. Roughly translated, it meant, "the face I show the outside world," as opposed to *Valodi-arcat*, or, "my true face." Being a pragmatic people, many wolflings chose to assume human form: Not only were humans a populous race whose settlements could be found throughout Valdara, but the Republic of Almaren, their ally and neighbor, was a predominantly human realm as well.

Some wolflings, however, decided on more exotic forms. During his time living among the Forest Lords, Eldan had seen wolflings transform into Aldatian river-sprites, complete with webbed feet and gills. He'd witnessed them shift into the forms of Zanbian claw warriors boasting thickly-carapaced torsos and double sets of arms ending in matched pairs of razor-sharp pincers. And finally, he'd watched in awe as an aged pack-dame, her pelt tattered and streaked with grey, became a wind dragon with a head the size of a wagon and a body bulking as large as a barn.

I wouldn't mind seeing that dragon overhead right now, Eldan thought to himself. He snorted. *Might as well wish for a squad of Blackstaffs while I'm at it. Not that a Border Watch company would rate one battle-mage, let alone a squad.*

He glanced over at Canus. His pack-brother had taken up position behind the boulder and was scanning the road for signs of the slavers. Looking around, Eldan couldn't see the rest of the company, but he could sense their presence. Confident. Eager. *Deadly.* The young lieutenant felt a surge of pride. *On second thought, a couple of battle-mages would only slow us down.*

Five minutes passed. Ten minutes turned into fifteen, then twenty. Just as Eldan started to worry the slavers had made camp for the night, he heard the faint sound of wagon wheels.

The other members of the company had heard as well. A hooded head rose from concealment to take a last look around. Tall grass moved against the breeze. Soft metallic clicks announced the cocking of crossbows.

Moments later, the Ssylarian wagons came into view. As Canus had reported, the first two were typical slave wagons: long, broad-wheeled vehicles with steel cages bolted onto tough bamboo frames. Capable of carrying up to a dozen captives, each wagon was drawn by a six-horse team and accompanied by a quartet of white-robed guards mounted on fleet desert ponies. Short and slender, with blunt snouts and plain beige-pebbled skin, the guards stood in stark contrast to the inhabitant of the open-top carriage trundling up behind them.

Oh, yes. That's definitely a Sand-Dancer, Eldan thought grimly as he studied the Ssylarian lounging in the back of the coach, noting the crimson ceremonial robe and talon-tipped fingers inlayed with runic markings. Though seated, Eldan estimated the blood mage would stand a good head taller than the any of the guards and his long reptilian face was covered in bright emerald scales showing the black-diamond patterning of the noblest Ssylarian bloodlines.

Which explains the carriage. Eldan shook his head. *Only a high-caste Ssylarian would insist on travelling in that monstrosity. Not that I'm complaining. It certainly made our job much easier.*

The carriage was a heavy, ornate affair constructed of black oak and decorated with gold leaf and ivory-carved panels. Drawn by a single pair of matched albino stallions, the coach might have made an impressive sight on the streets of Meridon but was wholly unsuited for use in the wilderness. The cumbersome vehicle had slowed the slavers' pace significantly, giving the company ample time to swing around ahead of them and prepare the ambush.

A cry of frustration drew Eldan's attention back to the slave wagons. A burly farmer was attempting to pry apart the bars of his cage by main strength. He attracted the attention of one of the guards riding alongside the wagon. Moving with deceptive speed, the Ssylarian brushed the tip of a slender glass rod against the man's hands. The farmer bellowed in pain, but refused to release the bars. A bored expression on his face, the lizardman applied the stun rod again, this time jamming it against the man's arm. The farmer convulsed, tiny green arcs of eldritch energy dancing over his body. His fingers opened involuntarily and he fell to the floor of the wagon, shuddering. Studying his handiwork with an air of clinical detachment, the guard gave the man another jolt. The farmer screamed. Satisfied, the Ssylarian moved away.

The casual brutality of the act enraged the young lieutenant. Bracing the small hand-held crossbow across his forearm, Eldan took aim at the slaver. Just as he was about to squeeze the trigger, a strong hand gripped his shoulder. Tearing his gaze away from the guard, Eldan found himself looking into Canus' eyes.

"Patience, my pack-brother, patience." The wolfling's mind-voice was stern. *"Have you forgotten the blade-sergeant? Would you risk alerting the blood mage before she's in position? Gamble the lives of your men to satisfy your sense of outrage?"* Canus sighed. When he continued, his tone was softer. *"Make no mistake, Eldan. Like you, my spirit cries out with the need to wreak vengeance upon these honorless creatures. Yet we are hunters. We need to put aside our emotions, to stalk our prey with a clear mind and a calm heart. Only then will we be able to bring Vadassa's justice down upon the heads of the rossz-zuzavae."*

Eldan lowered the crossbow. Rossz-zuzavae—roughly translated into Common as "defilers of the natural order"—meant beings too inherently malevolent to be capable of living in harmony with others. It was one of most deadly insults in the wolfling language. For Canus to label the Ssylarian slavers "rossz-zuzavae" showed the depths of the Forest Lord's anger. It also committed him to their destruction, even at the cost of his own life. And where one pack-brother led, another was bound to follow.

The two friends clasped arms in the wolfling manner, forearm to forearm. Canus intoned, *"May Vadassa bless our hunt—"*

"—and protect our pack." Eldan finished the prayer.

Both slave wagons were now past the ambush point and nearly even with Eldan's position. Eldan felt his pulse quicken. Forcing himself to take deep, steadying breaths, he targeted the driver of the first wagon.

As the blood mage's carriage reached the tree stump, Falla sprang the trap. The hiss of arrows and the deeper, angrier hum of a crossbow bolt split the air, accompanied by cries of "Almaren! Almaren! For the Republic and the Watch!"

Eldan loosed his bolt and saw it strike home, throwing the driver from the wagon. Around him, the other members of the company rose from concealment and released a well-aimed volley at the Ssylarians surrounding the slave wagons. Seconds later, the driver of the other wagon was down, as were two of the guards. A third slaver was slumped in his saddle, pawing weakly at the pair of arrows embedded in his stomach.

Eldan discarded the crossbow, drew his longsword, and charged the stunned survivors. Quick as he was, Canus was faster. Singling out the slaver nearest the wagons and the now cheering prisoners, the wolfling-turned-human bounded toward him, quarterstaff spinning.

The slaver, quicker to react than his companions, dropped his stun rod and unsheathed the pair of matched sabers hanging from his saddlebow. Urging his horse forward, the Ssylarian launched a whirlwind attack against the wolfling.

Though enthusiastic, the guard lacked the skill to fight with two blades. Canus easily deflected the blows with quick flicks of his staff, waiting for an opening. The Ssylarian extended himself once too often and Canus pounced. Batting the blades aside, the wolfling flipped his staff level and thrust it like a spear. The iron-capped butt of the heavy quarterstaff slammed into the slaver's chest, crushing his sternum. A bewildered look on his reptilian face, the lizardman toppled from the saddle and fell under the churning hoofs of his mount.

Eldan didn't have time to congratulate Canus on his performance. Another Ssylarian, this one on foot, was trying his best to skewer the young lieutenant. Unlike Canus' opponent, the guard wielded his sabers with the confidence of a practiced fighter. He was also fast, as fast as the duelmasters Eldan had trained under in his youth. Eldan was forced back; only his greater reach and the length of the longsword allowed him to fend off the slaver's flickering blades. Thinking quickly, he leapt backwards, snatched the dagger from his belt and threw it at the guard's face. Instinctively, the Ssylarian raised his blades to block, leaving his torso unguarded for a fraction of a second. More than enough time for Eldan to lunge forward and smoothly run him through.

Wrenching his blade free of the corpse, Eldan quickly surveyed the battle. The situation seemed well in hand. The injured slaver had succumbed to his wounds. Fallen from his horse, his body was draped across a moss-covered log, the arrows that killed him poking through white robes streaked with black Ssylarian blood. Two of the three remaining guards were dead as well, cut down by Corporal Aleena and the other members of the company who'd followed Eldan's charge. The final guard was—

"Down, chief!"

Eldan dropped and rolled to the left as an arrow whirred by, grazing his right arm. Hissing in pain, Eldan came to one knee and looked over his shoulder. Forty feet away, the last slaver was sitting astride his mount. Instead of fleeing, he was already fitting another arrow to the string of his bow.

Time seemed to slow. Canus was charging forward, roaring. Aleena was desperately trying to unsling her bow. Other members of the company were racing toward the guard. Eldan knew they would never reach him before he fired. The Ssylarian took careful aim...and fell backward off his mount as a crossbow bolt blossomed from the center of his forehead.

Stunned by his sudden reprieve, Eldan turned and saw Sergeant Falla hurrying toward him. Behind her were Raines and Crumb. Raines was rewinding his crossbow. The blade-private gave Eldan a laconic wave.

"Sir! Lieutenant! Are you okay?" Falla's voice was filled with concern.

Eldan laughed. "I'm much better now, Sergeant, thanks to you and your merry band." Sheathing his sword, he rose to his feet as Canus came bounding up, his face anxious. Eldan sent him a silent message of reassurance; his pack-brother tended to be a worrier where his friends were concerned.

"I'm sorry, sir. We would have been here sooner but we ran into a bit of trouble." The sergeant gestured back along the trail.

"The mage?" Eldan asked, examining his arm as he spoke. The arrow had left a four-inch gash across the outside of his bicep. Though shallow, the wound was bleeding freely. He retrieved a linen bandage from his belt-pouch and quickly wrapped the cut.

"No, he went down easily enough. It was the coachman. Someone missed an easy shot." Eldan noticed Crumb wince at the sergeant's biting tone. Falla continued, "He turned out to be quite good with a blade."

"I doubt he was an ordinary servant. More likely a bodyguard who doubled as a coachman. Remember, we're talking about a blood mage here. Assassination is the preferred method of advancement within their Order. I'm actually surprised he only had the one guard."

Eldan chuckled. "Or maybe I'm not. He probably felt safer traveling the wilds of Almaren than he did at home. In any case, that's neither here nor there. The blood mage is dead, as are the slavers. And we have some tidying up to do."

The blade-sergeant nodded. "Orders, sir?"

"We'll make camp right here. Take Raines, Crumb and Holmes. Free the captives and do what you can for the sick or injured. There's a stream nearby and they'll want to wash off the stench of those cages. That's fine. Just make sure one of you accompanies them—night is approaching and these mountains harbor dangers greater than Ssylarians."

"You've got it, Lieutenant." Falla trotted off, the three privates following in her wake.

"Corporal Aleena!"

"Sir!"

"Take Longshanks, Simms, Locksley and Marion. Search the Ssylarians. Any coin or jewelry you find, hand over to the farmers. It probably won't amount to much, but it should help them start rebuilding. The rest—weapons, horses, harness and tackle—go with us. Once you've finished with the Ssylarians, put their bodies in the wagons. We'll drop them off with the high constable in Breckinford. He can notify the Ssylarian ambassador that another "non-existent" slaving party has had an unfortunate accident."

"Yes, sir." The blade-corporal saluted and moved away.

Eldan looked at Canus. *"The rossz-zuzavae are destroyed, the blood mage slain, our pack members uninjured. Vadassa truly did bless our hunt."*

The wolfling turned his gaze to the slave wagons. Raines and Crumb had broken the bolts of the cages and were helping the captives to the ground. His reply was soft. *"She did indeed, pack-brother. She did indeed."*

The two friends stood in companionable silence, watching the happy scene. Farmers were embracing each other and their rescuers;

Falla had started a large campfire and two haunches of fresh venison—retrieved from the company's packs—were slowly roasting over the coals; Holmes was playing a jaunty tune on his ever-present lute, adding to the festive air.

After a time, Eldan shook himself. *"They'll need someone to escort them home. I'll have Sergeant Falla—"*

"Lieutenant Swayne! Sir!" Corporal Aleena was hurrying toward him.

"Yes, Corporal?"

"I'm sorry to interrupt you, sir, but we've found something you should see." She held out an intricately-carved wooden tube, a bit longer than her hand. "It was on the Sand-Dancer, hidden beneath his robes."

Eldan took the tube and examined it closely. He gave a low whistle. Pointing to a small engraving on the cap of the tube—a saber crossed with a lightning bolt—he said, "This scroll case bears the seal of the Sandlord, head of the blood mages."

Aleena shifted nervously. "Do you think it might be spelled, sir?"

"Canus, can you sense anything?"

"Nothing, chief."

"Canus says not." Eldan opened the case and removed a single scroll. "My Ssylarian is limited, but I'll be interested to see what type of message would be carried under the Sandlord's personal seal." Unrolling the parchment, he began to read.

A few minutes later, he finished. Rerolling the scroll, he carefully replaced it in the case, and then tied the case to his belt. In a quiet voice, he said, "Corporal Aleena, please ask the blade-sergeant to join us."

"Sir, what—"

Eldan held up a hand. "Please, just get the blade-sergeant."

"Yes, sir." Aleena ran off.

"What's going on, chief?"

"Not now, Canus."

A minute later, the blade-corporal returned, followed by Sergeant Falla. The blade-sergeant asked, "What's the rush, lieutenant?"

"There's been a change of plans." Eldan said shortly. "Canus and I will be riding immediately for Meridon."

"Sir?"

"Please don't ask. I'll—I'll try to answer later...if I can. What I need you to do now is listen carefully and follow my orders to the letter." He looked at his officers. "Believe me, I'd tell you if I could. You just need to trust me."

"We do, sir. Absolutely." Falla reply was quick and sure. Aleena nodded firmly in agreement.

"Good. Here's what I need you to do: First, you will destroy all evidence this ambush ever occurred. Burn everything remotely Ssylarian: the bodies, the wagons, weapons, supplies, even the coins and jewelry we were going to give the farmers. Scatter the ashes to the winds and then hide the remains of the fire. Second, we were going to escort the captives back to their village. You still will, but once there, you will make stay and sure they don't speak to anyone outside the village about what has occurred. If this requires you to place them under arrest and confine them to their homes, so be it."

"But sir, they're free citizens of the Republic!"

"I know, Sergeant. I know. I don't like it either, but you'll understand later." Eldan thought for a moment. "If it helps, tell them that I've ridden to the capital to ask the government to relocate them to a new hamlet, safe from slavers and closer to the main market towns. Let them know that the government will only agree to this if they don't talk about the raid. Make them think the Senate is concerned that news of slave raids might cause panic."

The blade-sergeant slowly nodded. "That might work. But what happens when they *aren't* relocated?"

"I'll just have to make sure that they are." Eldan's voice was grim.

"Sir, are you certain about all this?"

"Yes. Now, you have your orders and we must ride. Vadassa's blessings on you both."

"Thank you, sir. We won't fail you." Falla saluted and strode away, Aleena close behind.

Eldan started jogging toward the small, wooded copse where the company had hidden their mounts prior to the ambush. Canus quickly caught up.

"We need to get to Meridon as soon as possible and talk to my father."

"Your father? But you haven't spoken to him since you joined the Border Watch. He's—"

"He's an arrogant, ruthless old bastard. Yes. But he's also a patriot and the former Speaker of the Senate. He knows the government backwards and forwards and he'll know who we can trust."

"Trust? What are you talking about? What is going on?"

"As I said, my Ssylarian is limited. From what I could understand from the scroll, there's a conspiracy to overthrow the Republic. It's headed by a group of senators—no names—who call themselves "The Five." He fell silent.

"And?"

"And that's it—all I could understand. I did mention my Ssylarian is limited, didn't I?"

Not another word was exchanged until, as the pack-brothers spurred their horses northwest toward Meridon, Canus asked *"What are we going to do, chief?"*

"I don't know, pack-brother, I don't know."

∞∞∞∞

Man Tracker
by Kevin M. White

Arthur Bindell eased the '55 panel truck down the narrow mud strip that passed for a road near the Coquille marshes. The vehicle bounced and slid like a roller coaster car about to jump the tracks. This caused him to stab his upper lip with the tooth pick he was teething on.

"Son of a b-" he cursed as the wheel began to turn against his sweating hands. The brush to either side of the mud track seemed to press in as if waiting for him to slide from the road so it could grab the vehicle and pull it into the dense foliage.

The road dumped out into a grass clearing with gray light filtering down from above. A number of vehicles were parked haphazardly in the clearing like toys tossed in the middle of a room. A sheriff and about a dozen men stood around drinking coffee from thermoses or smoking cigarettes.

A low, guttural whine rose up from the darkness of the back of the panel truck and Arthur rapped the knuckles of his fist against the wire screen behind him.

"Shut up back there!" he bellowed.

The whining retreated in volume but didn't entirely cease.

As Arthur eased into the clearing, the sheriff turned from the crowd of men and slowly headed his way. He halted and rolled down the window as the sheriff snuffed out his cigarette a few feet away in the damp, trampled grass.

"Glad you could join us Mr. Bindell," the sheriff drawled.

"So am I," Arthur replied. "Somebody should have told me what passes for roads in these parts."

"Yeah," the sheriff said, scratching his neck as he nervously eyed the panel truck. "Once you get off the county roads it can be kind of tough to get around. You didn't have much trouble did you?"

Arthur waved his hand, dismissively, "I just hate being late that's all. It gets everyone riled up."

"I can't tell you how much we appreciate you coming down," the sheriff continued. "This fellow is a real bad one and I'd hate to lose any of my men trying to take him in."

"This is what I do," Arthur replied. "We take the risks so you don't have to."

The sheriff nodded. "You can park anywhere here. We'll get started when you're ready."

Arthur eased the truck forward and noted that the other men were spreading out, extinguishing their cigarettes and dumping out paper cups of coffee as they watched him pull into a spot a few yards away.

He turned off the ignition and eased his bulk out of the bench seat as the steady whine and grunts from the rear of the vehicle began to build in volume. Arthur paused halfway down the side of the vehicle before slapping the flat of his hand hard against the metal surface.

"Shut up in there!" he roared.

The men had formed a semi circle about twenty feet from the back of the vehicle and the sheriff was addressing the group by the time Arthur joined them.

"This is Arthur Bindell," the sheriff said. "He's one of the most successful man trackers in Coos County. We should have our fugitive rounded up in no time."

Several of the men nodded while stealing curious glances at the panel truck. Their faces registered everything from wonder to apprehension. It was the same everywhere he went. Just like kids watching the circus come to town.

"Would you like to say a few words before we get started?" the sheriff asked.

Arthur hiked up the waist of his faded jeans and removed the tooth pick from his mouth as he strolled over to the assembled men. "Some of you might know how this works, but for the benefit of those who don't there are a few rules."

A chuckle of nervous laughter rippled through the group before the sheriff's stern look returned the glade to silence.

"No smoking," Arthur began. "It spoils the scent and makes the tracker's job harder. Besides, they aren't keen on fire. Don't get in front of me once we head out. I need a clear scent line and believe me, once they get worked up, you don't want to get in the way."

A hearty round of laughter bubbled up, causing Arthur to pause and wait until it died down. This was what he wanted. Men at ease. There would be plenty of time for second thoughts and uncertainty later. "I assume you have an article of clothing or something that belonged to the fugitive?"

The sheriff nodded. "We have a sock and a shirt in the cruiser."

"Good enough," Arthur replied. "Now in a few minutes I am going to get the leashes from the front of the truck. I'll need some help laying them out. Fifteen feet of chain gets pretty heavy."

The men looked at the truck and then back and forth at each other.

"Nobody has to get near the back of the truck," Arthur said, still sizing the men up. "I won't be letting my boys out until everyone is safely back, so there's no need to worry about that."

After murmuring amongst themselves, two of the men came forward. Arthur turned away, barely suppressing a smile as he replaced the tooth pick. It was amazing how a group of grown men could be reduced to frightened schoolboys. He had to remind himself that he had been at this twenty years. What might seem normal to him would be a hellish nightmare to the average man.

Arthur opened up the passenger side door and grabbed a wood milk crate from the bench seat.

With a grunt, he lifted it out and set it on the wet grass. The two men that had stepped forward grabbed either end and hefted the box containing a coil of link chain back to the rear of the truck.

Arthur was joined by a third man who helped him bring the other wood box back where they set it down next to its twin before he addressed the men once more. In short order, the chains were laid out in the damp grass with a heavy lock looped through the end nearest the truck's doors.

"Now just step back. I'll handle the rest of this," Arthur said. "And sheriff, I'll need those scent items when I'm done."

Arthur turned to the panel truck's doors and produced the keys from his pocket. The door was double locked and as he slid a key into the first cylinder the back of the truck began to rock from side to side as its occupants started to howl and cry.

A murmur of panic rose up from behind him and, without turning, Arthur knew the men had stepped back even further from the truck. As he selected the second key and placed into the other lock, he also fished a small black box from his shirt pocket. A red button was centered on the top and two small, metal prongs jutted from the front panel.

The howling increased as the rear of the truck bounced up and down and the cries took on an almost human tone.

"Time to get things under control," Arthur muttered as he put away the keys before grabbing the door handle and turning it.

The door swung wide and the two beasts inside lunged at the steel reinforced cage. The door of the cage was secured by a heavy padlock, so he knew he was in no real danger. That didn't stop the predictable panic from unfolding behind him, however.

The creatures wore rags that might have once been shirts and pants. They had no shoes. Their skin was gray, mottled and bore evidence of old, unhealed wounds. Their eyes were clouded, lacking intellect or expression. Broken, rotted teeth showed each time their cracked lips opened to scream.

Arthur raised the box and pressed the red button. Immediately, the creatures dropped to the floor twitching and feebly grasping at the thick, leather collars around their necks which contained transmitters for the electrical shock that went into their nerves at the base of the neck.

He shook his head and pulled out the keys again to undo the padlock. The creatures lived only for flesh and understood only the need to eat and avoid pain. There was nothing like a little jolt to calm things down. Now he would have the next three or four minutes to free the lock and then hook them up to the chains before they regained semi-coherence.

There was no doubt that dealing with these man trackers was far more dangerous than using ordinary dogs. At best they moved like drunkards and their sense of smell was about on par with a good scent hound. They did, however, have one big advantage.

A killer might not think twice about slaying a deputy or a tracking dog if it meant a clear path to freedom, but even the most hardened con would think twice about taking on one of the living dead.

Though a vaccine had eventually been conceived, the zombie plague, as it was referred to in popular culture, had taught humanity one thing. There are some things worse than death.

∞∞∞∞

River Road
by Cary R. Ralin

Wanda Wilbur watched the paddle holster holding the grip-worn .38 Special slide onto the sturdy, sweat-stained leather belt. "You goin' out? You been patrolin' near every afternoon." Wanda took off her Buddy Holly glasses. "Who my s'posed to talk to?"

"Well, Miz Wilbur, lack of an audience has never bothered you before." He smiled to himself. That was a good one. "Missoura's now the meth capital a the United States accordin' to the Feds." He grimace-smiled this time. "Gotta keep the hopheads outa our backyard."

Wanda nodded and clicked her tongue as she rearranged a large bobby pin in her hair. "Well, lucky for us, we got six-term Sheriff R.T. Barnes on the trail."

The Sheriff ambled toward the fly-friendly screen door. "I'm gonna go cruise the river a bit. The wife calls, tell her I'll be home for supper at six."

Butler County had no towns over 200 people, so Black River, which crossed the county, had been the de facto activity center for as many generations as anyone could remember.

As the lone department cruiser crossed the rat-a-tat-tat bouncing boards of the canopied wooden bridge, it slowed so he could scan up and down the river for signs of miscreants. Nothing marred the tranquil shimmering of the flowing water and the forest of trees jutting out over the water, hanging onto the banks despite the earth being slowly eroded away by the winding and swirling currents below them.

He eased off the bridge, turning north onto the gravel road that roughly paralleled the riverbed. The artery had no name, but most called it River Road.

The car rolled to a slow stop next to a well-traveled path that ran down to Big Eddy, a popular swimming hole and party place on hot summer afternoons. He could hear laughing voices and giggles and the whoops of boys using the rope swing to show off.

The gabbing girls tanning on towels and the boys imitating Tarzan in their tighty whiteys didn't notice him until he was among them.

"Tommy McFadden! Get over here!" Tommy turned at the voice he recognized and shuffled his feet toward the sheriff. "Tommy, by my count, you're the only one here of drinkin' age." He made a show of scanning the scene. "And unless y'all is mighty hungry, those coolers there could hold 'bout two cases a beer." Tommy said nothing.

The Sheriff resumed. "I am forced by law to arrest underage drinkers and anyone who buys liquor for 'em. So. I'm gonna take a little break here for a smoke. When I'm back on duty, if I see any full cans that haven't been dumped into that river, y'all are gonna provide us a river detail." The sheriff saved the county money by using lawbreakers as free cleanup labor and the teens hated that worse than being hauled in.

After the break and a thorough chastising later, the sheriff turned over the Chevy's 450 and resumed his slow cruise. He tuned the radio to KLID Country. As his eyes came back up, he saw a flash of movement near the curve ahead as someone disappeared into the foliage. He reached the curve and got out to follow. Stepping carefully over and around poison ivy and dam'd sticker bushes, he worked toward the river.

When the sheriff broke through the brambles, he recognized the man stooped at the river's edge. "Eh, Jody," he called as he walked closer, "what brings you out here?"

"Aw, got me a litter a cats, Sheriff. You know, the damn critters go all feral on ya."

The sheriff could now see Jody was holding a tied, burlap feed bag just under the surface of the water. It was moving.

"Jesus, Jody," the sheriff was obviously uneasy, "that's kinda sick."

"It's God's way sheriff. Ya rather I shot 'em or smashed 'em with a ball peen?"

"Jeez. Maybe so. Drownin' has to be a bad way to go," RT said as he looked away. He changed the subject. "How's Mama and Betty?" Jody's wife and daughter.

"Mama's good, but Betty's feelin' poorly. She's eight months now. Never had a youngen before, so she's a hormone rolly coaster."

The sheriff grasped the excuse to leave. "I still got about an hour. Maybe I'll go check in on 'em."

Jody didn't turn from his task, but he said loud enough his voice echoed off the far bank, "That ain't necessary, RT. You know I don't like strangers at my place."

"I'm no stranger, Jody, and don't call me RT," RT said as he hustled back toward the black and white.

He sped up to forty to put some distance between Jody and himself. Two lefts and a right put him on the dark, tunnel-like road that led to Jody's and Mama's house.

Before the Chevy stopped completely, it was surrounded by three pit bull mixes that didn't bark; their bodies just paced back and forth while their heads swiveled to stay focused on RT and dared him to get out.

Mama came outside, corralled the canine guards and invited RT inside. As they stepped onto the uneven wooden porch together, "How you doin', Mama?"

"Oh, gettin' along, I guess." Her fingers twisted together like they hurt. "Things been kinda hard with Betty."

"You take her to the Doc, or a hospital?"

"No, no. She's here, in the back."

"Think I'll just step in for a minute," as he walked toward the only closed door.

"Sheriff! No. She's...she's come up with a miscarriage and don't feel like seeing no one."

He slowed, but then turned the doorknob anyway and stepped into the bedroom. Betty was lying on her back in a bed barely big enough for her. The thin gray sheet covering her clearly showed her flat stomach. "How you handling things, Betty?"

She didn't answer at first. Then, "Bad. Real bad." She looked at Mama.

RT removed his hat. "If you don't mind sayin', in what way, Betty?"

"I lost my baby girl. Guess she was stillborn."

"Really. Jody never said that."

Mama nervously jumped in. "How'd you come to see Jody?"

"Well, I just talked him down to Black River where he was drownin' a litter a cats."

Silence. Then, "Sheriff Barnes," Betty quietly spoke as she stared at the floor, "we don't have no cats."

∞∞∞

The Taller and Tumult
by Augustus Peake

We were there in your Garden of Eden. I believe it is documented; though I have never read the book. Documented, but misattributed. You called us, and continue to call us, 'the snake'. Understandable, I suppose - we do look rather similar - but somehow faintly disappointing. Don't get me wrong – all that ignominy and hatred wasn't something we craved. On the contrary, we were amused by your taxonomic incompetence. Still, some of us were and are a little peeved. I mean, to be over-looked for millennia can't be good for one's self-confidence, can it?

And just for the record, it was a pear.

You are shocked, I can tell. Which part shocks you? That the garden really existed? That it was a Taller?

That there were many beginnings?

In our family, there were some greats. Giants, really. That tree in Eden was not a highpoint, literally I mean. After all, pear trees tend not to be greater than 10 meters. But I had a grandfather, you know, who made it to Giza. Now, for you moderns, a trip from The Garden to Giza would be a short plane trip away. Not for us. For generations, we had talked of it and made it the object of our collective ambitions. And although it was Khafre's and not Khufu's, he was the first to get there, the first to tall one, the first to reach Tumult on one of your constructions. In our stories of him, he moves from stone and stone-cutter, to mule and mule driver, to slave to slave to slave up the face of the great stone edifice to its final stone. And when that final stone is laid, he is there for his Tumult. Blue with a hint of pineapple.

Tumult. What deep, contented joy it brings us. When one of us reaches it, we all feel it – though not as intensely as the Tumulter. Is there jealousy? Some, I won't deny it. So many try, so few succeed. Most of us meet the flat and flat-line. Simply put, the rise is our friend, the decline our fall.

Just do not talk to me about mountains. I do not want to discuss them. They are a sore point. Let us just say that height is good but snow is bad. How horribly ironic.

Later, a limb of my family moved from the old world to the new. An astonishing achievement when you think about it. Several cousins even made it to California. Need I say it was the wonderful sequoias? Perched on the upper-most branch of the park's tallest tree with a hapless tree surgeon from Oregon one cousin met Tumult. It was spectacularly peachy.

I can see you are struggling to comprehend what we are and what defines us. Perhaps an analogy will help. Your sharks are an approximate aquatic parallel. For water and thus oxygen read verticality. Let me explain: sharks swim, and by this act, they oxygenate their blood. We climb, and by this act, we reach tumult.

We call ourselves 'Tallers'. Does that help?

How did I get to be here with you? Now that is quite a story, and I am not sure you want to hear all of it. You seem, to say the least, a little preoccupied. Let us just say that my own talling began with a blade of grass and I was talled from there to a tree – fig I believe – to a sparrow that perched on the sill of an office window with an outstretched hand that fed an avian coterie, to a hand that rested casually on your shoulder - as your remarkable bonus was announced - to where we are now.

Canary Wharf Tower.

One foot from the edge.

I have a feeling my Tumult will be bright yellow with a hint of cinnamon.

∞∞∞∞

Clawbinder
by Marlena Frank

Her large leather boots crunched down onto the gritty earth. Saira could taste blood in her mouth from where the beast had slammed her into one of the rocky cliffs earlier. She held her breath, and lifted her eyes skyward, pushing her blonde hair aside and shielding her eyes from the glaring sun above. For a moment she saw nothing, but then the dark shape appeared over the rocky outcrop. The giant bird's wingspan easily blocked out the sun as it flew through the clear blue sky.

She let out her breath slowly, fighting off the cold terror in her chest and gritting her teeth in determination. She had thought she'd lost the fearsome creature known as Rajani, but as she watched its giant form tip in the sky she knew it was coming back around. For her. Saira moved quickly down the rocks, tiny pebbles skittering away from her feet. She could do this; it was what she'd been trained to do: fend off the Giant Ones such as Rajani. But in training they'd only been a fraction of her size and not nearly as clever. A single blast from the Power Crest would frighten the little ones off easily, but not the mighty Rajani. Saira doubted that even three blasts would prevent her from being torn asunder by the bird's giant claws.

Her left hand was shaking, clutching the large ruby of her amulet as she scaled down the cliffs. It was absorbing the energy well, but it had to be stronger if she had any hope of scaring Rajani away and she was running out of time. In front of her the giant shadow swept across the canyons and Saira heard herself whimpering with every breath. Rajani was moving closer, her wings slicing through the air above.

Just as the shadow came within meters, Saira leapt over what she thought was a stony crag. As she flew over it, she realized with drowning despair that the crag was actually a gully. There were many strewn across this desolate place, but she hadn't seen any as large as this one. Her brown eyes went wide as she started to fall into a dark pit far away from the sunlight above.

She pulled her left hand away from her chest and flexed the fingers out before her. "*Carpo!*" she cried, her shrill voice bouncing off the cavernous walls. Then a dark ruby light erupted from her palm and black hungry tendrils flung out into the walls all around her, securing themselves into the rocks. Her body was suddenly pulled to a halt and she blinked in shock as she realized what had happened. Her heart was still pumping madly in her chest, but the Power Crest had saved her. She started laughing to herself amid giddy gasps for air. What might have been her doom, the pit base, was far beyond the long reach of the sun; there was no telling how long she would have fallen before slamming to her death. The sides were craggy and the soil dark, meaning it had been here for some time. She looked back to the tendrils of the Power Crest, still gripping firm into the rock. They were strong but she wasn't sure how long they would last. Then the light within the tunnel was darkened, and she looked up already knowing what she'd find. Beyond the gaping opening she saw Rajani's huge form moving back and forth in front of the entrance.

"It is I be laughin' now, child!" Her deep voice flittered down on a breeze as her orange eyes narrowed. "You sure be a fool for comin' here – into my very home!" Rajani lifted her beak to the skies and let out a horrid screech to the winds. She pulled her massive body up and flapped her wings down at the cavern. Saira was bombarded with a wind so powerful that the tendrils were stretched taut against it. She looked helplessly to the anchors within the walls, but they held firm. She only hoped they would stay.

Finally Rajani relinquished her assault and crouched low. She poked her long beak slightly into the crag's entrance. "I be stayin' here all night, child. Just for you. And next when you plannin' to escape, I'll be waitin' right here!" She cawed into the blue sky, her eyes wide with glee and excitement. Saira could feel her own hot tears pouring down her cheeks before she knew she was crying.

"Please Rajani," Saira's voice sounded small and meek compared to her tormentor's. "Great ruler of the skies – please, I meant no harm!"

"No harm! You takin' Rajani for a fool?" She preened at a few stubborn breast feathers. "I do not believe in such lies. 'Specially not from a scrawny child come to steal my precious babies!"

Saira shook her head. The Giant One was right. She had attempted to steal an egg. One of the precious few that Rajani would create all year. But she had to think of something to tell her. Eventually the tendrils of the Power Crest would give out and she'd fall to the bottom of the gaping pit.

"Rajani, I did not plan to take your babies. In fact I was trying to save them."

The great bird had been pruning her tail feathers, but turned again to look at her prey with its lantern eyes. "Save them? From what? What could possibly kill them with me here?"

"Something you could not see even with your great sight, though you might be able to catch it without knowing."

Rajani blinked, "What? This be a riddle of some kind?"

Saira kept her eyes steady and watched the Great Rajani falter ever so slightly in her calm arrogance. "Sickness and disease, Rajani. Surely these things are familiar to you?" The look within Rajani's eyes told Saira that she was correct. "We've seen many Giant Ones fall to its will, mighty ones whose shadows far surpass yours, Rajani. We've watched them fall from the highest peaks, plunging weak and helpless to the ground."

Rajani shook her feathers, "This be a joke of some kind. We don't fall from skies, child. We rule them."

"But it doesn't end there," Saira wouldn't be cut off. "Only rarely do they take the larger ones. Usually they prefer them smaller, more helpless."

Rajani became perfectly still, watching Saira's eyes closely as fear crept into her own.

"Children, babies, even ... unborn ones. Yes, for they are the most helpless, and certainly the easiest of your kind to kill."

The great bird's feathers were ruffled all around her neck now as she bobbed her head, horrified by the girl's words. "But – but how do you know?"

"Surely you've noted how much your kind has dwindled, Rajani. Why do you think that is?"

Rajani's eyes narrowed but she didn't speak. She didn't have to.

"My babies..." she whispered, her feathers moving slightly in the breeze.

"Go look for yourself, Rajani. Check each of your babies carefully and listen for their tiny hearts beating. You'll find that one has already been taken." Saira locked her pale blue eyes with Rajani. It is said that few warriors are capable of withstanding the gaze of such a beast. Most men end up cowering beneath them, and though

Saira shivered from head to toe as she hung by one arm above that black pit, she kept her eyes locked and stern.

Rajani turned away finally and began pacing back and forth above the cavern, her giant claws dropping bits and pieces of debris down the chasm. Saira blinked at an annoying bit of dirt that got in her eye, but she kept her aching arm still and waited. At last, the giant bird turned her amber eyes into the cavern, studying her tiny prey carefully. "Alright, scrawny one," her voice was filled with more venom than a serpent. "I'll check them. But don't be gettin' any ideas now," and she took to the skies in a great rush of wind, the sky momentarily blocked by her pale white underbelly.

Saira released the breath she'd been holding, and turned her eyes to the tendrils still clinging to the walls. There wasn't time to be frightened. She had to move quickly knowing how fast Rajani could fly. "*Escensi!*" She whispered, and slowly the tendrils started to climb, yanking one slick black limb from a hole and dragging it upwards before working on the next. Her arm throbbed painfully as each limb moved, but Saira knew she had to keep quiet. The nest was not that far away and the Giant Ones had excellent hearing. It was a frustratingly slow process, but eventually the octopus tendrils had climbed her to the top of the pit, and Saira swung her body over to a ledge. The black ropelike pieces recessed back into her palm, and as soon as her dusty feet hit the earth she was running again through the cliffs. Up ahead were some tall jagged ravines through which she could pick her way, the width was perfect for a travelling group perhaps even a small pack of warriors. Rajani wouldn't be able to fit her large body within them to find her. Many of the passages were underneath rocky outcrops and were mazelike in design. A single path could diverge greatly beneath the rocky land above, so even Rajani's keen eyes wouldn't be able to locate her. In fact, by the time Rajani found out what had truly happened, Saira would be long gone.

Just as she reached the entrance to the rocky shelves, Saira heard a screech fill the skies. She ducked inside quickly and had moved several yards before deciding she could chance a break. She examined her hand first, which was covered with the remnants of the black tendrils. It was very stiff and was now throbbing to the beat of her heart, but she knew that a few days' rest would have it ready for battle. She wrapped it cautiously in the fine white linen gifted to her before her departure. That would mask the scent of the Power Crest while she was out in the Wilds. She couldn't risk attracting any hunters while carrying such prized cargo. Until then she'd have to rely on her wits and her speed to get home. She pulled out the dagger from her belt and smiled into the writing that was inscribed on the small blade. "Looks like it's just the two of us then, Talis. Think we can handle this?" The dagger hummed slightly as though it was thrumming for battle. "I thought so," she smiled, readjusting the sheath to be more accessible now that she wasn't running for her life. Then she turned to the prize.

Saira opened the leather pouch on her side and smiled at the giant egg that lay within. The magical charms would keep it warm until she was able to get back to the village – and the charmed rock she'd placed in Rajani's nest was an excellent idea, even if it was a little impromptu. She guessed Rajani must have been fooled for a little while, just long enough to allow Saira to get to safety. She pitied any who became the mighty one's prey this day, for her anger would know no bounds.

Patting the warm egg gingerly, she hummed the song of the Trainers, the victory song they'd sing upon her return. The most difficult part of her journey was over, but the journey back had its own difficulties. But soon she would be granted the title of Clawbinder, finally proving she could be a trainer and tamer of the skies. She had succeeded where few others had, and in the years to come she would raise this bird to be her own. One day she would ride him through the clouds high above the crags and gullies of this barren waste. They would be as one: Rider and Roc.

∞∞∞∞

What Philip Did in Tulsa
by Steve Lowe

The blindfold bit into Philip's face, cinched tight enough behind his head to pull hair out by the root.

"What is this?" He slurred his words, still groggy from whatever had been slipped into his drink.

The voice said nothing. Philip heard only grunts. The person attached to the voice was straining against something. Then the straining stopped and Philip heard exhalation. "There," the voice said. It was a man. "Ready. But you shouldn't be awake yet."

Something bit into Philip's bare shoulder and an electric jolt once again removed him from the world.

#

A little candle set inside a bottle glowed from a table in front of him. The flame waved inside the glass, pulling and stretching at the edges where the bottle curved. The way everything grows at the edges, larger than reality allows.

Philip smelled pizza and his stomach grumbled and kicked. His ass throbbed and he felt an intense urge from deep down in his guts to move his bowels. He realized he was bent over and strapped down to some kind of low bench, his numb arms pinned behind his back.

"Hi." The man stood in front of Philip and shook a pill bottle in his face. "These will keep you awake," he said. "We've got a lot to do today." The man plucked a syringe off the table and jabbed it into Philip's arm. "And this," the man said, "is some antibiotic so you don't get septic shock." He patted Philip on the back when he was done.

"What... why?" Philip choked on the cottony dryness in his mouth and gagged on the flavor of his own tongue. "Why are you doing this?"

"You can't be serious." The man bent down and looked at Philip, really studied his face. "Wow, you are. I can't believe you don't recognize me."

Philip jerked his head side to side to confirm that he indeed did not recognize the man standing over him with the sizzling poker in his hand. It was more of a metal bar, really, with a pointed end that glowed orange. The pressure in Philip's guts and backside pushed his stomach forward into his chest. Waves of nausea swept over him.

"Why, Philip, I'm Harvey. Jemison. From Tulsa." Harvey cocked his head and raised an eyebrow. "You have to remember Tulsa." It was a statement, not a question.

Philip did remember Tulsa. Every day, he remembered Tulsa. Every day, he ran from that town, and El Paso and Albuquerque and Mesa, too, but never seemed to get far enough away. He nodded his head to show that he did remember Tulsa.

"But you don't recognize me?"

Philip shook his head again.

"So, you must have skipped town by the time the trial started. You must have been long gone, huh?"

Up and down, the sweat flipped off of Philip's soaked hair. And in that moment, he suddenly figured it out.

"Well, formal introductions then." Harvey reached behind Philip's back and grasped his bound right hand. "Harvey Jemison. Ex-Marine, ex-tig welder, and now, ex-con. Can you guess why I'm an ex-con?" Harvey waited, clearly expecting an answer from Philip.

"Um... because you were in jail?"

"Give the man a prize! Oklahoma State Penitentiary in McAlester, to be exact." Harvey squatted in front of Philip and leaned in close. "Wanna take a stab at why I was in the Okie state pen?"

Philip thought of Miranda, her ghost floating through his head, with her tight red curls and her tight little ass and her horrible, high-pitched shrieking.

"Oh, wait... I think I see a light coming on." Harvey tapped Philip's forehead. "It's coming to you now, huh? You thinking about a nice girl? With curly red hair? Name of Miranda Hartley? Yeah, you know who I'm talking about."

It was a mistake. She wasn't supposed to die. None of them were. Philip had spent the past 19 years running from his mistakes. From Miranda. He tried to tell that to Harvey, that it was all a huge mistake, that he would fix it if he could, but the words caught in his parched throat.

"Well, since you missed the whole police investigation and trial and all that jazz, I'll fill you in." Harvey set the metal poker back into the fire pit with a steaming hiss and sat cross-legged on the bare floor in front of Philip, wincing as he bent down.

"Back's not been too good for some time," Harvey said. "Lot of things haven't been too good. That's what happens when you're in prison. You feel like you age a decade for every year you serve. Once you come out, you feel rejuvenated at first, but it don't last. Like when you was a kid and got the bubble gum from the little dispenser outside the store with the quarter you been saving. You pop it in your mouth and it's sweet and wonderful, but five minutes later your jaw hurts from chewing and the flavor's gone. All you're left with is a gray, tasteless hunk in your mouth. That's what it's like being an ex-con."

"I'm-"

Harvey hushed him. "Nope, don't say nothing. I'm getting there. OK, we were talking about Miranda Hartley. See, I didn't know the girl, but you obviously did. Long story short, nobody seemed to believe me that I never once met her while she was alive and kicking. They were so convinced that it was me what done them awful, horrible things to her, that it didn't matter what I told 'em. And since you were long gone by then, and the prosecutor fella didn't have nothing but a re-election staring him in the face, well..."

Harvey stared off at the tools hanging on the far wall to his right. Big, iron tools designed for shearing and sawing and pulverizing. "Nineteen years. I was in there for nineteen years. On account of you. In the beginning, I couldn't believe the things they accused me of. They shoved all them crime scene pictures in my face and said *I* did this. Said it was me sliced her up like that. Me that bashed her head into the floor so many times that they couldn't identify her from pictures. That I ravaged her so terribly that..."

Harvey put his hand to his mouth and bit a knuckle. Philip felt the air leave the room, like they were suddenly in a vacuum. Harvey cleared his throat and went on. "I just couldn't wrap my mind around how anyone could do them things you done to that girl. That a man could be possessed of such wickedness and violence as that." He looked at Philip again, his eyes stony and cold, distant. "But I got over all that pretty quick. Prison does that. Changes you real fast. And it's amazing, given the right combination of idle time and burning hate, what a man can begin to imagine doing to another man."

"I-I'm sorry. I..."

"Nah. Too late for that now." Harvey stood and looked down with an inquisitor's gaze. "My lawyer had them re-test the DNA and got them to admit that they botched their investigation in a couple places. But he never did get them to say they were sorry. The day I was set free, not one person in that courtroom believed it was because I was innocent. I wasn't a criminal when I went into prison, but I did the time of a criminal. Now that I'm out, I still feel like I'm doing time. Your time. I think it's only right I pay you back some of that."

Philip cried and shook his head. Speech failed him. Harvey walked back to the fire pit and pulled out the poker, the end now a fiery, crackling red. He pointed it at Philip to show him the end, but Philip's vision wavered. Abject fear assaulted his conscious mind.

"The first year in the stir, I was raped five times." Harvey held up his left hand with all four fingers and thumb splayed out and whispered, "Five."

He strolled around the table behind Philip. There was a clang of chains and a cinching around his waist that caused him to heave. The pressure in his intestines felt near to bursting.

"Nineteen years is a long time. I don't have that kind of time anymore to just waste it, so we've got a lot of catching up to do."

Philip cried out, "Please, no!"

A door crashed open somewhere behind him. Men shouted and Harvey shouted back. Philip felt a cool breeze rush over his bare skin. He couldn't make out a word amid the frenzied din and fainted when the shooting started.

#

The detective with the pencil-thin moustache patted Philip's shoulder. A uniformed officer stood behind the detective. The officer was staring past Philip, toward his rear end, watching and wincing. He looked ill.

"Right here, Philip, look at me." The detective squatted and snapped his fingers in Philip's face. "Concentrate on me, don't worry about that."

The searing, ripping pain made Philip sick. The detective jumped out of the way. "It's OK, we'll make you right. Don't worry. There's doctors waiting for you once we get you free. You don't know how lucky you are that we got here in time."

The detective looked Philip in the eye with an earnest intensity. "The man that kidnapped you was a convicted killer. I've kept my eye on him since he was released because I knew he wasn't done yet." The inspector looked down at his feet and shook his head and smoothed out the narrow, sculpted facial hair around his lips. "I knew we never should have let that monster out. Not after what he did to that poor girl." He looked up at Philip again. "But we got him this time. Everything's going to be fine. You just hang on."

Philip tried to smile.

∞∞∞

Funeral Flowers
by Edoardo Albert

The taxi driver knew where to go.

The man paid him and then watched as the cab drove away. The driver had not spoken during the journey. The man had sat in the back, looking out, but not seeing.

He was going to bury his father.

The building he stood in front of did not look like an undertaker's office. Plate glass windows held him in reflection but he did not look as he remembered.

He couldn't see a door. He looked around, but there did not seem to be any other way in so he stepped closer to the building and stopped. A section of the glass slid open. The reception was glass and marble and steel and the receptionist was their human equivalent: clear, calm and cool. And, of course, beautiful.

He went in, and the glass slid closed behind him. He could not see out through it. Instead he saw himself, repeated again and again, disappearing into infinity.

He sniffed. The air was perfumed, a distant hint of summer meadows sleeping in the sun. Not what he had expected of an undertaker. But even death was corporate now.

"How can I help you?" the receptionist asked. Her tongue flicked, dampening her lips. Saliva glittered like diamonds on the lip gloss.

"I have an appointment," he said. "About my... my father."

"Oh, of course. Mr. Evans. We've been expecting you. If you would like to go through, Mr Singer will see you right away." She nodded towards the corridor that disappeared behind her into a haze of fluorescent light.

"Right. Thank you."

"Mr. Evans, we're all very sorry, but we are here to ensure that your father will never be lost to you."

"Pardon?"

"If you go through, Mr. Singer will explain everything." She turned back to her desk.

Mr. Evans walked past the receptionist and down the corridor. There was a door at the end. It was closed, but as he neared it the door opened and he saw a man standing there.

"Mr. Evans?"

"Yes, that's right. I have an appointment."

"Of course. Please, come in. Sit down." Mr. Evans made the first movement towards shaking hands, but Mr. Singer had already retreated to his side of the desk. No other option left, Mr Evans sat down. Mr. Singer leaned forward with his fingers interlaced.

They were beautiful fingers. Long, but not thin. Perfect nails too, pink to their tips and their quicks.

"You're not married?" Mr. Evans asked, then wondered why.

"Very observant," said Mr. Singer. "Normally it is only the ladies who notice such things. No, it is true that I have never married. I have chosen to dedicate myself to my work."

"I'm sorry. It was rude to ask."

"Nonsense, Mr. Evans, nonsense. This is a difficult time for you. I appreciate that. May I get you something?"

"No, thank you very much."

"Maybe later?"

"Maybe." The smell was even stronger in here. He couldn't place it. It had something of spring to it, and something of summer.

"Ah, I see you have noticed?" Mr. Singer smiled.

"Noticed what?"

"The particular aroma that blesses our establishment." He smiled again. "At first we tried to remove it but now I fear my employees would be most upset if I found some way of masking it."

"What is it? I can't place it."

"Can't you guess? No, what am I saying, of course you can't. I remember from our talk yesterday on the telephone that you are unaware of the particular character of our business. But I can assure you that your father had satisfied himself as to our bona fides before making this a stipulation of his will."

"I'm sorry, I don't understand."

Mr Singer stood up, came round from behind the desk and perched himself on its edge.

"May I ask your first name, Mr. Evans?"

"It's Gerald."

"Gerald. It suits you. Well, Gerald...?"

Gerald nodded. He had no objection to his first name being used.

"Gerald, then. We are not a normal place of rest, as you can no doubt appreciate."

"I didn't think it was an undertakers when I arrived."

"Precisely. We are not undertakers. Our philosophy here is very different. We do not burn people. We do not bury them. This is the modern day, and yet those barbarous customs still survive. Here, we believe the departed should be treated with respect. Here, we strive to preserve the departed as their loved ones remember them."

"Preserve? You don't mean taxidermy?"

"Nothing so old fashioned as that. Perhaps it would be best if I showed you some pictures from our catalogue. It was seeing this that made your father decide to commit himself into our hands."

Mr. Singer picked up the heavy book that lay on the desk and placed it open in front of Gerald. There was a picture of a man, lying down as if he slept for a few moments and would soon wake.

Gerald looked up at Mr. Singer.

"He's dead?" he asked.

"Departed, Gerald, departed. Nobody is truly dead while we keep them in our hearts." He gestured at the book. "Take a look. Satisfy yourself that your father will be in safe hands. Now, are you sure about that cup of tea?"

Gerald looked up, distracted from the picture of the dead man. "What? Oh, yes. Thank you. I will."

Mr Singer left the room. He moved as if no mark would be left whatever the surface he walked upon. Gerald went back to looking at the pictures in the book.

He would not have believed that these people were dead. But they were, and he leafed through the pages of the book, staring at each new body, more perfect, more beautiful than the one before.

Gerald put the catalogue down and took a deep breath. His eyes scanned the room but they were not looking for anything. Memory searched for the image of his father but he could not picture him. Details, fragments, yes. But not the whole man. Already the memory was fading.

A spider crawled across the desk and stopped next to Gerald's hand, its two front legs feeling the air, tasting the scent it carried.

Gerald did not see it. His memory was hoarding everything it could find of his father, pulling out memories from where they had been hidden, looking at them again and then packing them away somewhere safer.

Then he saw the spider. Gerald jerked his hand away, but the spider did not move. Its front legs tasted the air currents, but it did not run.

Gerald looked for something to hit it with, but there was only the book on the desk. He looked around the office, but it was bare and functional.

When he looked back the spider had disappeared.

He leaned over, peering at the floor, trying to see where the spider had gone. He did not like the idea of it crawling around down there, but he saw nothing.

Behind him, the door opened. He twisted around and saw Mr. Singer coming in carrying a tray with two cups upon it.

"Your tea," he said, setting the tray down.

"There was a spider in here."

"Really? Where?"

"It's gone now. It was on the desk."

"Don't you like spiders, Gerald?"

"I don't care for them."

"Wonderful beasts we think here. Did you avail yourself of the opportunity to look through the catalogue?"

"Yes, I did. It was... impressive."

"So you can see, Gerald, that you need have no qualms about putting your father into our care."

"I suppose not. But how do you do it?"

"Do what?"

"You know, preserve them. How do you do it?"

Mr. Singer smiled again. His teeth were very white.

"I see you have not yet looked at all of our book. There is an explanation of the process at the end." Mr. Singer nodded towards the catalogue. "If you would like to turn to page 217..."

Gerald leaned forward, picked up the book and started flicking through the pages. He half listened to Mr. Singer while he looked for the correct page.

"The process by which we preserve the departed is entirely new. Indeed, we venture to say that many of our clients have never looked better than they do now."

Gerald found page 217. It was the same as the others. A picture of a man, a half smile on his face, sleeping. Sleeping the sleep with no waking. Gerald looked up at Mr. Singer, the question on his face.

"You've found it. Now if you look closely you will see a circle has been inscribed on the photograph of our client. Turning the page over will show you a series of magnifications of that area of our client's skin. Please go ahead, Gerald. Turn the page."

Gerald looked back at the book. His hands seemed far away. He watched as they turned the page of the book.

"You remarked earlier about the perfume. Well, now you can see the reason for it."

Gerald looked at the pictures. A series of magnifications of the dead man's skin.

But it was not skin.

Fields of flowers, tiny flowers. Flowers packed, crushed together. And each flower a face, its mouth agape, staring up at him although it had no eyes. Tiny flowers where skin should be, a sunflower head made into hands and face and arms.

The dead man was made of flowers.

Gerald looked up at Mr. Singer. His mouth was open but no words came out.

"It's beautiful, don't you think? No wonder our clients look so wonderful after the process is complete. And now you know the reason for the smell. With all these millions of flowers surrounding us all the time, we could hardly avoid perfuming the air."

Gerald's gaze dropped away from Mr. Singer's face. His smile was too bright, too white. His eyes too dark. They swallowed.

"How... How do you do this?"

"With these."

Mr. Singer's hands opened and the fingers, the beautiful, long fingers, unlaced from each other and the cup of flesh was full of spiders.

"This is how we do it. With our little friends. Truly creatures of marvel. When a new client is brought to us, after certain preliminary work, we introduce these extraordinary little creatures to the body of the departed."

Gerald could not move. His mouth opened and closed but no words came out and his breath stank of flowers.

"Then comes the most marvelous part of our work. The transformation occurs when the spiders inject each cell with an extraordinary chemical that turns it into a flower."

The cup of flesh was offered to Gerald, offered across the desk so that he might see. A single spider emerged from the mass, standing upon the bodies below. The spider reared up upon its back legs and Gerald saw that its belly was a mouth and from that mouth came a tongue and the tongue was sharp.

"The result you have seen. You must excuse me if I seem over-enthusiastic, but even after years of working at this establishment the process never ceases to amaze me."

The spider's tongue flicked out and probed Mr Singer's flesh. Gerald opened his mouth to warn him but his throat was ash and his lungs were dry and he had no voice.

"It was no surprise to me that you saw one of our spiders earlier. They do get everywhere."

The hands stopped beneath Gerald's face.

"Take a good look."

Gerald squinted. There was something he could not make out. He looked closer.

All the spiders were feeding on Mr. Singer.

He jerked back but the chair would not move.

"Is something wrong?"

Mr Singer was very close to him. Smiling.

He smelled. He smelled of flowers.

Gerald looked at his skin, at the beautiful, flawless skin.

Fields of flowers spread across the face. Tiny white flowers. Each a mouth, open and gaping.

"Not trying to leave, are you Gerald?" Mr. Singer, still smiling his white, white smile, raised his hands into the air and opened them.

Gerald found his voice. He screamed.

Spiders, spiders everywhere, falling onto him, crawling over his sleeves, looking for flesh. Hands spasmed over his chest and arms and head, brushing off spiders.

He fell from his chair and then he saw the spiders skittering over the floor. Flailing upwards, he made for the door.

"Surely you're not leaving, Gerald?"

The smell. The smell, everywhere. In his lungs, on his skin, in his eyes. He was choking on it.

"Don't go."

Bodies beneath his feet, crunching into the floor. But he could still get out. No one was coming after him. He just had to get to the door. Then it was a clear run. The woman would not stop him. He'd get out of here. Just get to the door. The door.

He grabbed the handle.

"You can't go." The voice was quiet now.

Gerald looked down at where his hand had been.

Flowers. Tiny white flowers floating through the air.

The perfume of his flesh filled the air.

∞∞∞

The Cromera
by Lydia Kurnia

Shilvana was six when the masters first severed her hand.

She had been waiting for this day. After all, that was their purpose: food for the Cromera. If her body parts meant safety for the elves of Farizia, then this was nothing but an honourable sacrifice.

The Cromera protected all, weathering the storms that forever threatened the city. In return, the masters would sustain Her with the younglings. Before puberty, Shilvana's kind had the gift to regenerate. Her hand would grow back in a matter of days.

She just did not know it would hurt so bad.

She was fortunate. The Cromera only wanted her hand. Her best friend Erikh had almost died from bleeding when he lost both his arms at previous feeding. The masters would always try to negotiate, knowing there was limited supply of younglings for the Cromera to feed on. She must not be too greedy—Goddess or not. But Shilvana knew at the end of the day: what the Cromera wanted, She got.

Shilvana had never seen the Cromera. The masters would never let the younglings near Her. In the dining hall, the younglings would gossip about what She might look like. They made it a competition: whoever came up with the worst would get the top bunk at the quarter. Shilvana had won once, when she told them the Cromera had several heads—each made of thousands of mouths and stomachs—that was why the Goddess was always hungry. The top bunk was not as worthy a prize as she had imagined, but Shilvana was proud to have made the other younglings flinch.

Erikh had a different idea about the Cromera. He told Shilvana that in his mind, the Goddess was beautiful, with hair flowing about Her like a halo and eyes so bright they blinked like the stars. Shilvana rolled her eyes. Erikh had a way to romanticise everything. But that was why she liked him so much. Erikh was always impossibly positive.

The Cromera was a mystery. But unlike Her form, the younglings all agreed about one thing: the beauty of Her voice. It was mesmerizing, thin like the wind of a flute, but with strength that could break even the toughest of hearts. Sometimes She would sound like a choir: thousands of Cromera, all singing in unison, making the trees dance in harmony with Her tunes. At night, Shilvana and Erikh would sit by the window listening to the Cromera, forever Her loyal entranced audience.

At least She provided superb entertainment.

Erikh often had tears in his eyes as he sat there gazing at the wall behind which the Cromera would be. Shilvana never cried, although she always felt a lump in her throat every time the Cromera sang.

It was not until Shilvana was older that she understood why.

But by that time, it was too late to shed a tear.

#

That afternoon, they all celebrated Marizka's release.

Shilvana didn't know her well. Marizka was a shy one, always hiding behind the books as if willing herself to melt with the pages. She was very beautiful—the oldest of the younglings with all the right curves that made the boys tremble like the Bogimashes when she was near.

Erikh was in love with her.

Marizka was fifteen today. A lady. This day marked the end of her service in the Dorm—or what the masters affectionately called the Cromera's grocery barn. Marizka had earned her freedom, with scars and smiles to prove it. Tomorrow, she would start a new life amongst the elves in Farizia.

They all gathered in the dining hall. The masters had cooked up a feast: vegetable pies, chocolate rolls, taro crispies—celebratory food beyond their imagination. The masters even brought out the Bogimashes.

Everybody squealed in delight. They all knew what that meant: there would be music and dancing tonight. Shilvana noted fifteen Bogimashes as the masters hung their long, slithery bodies about the northern corner of the dining hall. Fifteen. One for each cycle that Marizka was here for.

The younglings crowded around these slinky creatures, stroking and nudging at their translucent bodies. The Bogimashes wiggled and blinking lights burst about the space, reflecting myriads of colours on the glass floor. Gasps broke in the air, followed by laughter as the Bogimashes hammered the rhythm of the first dance beat.

Everyone was in festive mood except for Erikh. He had turned all glum and silent. Shilvana thought he was selfish for sulking like that. Erikh should be happy for Marizka who would no longer be subjected to cruel amputations for the sake of a monster's appetite. Erikh scowled at her when she said that and Shilvana grinned. She knew Erikh was not upset because of that.

She changed the subject and talked about Farizia. Like the Cromera, they had never seen this city of dreams, but they'd heard so much about it from the masters. There were only five masters in the Dorm. Shilvana imagined a city full of them and could not help but wonder how they'd survive. Elves were funny creatures, she thought, very inflexible and weak. She remembered the day one of the masters burned his finger while barbequing the sausages. He had screamed like a baby and there was not even blood where he had burned. Elves could not regenerate like they did. Shilvana imagined the buildings in Farizia, they must all be covered with padded walls.

But apart from that, there was little else physically different about them. Someone like Marizka would appeal to both elves and her kind alike. That must be what was bothering Erikh. Maybe a dance with the lady of the night would fix that. Erikh beamed and when the beats changed, walked over to Marizka who shyly took his hand and followed him to the dance floor.

Shilvana watched them dance. What a beautiful sight. They looked so happy, it was heartbreaking. She hoped one day they would meet again. She wondered if that day would be as beautiful as today. She hoped Farizia was as wondrous as the masters described it.

Shilvana glanced at the masters watching the younglings shake their posteriors on the dance floor. The masters had smiles on their lips, but there was something dark in the way they lingered.

She drank her juice. Perhaps she was just imagining it.

#

To date—Shilvana noted—the only body part of hers the Cromera had not tasted was her head.

Erikh topped it off by disclosing that he had given his ears and tongue to the Cromera. Shilvana was not certain if she should laugh or cry. There was something humorously candid in the way he had said it, but she knew very well the pain that followed and could not help but cringe at the thought.

It was a sad night. Tomorrow, Erikh would reach puberty and leave her. After that, Shilvana would still have a cycle before her own freedom. Erikh had always been there for her after the feeding. His presence made her forget the pain. Shilvana wondered how she would survive without her best friend.

The younglings never talked about the pain. It was sacrilege to put it in words. There were times Shilvana wanted to, not so much the physical, but the pain inside. It had not mattered as much when she was younger, but after all these cycles, she could not help but realise there were questions she needed answered.

She had gotten herself in trouble many times for bringing these up with the masters. Fifty lashes and a night or two chained up in the dungeon. Shilvana did not mind the punishment, but she knew Erikh did. She had seen the devastation on his face, and when she was out, Erikh would give her the silent treatment which was the part she could not bear.

The Cromera sang. Erikh turned his head to the walls, tears welled up in his eyes. One night. One night before he would leave her. This could be the last chance he had to ever see the Cromera. Shilvana knew he wanted to. He—they—had the right to know what it was that had placed them in this predicament, honourably or not.

Without a word, she grabbed Erikh's hand and led him out of the quarter. He was protesting under his breath but she did not care. Shilvana ran along the corridor and paused behind the partition before the stairs. Erikh hesitated, but not for long. Shilvana knew he had guessed where they were going.

They tiptoed down the stairs, past the common area, the kitchen, the dining hall, past the library, down more stairs to the masters' area and finally, the main gate. It was locked, so they crawled up the big window and leaped through it out to the garden.

Two masters were guarding the gate to the Cromera. Shilvana led Erikh to the bushes nearby. Her hand touched a rock and an idea formed in her mind. She gave one to Erikh before mimicking a throw aimed at the masters' heads. *Just like Puka balls.* Erikh shivered and opened his mouth to protest. Shilvana slapped him impatiently. This was no time to be a wimp.

One, two, three. They threw the rocks.

Shilvana's hit the master's head squarely. Erikh's missed. Without preamble, Shilvana charged forward and butted the bewildered master's stomach with her head. They both fell. Erikh was soon on top of them, his shoe in his hand.

Smack!

She wasn't certain if it was her punch or his shoe that had rendered the master unconscious. It didn't matter. They must move fast before they woke the others.

The two younglings dropped away, panting with excitement and disbelief. Shilvana looked around. Nobody had heard the commotion. She crawled to the gate and found it was locked. She cursed inwardly.

Silence.

She realised then that the Cromera had stopped singing. Shilvana turned around, but Erikh was no longer by the fallen masters. She looked about in panic only to find her friend standing by the wall, glaring wide-eyed through a fist-sized gap, shimmering light bright about his pale face.

Shilvana called him, but he wouldn't budge, as if entranced by the view. She crawled and craned her neck beside him. It was bright. She had to shield her eyes with her hand before she could properly peek through the gap.

The Cromera.

There were—there were twenty of them, all chained to beds positioned in rows like a hospice. A large awning suspended over them with a wooden sign plastered on each side: *Harvesting ground 52*. They had tears gleaming on their faces—all female, all pregnant. Elves or her kind, she could not tell.

Shilvana scanned their faces in woeful disgust. Her heart pulled when she saw one she recognised. There, at the far corner of the camp, was Marizka. Next to her pregnant form sat a master, stroking her hair affectionately while she glared at him with hatred shining in her eyes. She was gagged. She was crying. She was... miserable.

The master walked to the table not far from her, and grabbed a plate where a severed hand—still fresh and bloody—lay on the surface. Casually, he picked up a fork and began eating. He even fed Marizka with pieces of the flesh.

A thousand knives grazed at Shilvana's heart. There were no elves. No Farizia. The Cromera was their future, where the males became masters and the females bred the younglings for food.

She felt Erikh drop to the ground, curling into a ball and sobbing uncontrollably next to her.

Her best friend. Her future enemy.
Shilvana vomited.

∞∞∞

Bootleggers
by Dale Phillips

The line of bums looked like scarecrows in the rain, and I had to laugh. Here I was, smoking a cigarette, warm and dry in my car, while they waited for a handout bowl of soup. Since the stock market crash, a lot of guys couldn't find work or enough to eat. But not me, I was smart and doing better than ever. Because I was a bootlegger, running illegal hooch to anybody who could pay. And the tougher the times, the more people drank to forget their troubles.

Business was so good, in fact, that I needed some extra help with a new job. I'd picked Davy Donaldson to be my new sucker. He had a good strong back and he could run a boat. He'd been fishing these coastal Maine waters for over ten years, before the bank foreclosed on him. That was why he was out here with the other bums.

The First National Bank in Rockport had sent Sheriff Powell and his deputy to throw Donaldson off his own boat, but Donaldson had thrown them off instead, right into the harbor. Then he went down to Rockport and slugged that banker, so they gave him six months in jail, and took everything he had. I'd have been smarter, and sapped the guy in an alley, with no witnesses.

Since Prohibition created competitors, I also needed someone who wouldn't go all to pieces if we got shot at. You couldn't be too careful in this business, and I always carried a pistol, just in case. Donaldson had served with Black Jack Pershing in the Argonne Forest, so I knew he had some guts.

I adjusted my cap, got out, and went up to him in the line.

"Take a walk with me Donaldson. Got something to talk to you about."

His shoulders were hunched, his head down against the weather. He couldn't look at me.

"I'm kind of hungry, Billy."

Him and his damned soup. I didn't like to ask twice.

"Don't you worry about that. Come on, let's go."

He gave a look at the church door, then followed me back to my black Model T. Maybe it had a headlight missing and looked like a falling-down chicken coop on wheels, but it was all mine, and I wasn't waiting in the rain for a handout.

I drove us to Neptune's Landing. Before things went bad, everybody had eaten there, but now it was just for smart guys like me, the ones with money. I lit another cigarette while Donaldson looked around as if it was all new.

"Order anything you want," I said. "Anything at all." I smiled. "You don't even have to get the fish."

He had a steak and a big pile of fried potatoes. I could eat steak any damn time I wanted, so I just had a hamburger sandwich. Before I was even halfway done, he'd polished off that big plate of food. I had the waitress bring him a thick wedge of fresh apple pie and some coffee, so he'd see what a sport I was. The first good meal he'd had in some time, and he owed it all to me.

Some color came back into his face, and he was quiet. He was ready for my pitch.

"That was pretty bad when they took your boat away, Davy. Bankers don't fish, what do they need with a fishing boat? What was her name again?"

"The *Mimi*," he said.

"Ah, yeah. That's it. Who's Mimi?"

"A girl I liked in France."

I knew the kind of woman a soldier met over there, but I didn't say anything. No reason to rile him up.

"Well your luck's about to change, Davy boy. I'm going to do you a big favor."

I lit up another cigarette, and even offered him one, like I was his friend.

"You know that Cain guy, the one from away? Bought that big old Harrington place down by the shore?"

He nodded. "That house was in their family for four generations. They got foreclosed on, too."

I waved my hand, dismissing his words.

"Yeah, well, it's his now."

"Nobody has anything nice to say about him. Some kind of crook, isn't he?"

"You may not like the guy or what he does, but he pays in cash money. Want some?"

"For what?"

"For helping me bring in a few cases of whiskey for him."

"He likes whiskey that much?"

"He likes *money* that much." I shook my head. "We resell it."

He smiled, kind of sad.

"I'm no bootlegger. Why me?"

I blew a ring of smoke. "You know every inch of this coast for twenty miles each way. You could probably run it blind." I said. "And you ain't got no family to ask questions about when you work or what you do."

While Donaldson was fighting in the War, we got that big storm. Bodies and wrecked boats washed up on the shore for weeks. His people were fishermen, and all the men old enough to work a boat were gone in that one night. If I'd been dumb enough to settle for that life, I'd have been gone as well.

After he returned, the Influenza epidemic took the rest of his family. So he got a loan for the *Mimi* and spent ten years fishing these waters, all by himself. He could disappear tonight and nobody would come looking for him.

"The pay's good, real good," I said. "We take a short boat ride at night, grab the stuff and unload it at Cain's."

He didn't say anything, just turned the thick china mug in his hands. He had big hands, scarred from working a fishing boat. Only suckers work that hard.

"What about the Coast Guard?" He finally said.

I laughed. "Cain's got a rumrunner built by Will Frost."

He finally looked interested, and I knew I had him hooked at last. Frost was called "The Wizard of Beals," and every fisherman on this coast wanted to helm one of his creations.

"She's got a flat aft and a torpedo stern. Cuts the water like it was air. They'll never get near us."

He thought it over some more. "I guess I've got nothing else."

"That's right," I said. "Right as rain. This is your big chance. You listen to me, and you can do okay. I'll take you by tomorrow, so he can look you over."

#

The next afternoon I picked him up at his shack and drove us out to the Seaside Meadows Country Club. I chuckled at the look on his face. This place was for swells. They didn't let guys like us on the grounds, unless we were mowing the grass. But someday I was gonna belong here, and then all these monkeys could line up to bow down to me.

I breezed over to the guy in charge and told him to take me to Cain. He personally escorted us over. Cain was walking to the clubhouse with some big-britches friend. I took off my cap and nudged Donaldson to do the same. Cain saw us and tossed his golf club to the side, and it was funny to see his caddy scramble to grab it before it hit the ground.

Cain had black hair that was slicked back, and a triangular face and pointed little chin that reminded me of a weasel. He looked Donaldson up and down and took the cigar out of his mouth.

"This is the guy, eh, Billy?"

"Yes, sir, Mr. Cain. He's strong, and he knows how to keep his mouth shut."

Cain flicked ash off his cigar and studied the stub. "But is he tough, Billy? I need a tough guy."

I shrugged. "Pershing gave him a medal."

Cain stepped in close to Donaldson, just as a couple of women came over from the clubhouse. I recognized Cain's wife, who was at least thirty years younger than him and a real looker. Too bad, I didn't want them to see what came next.

"Are you a tough guy?" I heard Cain say.

"Tough enough," Donaldson replied.

Cain half turned away, and then swung his arm in a punch that caught Donaldson full in the gut. Donaldson just grunted and stood there. Cain nodded and looked at me. "He'll do. Let's talk."

I stepped to the side with him as Mrs. Cain went over to Donaldson, looking concerned. Cain gave me some instructions for the next day, but I barely heard him, afraid that dumb fisherman would say something to ruin the deal. She walked away with a sour look on her face. When Cain had finished, I ran over to Donaldson.

"What'd she say to you?" I asked him.

"She wanted to know why her husband hit me. I told her it was to see how I'd react, so he'd know whether or not to hire me. Then she asked me why I'd work for a man like that."

"What'd you say?" I hoped he hadn't given any lip against Cain.

"I told her for the money."

"Dizzy dame. Of course it's for the money. That's why she married him, right?"

"I guess."

"Hey, Donaldson, lemme give you some advice. Don't mess up the job mooning over a pretty face."

"Don't worry. She's not my type."

I picked Donaldson up at ten the next night and drove us to Cain's place. All my runs up until now had been on land, but we were trying something new. I took us down to the private dock where Taft, Cain's hired gun, was waiting for us. I didn't like Taft, and I don't think anyone else did, either. Looking at him reminded me of the jagged black rocks in shallow water, the kind that rip the bottom out of your boat before you know it. Even his voice was dangerous, and too smooth, like a snake with human speech.

There was an electric light on a pole, and I could see Taft's eyes as he looked at Donaldson. I hoped there wouldn't be trouble. Taft liked to be the big dog.

"So this is the new guy, huh?" Taft smiled like a wolf seeing a big, juicy rabbit. He stepped in close to poke a finger in Donaldson's chest.

"You remember this," Taft said. "You follow orders and keep your mouth shut. You got that?"

Donaldson was smart enough to say nothing, and just nodded.

"Good. 'Cause the last guy didn't end up so good when he forgot that."

I shuddered, not wanting to know any more. Elias Norwell had been helping me make some runs around town, but he got to sampling some of the stuff and started shooting his mouth off about how he made his money. Nobody had seen him for over a week now.

We followed Taft down to a 24-foot white motor launch, with an enclosed cabin in front. Donaldson looked like a kid at Christmas. He took the wheel and fired up the big twin diesel engines, and they made a nice rumble. This little beauty had some speed and handled well, taking the roll of the waves smoothly.

It was clear and the stars were out, so we could see where we were going. Taft told Donaldson to go around back of Little Seal Island, just past the three-mile limit. We passed Caswell Point, Federal Cove, and Pine Inlet, and before long were between Big Seal and Little Seal Islands. Donaldson kept to the deep part of the channel and eased around the headland to the back of Little Seal.

In a sheltered lee was a cutter that Taft said was the *Dangereuse*. He flashed a signal, two times, two times, and once more. He got a response and told Donaldson to cut the engines. We drifted in silence, waves lapping at the side of the launch.

A voice came through the night. "It's on the beach." The beam of a searchlight cut a path from the cutter to the shore of Little Seal. I saw a stack of crates on the tiny strip of land.

Taft chuckled. "Sounds like they don't trust us. Go ahead, take us in."

Donaldson turned the engines on and nudged us toward the beach. We stopped a few yards out and gently drifted in until the bow of the launch scraped on the gravel. Donaldson jumped down, his sea boots splashing, and pulled us closer.

Taft handed him the lantern, and Donaldson went over to the pile. I could see the official maple leaf mark stamped on the side of the crates.

He set down the lantern and hefted the first one. He brought it back slow, walking carefully across the slippery gravel. He passed the first case aboard. We were real careful not to drop it.

We got the rest of the cases stowed, and after the last one, Taft handed Donaldson a burlap sack.

"Put it on the beach."

I itched to know just how much money was in that bag. Donaldson set it on the gravel and returned with the lantern. He pushed us off the beach and jumped aboard.

Taft growled to us in a low voice.

"Wait."

We stayed there bobbing up and down, and a dinghy passed us, the oars dipping and splashing. They grounded on the beach. Someone jumped out, retrieved the sack, and got back in. They rowed past us again, toward the cutter, without a word. Once the dinghy had made it back to the cutter, Taft gave the word, and Donaldson fired up the engines. We chugged out of the lee into the channel, and I let out my breath.

We motored through the night back to the house. As we came up to the dock, I saw someone watching us from the upstairs window. The light went out when Cain came down to the dock in a coat, rubbing his hands. He looked at Taft.

"Any problems?"

"Milk run. Easy, just like you said."

"Excellent. You boys bring those cases up. And be careful with them."

Taft and me carried one case between us, and each trip Donaldson got one by himself. Cain took us around back to a cellar door, and we stacked them against a wall.

When we were done, Taft gave me the envelopes. Donaldson's cut was fifty bucks, but I took ten for my fee and handed him the rest. It was more money than he'd seen in awhile, and I thought he was going to faint. And he owed it all to me for making him a bootlegger.

#

We made more runs, with only slight changes. After the Canadians on the cutter had seen us a few times, they dropped the beach nonsense. They didn't want to do any more work than they had to. Instead, they had us pull up alongside, and Donaldson would board the cutter and go below to bring up the cases. They got more relaxed with every run, and we saw fewer guns each time.

Things went well until the night of the storm. Donaldson had said we shouldn't go, but when Cain wanted whiskey brought in, you didn't argue.

So there we were, chugging along as the launch rocked every which way, and the waves threatened to broadside us. When we reached the cutter, I saw the storm was knocking her around as well. The crew was hanging on to whatever they could. It was damned hard loading the cases with everything soaked and slippery, and the deck pitching from side to side.

Once out of the protection of Little Seal, the wind hit us hard. There was no way we were going to survive that run across the open water, so Donaldson turned the launch to hug the shore of Big Seal. We set out the sea anchors in a cove and waited it out.

It was a wet, rough night, and a cold one. Taft and I stayed in the cabin, drinking from our flasks, while Donaldson kept watch until dawn. We finally made our way through the chop back to Cain's. The light was in the sky and Cain stood outside as we pulled up. He stormed down to the dock, looking furious.

"Damnit, Taft, where the hell were you?"

"Storm. We'd a sunk if we'd tried before now."

"We have to get that whiskey out now. Hurry up, before someone sees."

We sweated and slipped as we loaded the crates from the launch into two shiny new Packards. Donaldson must have caught a chill in the night, because he was all white. Twice he almost dropped a case. Cain looked at him and shook his head, then looked at me.

"Come with us."

I jerked my head at Donaldson, who looked barely able to stand. "What about him?"

"He can wait here until we get back."

I didn't give him another thought. I guess that's where the trouble started.

#

Donaldson came down sick from that night, and I went to check on him to see if he could still work. My heart just about stopped when I saw Cain's wife leaving his place.

Inside, Donaldson was in bed. He looked like holy hell, but he was smiling.

I started yelling. "You stupid jerk! What the hell are you doing? What was she doing here?"

"Serena?"

"Who? Oh, God, no. Are you trying to get killed? If Cain finds out—"

"Then he better not find out."

"Dammit, Donaldson, you know in a hick town like this there's no secrets. What if someone tells him?" I hoped to God no one would be stupid enough. I sat down and made him tell me the whole damn story.

When we'd left him at Cain's, the missus saw him standing outside and took pity on him, like you would a wet dog, I suppose. Of course she took him in and let him warm up. They talked for a long time, he said. I held my head in my hands. Donaldson didn't know much about women, and here he'd gone and fallen for the wrong dame.

"Donaldson, you gotta tell her she can't ever come back here. It ain't safe. He'll kill you."

Donaldson was quiet, staring up at the ceiling.

"Everything I've ever loved has been taken away from me." He rolled away to face the wall. He hadn't heard a word I'd said.

#

It was all going to hell. We got word that some other gang was trying to muscle in on our action, so we kept a spare pistol and a shotgun stashed in oilcloth in the cabin, and packed sandbags inside in case there was shooting. I tried to get Donaldson to carry a gun, but he was too much of a dope. Said he'd killed enough people in the war.

Then one night when we went to pick up Taft, Cain and his wife were yelling at each other. We were standing inside, by the kitchen door. She ran in and Cain came after her, still yelling, even when he saw us. He grabbed her wrist, and when she tried to pull away, he slapped her. Donaldson started to move, but Taft stood in his way with his hand inside his coat.

"You don't want to do anything stupid."

"You better not do that again," Donaldson said to Cain.

"WHAT?" Cain bellowed. "You dare speak to me like that? You work for me! You're just the hired help." Cain panted and wiped his sleeve across his mouth. His eyes glinted as he looked at Taft.

"Get him out of here. Take care of this."

"Mr. Cain," said Taft. "I see no reason why we can't make our run tonight. I can move things up a bit."

Cain actually smiled. That was when I got worried.

"Yeah, good. Get it done tonight, then."

I hustled Donaldson out of there. Suddenly I didn't feel so smart.

A fog was coming in, and Donaldson put the running lights on. I was thinking about what Cain and Taft had said, and my stomach hurt. After what he'd said, I knew Donaldson wasn't coming back from this trip, but I didn't know if I would be, either.

My teeth were chattering as we cruised out to Little Seal and made it to the cutter. Taft made me go get the shotgun, telling me there was going to be trouble. Hands shaking, I got the gun and made sure it was loaded, and tucked it under my coat.

We pulled up alongside. Donaldson secured the launch and went aboard the cutter. Taft stepped on board and offered up his flask.

Next thing I knew, the shooting started. One of the cutter's crew looked at me and reached for something, but I got the shotgun out first and fired at him. He tumbled back, but a bullet hit my leg. It felt like someone had smacked me with a baseball bat. I fell to the deck and saw someone else fire at me. I let loose with the other barrel and he disappeared.

Then there was silence.

"Donaldson," I groaned, trying to hold my blood in with my hands. He came to the cutter's rail and returned to the launch. He had blood all over him and some bad-looking wounds.

"What happened?" I said.

"Taft. He just pulled out his gun and started shooting. The other guy jumped me. He knifed me, but I got him down. Taft shot the last guy in the stomach. He had his hands up, but Taft shot him anyway."

Donaldson started tying a bandage around my leg, which was hurting like hell. I thought I heard the sound of an engine somewhere out in the fog, which had closed in around us like a gray blanket.

A muffled shot came from belowdecks on the cutter. A minute later Taft came up to the rail above us, a leather satchel in his hands.

"Where's the other guy?" Donaldson asked.

"Didn't need him after he opened the safe." Taft held up the satchel. "Know how much is in here? More than you two will ever make in your life."

I figured that was especially true right about now. Here we were out on the deck, with nowhere to go. I was hoping Taft would shoot Donaldson first, so I might be able to pull my gun.

Taft had the satchel in one hand, and his pistol in the other. He looked like he was about to speak, when the night erupted in explosions. Taft jerked like a marionette, the satchel and pistol falling onto the launch. Taft sprawled against the rail of the cutter, his mouth working soundlessly.

A ghostly voice came from the fog on the other side of the cutter. "Anybody left?"

We said nothing and Donaldson untied the line, pushing us away.

"I think they're all dead," came another voice, deeper than the first.

"Let's make sure, then we can go finish off Cain."

"I never burned a place before."

"Yeah, well, boss wants to send a message."

"What about the boat here?"

"It ain't going nowhere in this fog. We'll make sure and come back for it tomorrow."

We had the cutter between us and them. Since we were near the rocks, Donaldson started the engines. They roared to life, and he pushed on the throttle to get us out of there, heading for the channel.

I didn't know what they had for a boat, but it must have been as fast as ours. We heard them coming after us, and they started shooting. A series of dull thuds smacked into the launch. Splinters ripped through the air, and one sliced my cheek open.

I thought they had us, but the fog threw them off. I could hear them motoring around, and they fired more shots, but no more came near.

"Get me a doctor." I said. My head was swimming.

"We have to get to Serena first."

"Donaldson, no, we gotta—"

"I have to. They're going there to kill them. I have to get her out of there."

I tried to argue, but blacked out. When I came to, the boat wasn't moving, and Donaldson didn't answer when I called. I didn't know how long I'd been out. I pulled myself up and saw that we were at Cain's dock. If that other crew got here, I'd be a dead man. I picked up the shotgun and used it to push myself up to stand on my good leg. Gritting my teeth, I could get along with the shotgun as a crutch.

The fog had thinned some, and I saw the lights from the house. I started for them, and almost tripped over the satchel Taft had dropped. That fool Donaldson had thought more of the dame than the money. I was no fool, and took it with me. It wasn't easy, but I wasn't about to leave it behind.

Inside the house I heard voices arguing, and I called out for Donaldson. I followed the sound, and found the three of them all standing in a room like they didn't know what to do.

Donaldson had a gun on Cain. He looked dangerous, and I wondered if he'd had that same look when he was fighting the Germans.

I collapsed into a chair, dropping the shotgun, but holding on to the money. My leg was bleeding again, and Cain looked blurry as he stood by his desk.

"You won't shoot me in cold blood. And that guy looks dead already."

Donaldson turned to look at me. I saw Cain reach inside a drawer and come up with a pistol. There was a hellishly loud sound in the room. Cain fell back against the wall and there was a scream. I blacked out with the shot still ringing in my ears.

#

I woke up in a hospital bed after they'd removed the bullet from my leg. Donaldson had called the cops before he took me to the doctor, and they'd shown up at Cain's with an armed posse. They'd caught the other gang just after they'd set fire to the house, and that was it for our competition, all four of them shot down like dogs. There was no trace of Donaldson, Mrs. Cain, or the satchel of money, but one of Cain's Packards had gone missing.

They sent me to jail, and about a year later I got a letter from somewhere down in Mexico, it didn't say where. Donaldson and the widow Cain had bought a small fishing boat, and a little house close to the shore.

I held the letter and looked out through the bars to the open sky beyond. I guess he was the smart one after all.

∞∞∞∞

The Brokenhearted Leper
by William Knight

Froth was my cellmate. He was a leper. Not the contagious kind. The kind of man kept alive for the sport of nasty children, and dismissive nobles--who shunned his outstretched hand as if it brandished a dagger.

"She was a sight, my lad. A true beauty," he said longingly.

I nodded, feigning interest in his oft-told tale.

"If it wasn't for this accursed affliction."

Light seeped through the bars, illuminated Froth's deformity in a dazzling ochre haze. I tried not to flinch, but failed. Froth noticed and clammed up, his one good eye leaking betrayal.

Somewhere, in another cell, a woman cried. Her incessant wailing clamored off the moss-bitten stone walls. In reply, a heartless soul yelled for her to "pipe down."

I hunkered down in the dirty straw and pulled the flea-riddled blanket tight around my shoulders.

A rat lazily tracked a course outside the bars, stopping to sniff in my direction, as if mocking my incapacitation. A pockmarked hand darted out of the shadows, snared the rat, and it disappeared in a fit of furious squealing to become a desperate prisoner's meal.

Froth sighed reluctantly. Obviously he'd decided to forgive my effrontery and continue with his well-heeled yarn.

"Hair the color of golden wheat, skin unblemished as a babe's. And the sound of her voice, ah..." He scratched at a knobby pustule under his occluded eye. "I'd wager it was the loveliest in the known world. I can hear it now. La, la, la..."

I buried my face in the blanket. No doubt it lost something in the translation, but Froth's wine-soaked pipes did little to curry favor for his erstwhile love's singing acumen.

The singing ended abruptly with a wealth of wet hacking.

I heard more than saw, Froth roll into his dirty mound of hay. His blanket was cleaner than mine, the stitching given less to abandon. It used to belong to me. He'd 'accidentally' wrapped himself in it one morning while I was sleeping. He could keep it--contagious or no.

Froth hummed quietly to himself.

I was left to make peace with sleep as best I saw fit. No easy task. Thoughts flowed like wine from a smashed cask.

I pictured the woman I'd had the audacity to become enamored with. Unlike Froth's long begotten mistress, mine had dark hair, and skin the color of cinnamon.

"Untouchable," was my mother's warning.

I did not heed.

#

Click, clack. Click, clack, came the sound of the guard's interminably slow slog.

Fate had conspired to berth me in a cell at the very end of the aisle.

Sometimes the footsteps reached our far flung quarters, though more often than not the slop bucket ran dry and we were left with only pangs of hunger for company.

When hungry, Froth became quite loquacious, and I less keen to hear his wistful reminiscences.

Click, clack. Click, clack.

A little more. I could smell the moldy broth. The clacking was so loud against the stone flags I could swallow it. Taste it in my mouth.

I heard greedy fingers claw at one of the earthen bowls proffered to prisoners.

Then the footsteps grew fainter. No! I squeezed my face against the bars and briefly caught the image of a receding sea-green tabard. Then the ungentlemanly bastard began to whistle.

Never mind us! Go back to your game of crook-hand, you knave. We'll be fine here with the greasy straw. We'll just chew on it like hobbled donkeys!

Froth released a plume of acquiescent air, akin to a spoken "Oh, well."

"Did I ever tell you about her horsemanship, lad? Well..."

My white knuckles stood out on the bars as prominently as the winter moon in a cloudless sky.

#

Warm sunlight ribboned through the barred window, cast even Froth's squalid skin in a healthy glow.

I stared at his moving mouth, hearing no words. His fingers, bubbled like leeward render, gesticulated as he spoke.

My temperate pity slowly gave way to loathing.

"Why are you here, Froth?" I asked.

His monologue ceased and he chewed his bloated lower lip. When he finally spoke, the words were flat and stilted like remembered verse.

"I had a bit too much to drink one morning, Yilkem. I'm afraid my penchant for plum wine has landed me in this pickle."

"You were thrown in the Tower of Chains for being wine-addled? Surely such a benign infraction is the province of the gaolers, not the Royal Guard?"

For once, Froth was silent.

#

The Tower of Chains abutted a fencing green. Bright green grass gave way to traipsing nobles in gilded raiment, leisurely sipping libations to the consternation of the many dispirited eyes watching their every move. Sometimes they doused themselves with water from leather jackets to the forlorn moaning of the parched prisoners.

Duke Tyril often frequented the green, flashing around in a powder-blue waistcoat with layered tails; looking for the entire world like a frilly-papered lamb chop. His gold-weaved, basket-hilted saber reflected the sunlight as he twirled, parried, and riposted.

Occasionally Duke Tyril would glance wistfully at the Tower of Chains, a smirk alighting on his handsome features.

I knew, despite the countless peering eyes, that his smirk was meant for me.

#

Froth's occluded eye is nestled between harsh-veined scar tissue. It stares out at me, night after night, catching the transient moonlight as it plies its trade.

Some nights I cannot sleep. I lie awake for countless hours staring at the opalescent deformation.

I wonder at times--does Froth know his malfunctioning eye so disturbs me? Why doesn't he sleep facing the wall?

I believe he does it to irritate me, to fray my slowly unraveling nerves.

A tumoral growth overhangs the loathsome eye, like a distended lintel.

Sometimes, though I know it is crazy, I think I see a sentient glint in the eye. As if it's dissecting my movements, keeping tabs on me.

The Tower of Chains is a place where paranoia is allowed to fester. Like Froth's diseased skin, it will make abominations of us all.

#

"Tell me about your lady," said Froth.

I didn't respond at first. Instead I mulled over the proposition. I had no desire to dangle sentences before the leper, just so he could augment his own tedious stories.

"She is not my lady," I decided to say.

"Ah, jilted love. I know it well, Yilkem..." he began.

"Kensha did not jilt me," I said. I was angered by his presumption. As if he could understand the complexities of my affair. Always the old mistake experience for wisdom.

Froth reached out with the greasy spikelet's he called fingers and pawed the air. "I apologize, Master Yilkem. No offense intended, I assure you." His voice warbled and pitched with the theatricality of a performing minstrel, and I was not assured of the sincerity of his apology.

I turned away and stared at the small square of light, which teased us with the morning sky.

"Fine," I muttered at last--more to quiet the old fool than out of honest forgiveness.

"Kensha, you say? A lovely name, for a no doubt lovely maiden."

I smiled despite myself. I'm ashamed to admit that I'd forgotten the name of Froth's long lost love. Had he ever mentioned it? I wasn't certain. I asked.

Froth seethed with rage; his puckered skin alighted with crimson. Is he angry at my ignorance?

I apologized, but he turned it away with a venomous wave.

He muttered belligerently and turned to face the wall.

For once, his obscene eye is cloistered from view. And yet, I was still uneasy   "You'll see," he spit out. "By the Gods, you *will* see!"

#

I pressed my face to the rust-flecked bars. Two guards were removing a prisoner in a shoddy wheelbarrow. One held a lantern at arms reach, his mouth swathed in linen.

They were laughing. The faint remonstrance echoed uneasily on the ashlar walls of the cell, which were so unused to the cheery sound.

They unceremoniously dumped the recently departed in the barrow the tower's prisoners had dubbed 'clemency.'

The prisoner was wheeled away. Finally free from the Tower of Chains. Many eyes that watched the scene unfold, including mine, are full of envy.

#

"I can't remember her name," said Froth. He pounded a scab-crusted fist against his lumpy forehead. "I can't." His voice was beseeching.

I nodded. Froth hadn't spoken in over two days. For some reason it was a pleasure just to hear his raspy voice once more.

"What happened?" I asked.

He lowered his head and it disappeared into his soiled blanket.

"It was spring," he said. "Dying heather dusted the air; the scent of pine-risen was a rich companion. We had a cottage, I think. She was there one day, gone the next. Fell into some mischief. I searched for her for ages. I called her name. I called..."

He started to cry. His shoulders heaved and ebbed, imploring a comforting arm to hold them tight.

I remained where I was, and courteously ignored the tears.

As if Froth's sobbing were the enticing keening of a dog, a prisoner in the adjacent cell joined in and began to weep.

Tears were free in the tower. They're the only things that are.

#

Lurker inhabits the cell across from ours. His appellation is duly earned. All day long he traversed his miniscule quarters. Back and forth, back and forth. Sometimes he would pause and giggle like a man possessed, the sinews standing out on his neck in sharp relief to the pallid skin.

His cellmate didn't seem to mind, though. His cellmate is dead.

They've yet to remove the body. Apparently Lurker's sin against the crown is on par with my own. He gets a corpse for company, I get a leper.

The smell is stupefying, and I could easily commiserate with Lurker.

His sin must have been great indeed.

#

Kensha. As I languished away in the moldering cell with the diseased Froth, I tried hard to forget her.

She was lost to me. As sure as I would never feel the warm spring rain again, I would never hold her in my arms. Never smell her, never touch her. She smelled of alyssum, and her skin was smooth as silk.

Parthic warned me to be cautious. I ignored his warning to my eternal damnation.

In the cell across from ours, a rope was tied to the stubby iron bars of the window. Lurker swung from the end of the rope, his eyes bulging, a maniacal grin etched for all eternity on his face.

He is still at last.

#

"Hair the color of golden wheat, Yilkem. Have I told you?"

"Yes. You've told me. Many times, Froth. Many times."

"Oh." He cackled, his one good tooth standing out in its isolation. "Guess I must have. Tell me of your woman."

"I've told you. She is mine no longer." Perhaps she never was. She was Duke Tyril's as sure as the sky belonged to the ravens.

"Duke Tyril?"

Had I spoken the thought aloud? I shifted uncomfortably.

"Please." Froth leaned forward, his fetid breath an invading force upon my senses. "I love stories of courtly intrigue."

I had no desire to relive my naivety, but something in Froth's anticipatory countenance changed my mind. "I became enamored with the Duke's mistress."

"Ha! The foolishness of youth."

Nice of him to put it so subtly. "At least I remember her name."

Froth's mouth dropped open. He turned to the wall. "You'll see!"

"What will I see, Froth?"

He turned to face me, a cruel sneer contorting his face. "You'll *see*."

#

Froth rarely spoke to me anymore. Occasionally I would catch him sneering in my direction, but for the most part we ignored each other.

The spring had turned to winter, and a cold, biting wind howled through the small window. Sometimes it brought with it crystalline flakes of snow. They settled uneasily on the soot stained floor.

The blankets prisoners were afforded in the Tower of Chains are of poor quality and I'd spend the entire night shivering. Froth for his part seemed unaffected by the abysmal weather. Maybe it had something to do with his condition.

I wondered why he was still here. Maybe he'd lied to me about the manner of his incarceration.

Lurker still hung from his escapist rope, the eyes still bulged. Why didn't they take him away?

#

"What was her name, Froth?"

He snarled at me and dug his bony fingers into his bowl of slop. My own bowl of lukewarm soup remained forgotten beside me. I will get my answers.

"Tell me," I holler. The shout echoes off the riven walls.

"Leave me alone," he said.

I leaped over and grabbed him by the collar of his greasy tunic. His one good eye went wide with shock and the clay bowl tumbled to the floor, its priceless contents draining away into the mortared cracks.

"Tell me!"

He licked his lips. "Dreva."

"What happened to her?"

"She went missing, I told you."

"No!" I shook him roughly and he moaned in agony. I could almost hear his old bones clicking in response. "She didn't."

Tears started to roll down his cheeks. "No. Please." He voice was tinged with sorrow. "I beg of you."

"Tell me what happened, leper."

"I...I killed her."

I released him and he slumped to the floor. He clutched at the dirty straw and sobbed quietly.

Stunned, I stepped backwards; leaned against the wall. "Why?"

"She was unfaithful. My precious Dreva. I tried to apologize. I begged the Gods to bring her back, but it was too late." He held up his hands as if they were the ones to blame. "I loved her."

"But she didn't love you?"

"No," he said quietly. "Not enough."

#

The harsh snow made a mockery of the sun. It hid behind the clouds and Froth and I were left to languish in the shadows.

He continued to talk about his love as though he'd never admitted to me that he'd killed her.

"Someday I'll find her," he said. "Soon I'll be free from these bars."

"Maybe," I said noncommittally. I could leave Froth with his delusions; he had little else, after all.

"Soon the Duke will come for me."

I sat up. "Duke? What duke?"

He spluttered and shook his head. "I misspoke." He turned and buried his face in the blanket and hay.

I eyed him warily. The leper had more secrets.

#

It was the middle of the night. The moon was a frozen disc in the night sky and a layer of hoarfrost coated the floor of the cell. I crept over to Froth. He muttered lightly in his sleep, imploring some unknown threat for leniency.

I ripped off the blanket and grabbed him around the neck, cringing at the feel of his slimy, spongy skin.

"Wha…" he started.

I squeezed. Froth hacked violently, his palsied fingers scratching wildly.

"Why are you here?" I whispered. I eased my grip just a fraction.

"Please."

"Why?"

"I was drunk one night..."

"No." I smacked him across the face. He whimpered and tried to wiggle free. "Tell me the truth, leper."

"Murder," he finally choked out.

"I know that. I know you strangled your love. Dreva, was it? You deserve your fate, murderer. Why did Duke Tyril send you?"

I held his gaze for half a minute. His gleaming eye examined me. Finally he relented. "To infect you, Yilkem."

"What?" I released him and stumbled backwards, my heart racing, my senses dulled with fear.

Froth shakily pulled himself to his knees. A cruel laugh percolated out of his throat. "I am the punishment for your sin."

I screamed. "No! You're not contagious."

"A lie. Sorry, lad. It's too late. You're surely infected by now." He laughed harder. "I warned you. You'll see, I said. Remember?"

"Why?"

"Ah, that's the most beautiful part. Duke Tyril promised to set me free. Said he'd have his mage heal me. They'll remove this diseased husk and I'll be cured." He cackled anew.

I moved forward as if in a daze. Froth continued his throaty laughing until I bore down on him. My hands gripped his throat of their own volition. I squeezed.

Froth struggled futilely.

Soon he was limp. One lifeless eye. His torment over.

#

My cellmate's name is Banson. He hides from me in the corner and screams when I come near.

I am a leper. I understand his hesitation.

"Have I ever told you of Kensha?" I asked him. "Hair the color of the night sky..."

∞∞∞∞

Eye Quest
by Jeffrey Freedman

Eyes—all he could see were her eyes and eyebrows, nothing else. Cat-like eyes. Seductive, beautiful eyes, green eyes below sharp, straight jet-black eyebrows. He could spend an eternity staring into those hypnotic eyes. They began to move away, and he followed them. He saw the flash of her inviting mouth, and he chased. Long flowing blonde hair bounced off her bare neck. He reached and missed. Two perfect breasts flashed before his eyes, and then her discarded negligee flew into his face. He pulled it away from his face…and stared at a green translucent rectangular thing in the center of his dish.

I know what that is. I'm sure I know what that is. He tapped the side of the plate, and the vibration jiggled the green square. *What is it called? I know it. I know, I know what it is, but I can't remember.*

A tall man in a white lab jacket entered the room, escorting a young woman dressed in a red blouse and skirt. She smiled and held out her hands. "Mother," he sobbed as she enfolded him in her arms. He looked up and saw the garbage truck careening toward the driver's side door, her door. "Look!" he yelled, pointing. But she wasn't looking, and she wasn't listening. Instead, she yelled, "No, you listen to me—" Everything moved in slow motion. He could see her hand pointing aggressively and a hint of a blue sleeve. Then his world imploded.

"Aaaaa!" Bob screamed, shooting up out of bed. His body straightened, and pain radiated down his back. As he rotated his shoulders, the pain intensified and travelled up his spine. He looked out the window, but it was still dark. Then he glanced at the clock on the end table.

Damn. It was just past 3:00 a.m.

He closed his eyes and tried to remember the dream. This time, he had seen her breasts, lovely, beautiful breasts. He closed his eyes and tried to picture them again, but the memory was fading fast. He picked up a pencil and pad and began to sketch quickly before the memory faded. He had seen her in more detail. Dozens of images of the same catlike eyes hung about the room, as if all watching to observe Bob's progress. Some were partial faces, which included lips and hair. A few even had chins and cheeks.

He put the pencil down and examined his new masterpiece. This time, he had also sketched the curve of her neck, her long flowing hair, and those perfect breasts. This was his best sketch yet, with by far the most detail. He studied the sketch carefully and wondered who she was. *How could have I remembered her breasts?* he wondered. *Could she have been my lover?* He must have known her just before the accident. He couldn't remember, but he intuitively felt the connection. If his mother knew anything, she didn't want him to know the truth. But he thought that he had seen a hint of recognition in his mother's eyes when he'd asked and she'd denied knowing anything about the girl. Bob remembered his mother awkwardly avoiding eye contact and looking uncomfortably at her hands— highly suspicious, but not definitive proof.

It was possible he'd had a crush on the girl from afar, but he knew his feelings were real. Every time he stared into her eyes, his heart ached, and his body yearned for her. If only he could remember who she was, perhaps he could find her. But his mother seemed to be hiding all evidence of the girl. They had moved across the country immediately after the accident, and he couldn't persuade his mother to visit their old neighborhood. She had insisted that he was too weak to travel and that she was just trying to protect him. He found that impossible to believe.

Bob looked again at the clock—it was 3:35 a.m.—and he thought about the room. He smiled. He could search the room today. His heart raced at the thought. He carefully put the sketch under his mattress, stumbled out of bed and pulled on a pair of pants.

His mother always kept the room locked. There had to be something great hidden inside. *Why else would she have locked it?* She claimed she was storing her grandfather's stuff while he was being cared for in a nursing home, and she wanted to respect his privacy. *Maybe.* But Bob intuitively felt that clues to his past were hidden behind those doors. Perhaps there was some information about his father. Perhaps there were pictures of his dream girl. Bob didn't know, but he had to find out.

He had originally planned to get into the room during the day by faking an illness to stay home from school. A year ago, he wouldn't have considered missing a class, but now school was easy. After his car accident, he had been virtually a vegetable. All memories of his life before the accident had been erased. The doctors called it a traumatic brain injury. But he had gone through extensive rehabilitative therapy for his body and his mind. After one year, he had relearned how to read, write, and do basic math. By the end of the second year, he was already better at math and physics than his teachers. Concepts came quickly to him. It was almost as if the injuries to his brain had somehow enhanced his abilities and transformed him from an ordinary student before the accident into a genius afterward. He didn't need school. He was smarter than all his teachers.

However, in the end, he had decided against staying home from school. His mother kept the motion detectors in the attic activated during the day. It was only in the evening when she was home that she turned off the alarm. That meant he would have to break in at night while she was asleep. And this could be the night. His heart raced at the thought. He imagined finding an address, buying a plane ticket, and travelling across the country to meet his dream girl. They would tear off each other's clothes and…Bob shook his head. He had to stop daydreaming and get into the room before his mother woke up.

He opened the top drawer of his oak dresser and pulled out a six-inch by three-inch metal plate labeled "Flat Monkey". Bob put the monkey in his pocket and carefully walked into the hallway. As quietly as he could, he crept up the wooden staircase. The top of the staircase opened up into an unfinished room with slanted rafters that gave it the look of a prism with pink insulation stapled between the joists in and on the floor. Bob walked as quietly as he could along a narrow plank in the center that prevented him from stepping through the ceiling. He reached the door at the end of the room and carefully placed the monkey at the foot of the door. In its current configuration, the monkey looked like a rectangular block of metal only half an inch thick, but when Bob touched the back, a tiny leg popped out of each of the four corners. Bob put on his control glasses and clicked on the arm to initiate the motion. Inside the glasses, he could see everything the monkey saw. He controlled the monkey using hand gestures and head movements as observed by the control glasses, which he had used many times to control his *Dragon Destroyer* video games. With no dragons to battle, controlling the monkey was easy.

Bob maneuvered the monkey under the door. Once on the other side, the monkey unfolded into a one-foot-tall, fully articulated robot with two legs, two arms, two hands, and a camera for a head. The monkey climbed up a two-by-four and leapt onto the door handle. Then it unlocked the door. Bob's heart raced as he carefully pushed the door open and looked inside. He dared not turn on the light. Instead, he pulled the monkey off the door and shone its pencil light around the room. Boxes of all shapes and sizes filled the interior. *This was it!* His past was almost certainly hidden in one of these boxes.

Bob saw a box that looked different from the others. It was newer, and a different shape. Curious, Bob opened it, looked inside and began to riffle through the papers and junk in the box. Bob picked up a picture frame and slowly flipped it over, expecting to see an image of his mother and his real father. But it was a picture of a group of three young men, two women, and a small child congregated in front of a brick house. Bob didn't recognize any of them, but the house seemed familiar.

He picked up what looked like a small white jewelry box. He opened it and saw a gold chain necklace attached to a flat circular gold compass with its needle pointing to his left. Next to the needle, a red light blinked slowly. Under the light was the number 33. Bob turned the compass in his hand, and the needle rotated so that it continued to point to his left. *Very strange,* Bob thought. North was to his back, not to his left. He noticed a small clasp on the bottom of the compass, like a locket, and carefully opened it. His heart skipped a beat. Inside he saw catlike eyes staring back at him as if from his dreams. He wanted to reach out and caress her cheek and her beautiful blonde hair. A flood of remembered emotions overwhelmed him. He could not remember specific events, but he felt joy, longing, and despair at not being with her. He closed his eyes and could almost smell her. He had no doubt that this was her, the woman in his dreams. Beneath the photo of her amazing angelic face, he read the inscription:

**Robert,
I am yours forever.
Love,
Cindy**

Cindy. Yes. That was right. The name felt right. Bob smiled. Now he had a name to go with the face. They had been lovers, he remembered. He closed his eyes and remembered her naked in bed at his side, smiling seductively. He had to have her. He had to touch her. He had to be near her. Then, with a sudden jolt, he realized that he could find her. He could find her today. The compass pointed the way. Thirty-three meant that she was only 33 miles away. She wore an identical compass around her neck, and they pointed toward each other. His heart raced. He would ride his bicycle to the ends of the Earth to find her.

#

Cathy stumbled out of her room and paused in the doorway, trying to force her body to wake up. She casually glanced at her watch. *Damn.* She'd never make it to the meeting on time. *Why the hell did I wake up so late?* Usually, Bob woke her up as he scrounged around in the kitchen for breakfast. That boy could wake the dead with all the racket he made. Cathy smiled, thinking about Bob. She could see dramatic improvements every day. He was already brilliant again. Now she was certain that she had done the right thing. She was actually starting to think of him as her real son. Now they were a family, and she hoped he would never find out or remember the truth.

Bob's door was still closed. *That's odd. He must have slept in.* She knocked. "Bob," she called. "Wake up! You have to get ready for school. You only have another 10 minutes…Bob?"

Cathy opened the door and saw his empty bed. "Bob!" she yelled. No answer.

She went back into her bedroom and sat down at her computer console. She typed a few keys and activated the tracking system that located the GPS chip embedded under Bob's skin. The map on the screen zoomed out from her house so that she could see a detailed map from space. *Where the hell are you?* she wondered. Then she saw a red dot flashing on the map. Terror rose through her body.

Oh God! No. He must have remembered something from his past. He was heading toward the home he had lived in for most of his life. What would happen to him when he got there? Cathy closed her eyes and imagined him finding out the truth. Her stomach tightened into a knot. *I can't let that happen!* Somehow she had to find him and stop him.

#

Dressed in shorts and a bike helmet, Bob raced his bike down the suburban street, following the compass heading. The trip odometer read 40 miles and, according to the compass, he still had another 10 to go. It was difficult navigating with only "as the crow flies" directions to guide him. He had a GPS attached to his steering wheel, but he didn't have a destination to enter. He had already run into several cul-de-sacs.

Bob looked at the street sign and stopped to study the GPS map to see if turning left would lead to a dead end. A young boy and a girl chased a ball around a yard shaded by a brick Mae West house. The ball bounced across the sidewalk, and Bob stopped it with his foot. As he bent over, pain shot up through his back. He used the bike to push himself to an upright position and tossed the ball to the children. He looked at the other children playing in the other yards and wondered what it would be like to live the rest of his life with Cindy.

An eclectic mix of Mae West homes filled the community. The builder had designed each house in a different style. Several had brick exteriors, others had a more contemporary look, and Bob had even seen one built in a Tudor style. However, they all had the same basic shape that maximized outdoor yard space and indoor floor space. Like Mae West herself, the buildings curved in at the waist, although you had to imagine that the below-ground basement represented her hips. Bob had seen a picture of the interior of a Mae West house in a magazine. The ground floor was nothing more than staircases that led up to the second floor and down to the basement. It was only about ten feet wide by fifteen feet deep, leaving plenty of room for outdoor yard space.

Anticipating his meeting with Cindy, he began to feel nervousness in the pit of his stomach. Had someone told her he was dead? Had she gone on with her life? It was a distinct possibility. She had apparently never tried to find him. Or perhaps she had tried but couldn't. Maybe she had searched fruitlessly and had found no trace of him. Then Bob thought about the compass. *She must have known where I was. Why didn't she visit?*

Bob opened the compass. Studying her face, he realized that she looked older than a 15-year-old girl. Much older. She looked more like 20 or maybe even 30. Bob had a sudden revelation. *He had been dating his teacher. That explained everything.* He had read about students having affairs with their teachers. That was why his mother had hidden the past from him. That was why Cindy hadn't come to find him. They had been secret lovers. It all made sense now. Bob's heart soared now that he had finally figured out the truth. Once he found her, they'd have to escape to a foreign country with less strict morality laws. Maybe Tahiti. It didn't matter as long as they were together.

#

Cathy gripped the steering wheel so tightly her fingers turned white. She had to find Bob before anything happened, before he found out anything. All she cared about was finding Bob, bringing him home safely, and preventing him from finding out the truth. Her son, Bob. Yes, damn it, her son.

She pulled the car into the intelligent highway's acceleration lane, and the car took control. The car accelerated to 120 and pulled into the fast lane. Cathy pried her hands off the steering wheel and lay back in the seat.

Cathy closed her eyes and prayed that Bob was still okay. *Why now?* He was so happy and finally fitting in at school. Almost normal. Cathy held her face in her hands. *How much of the truth did he remember?*

She recalled that day three years earlier when she had first entered the mental rehabilitation center. A dozen children, all with traumatic brain injuries, filled the first room she passed. From the outside, at least, they appeared happy, all playing together in some kind of supervised recess.

Cathy held her head in her hand and tried not to think about it. *What would happen if he learned the truth?* She knew that he didn't have much time left, and she prayed with all her soul that his last years would be happy years.

#

Bob saw the small brick building, stopped the bike, and looked at the compass. He had another half mile to go, but he recognized the building. It was the building in the photo he had found in the box. Bob stared at the house and began to imagine himself walking through the doorway. He crossed the foyer and saw a nondescript woman wearing an apron walking into the kitchen. On the table, he saw three cooked chickens, a bowl of mashed potatoes, and a salad. The countertops were covered with cakes, cookies, pastries, candies, and chocolates.

The woman in the apron picked up a plate of chicken and began to walk toward him, but he couldn't see her face. A dozen small children raced by, pushing him aside. Someone bumped against him, and he turned to see an infectious smile. His mother's smile...but it wasn't his mother. Bob clearly pictured a young child with his mother's face racing away through a familiar home. *How can that be?*

He remembered the child. *Cathy?* As the realization of the truth flooded his thoughts his face fell.

He looked at the compass, which told him only half a mile further. He now knew what he would find a half a mile away in the direction of the arrow. *No...please, no...it can't be.* Bob felt as if his world were collapsing around him.

He got on his bike and raced as fast as he could down the street. He didn't bother looking at the compass. He knew instinctively where to go. He rode up the driveway surrounded by the large metal gates. Bob looked at the compass, and his heart sank. He was less than a tenth of a mile from her. He pedalled down the path and stopped at the site. He awkwardly got off the bike and let it fall to the ground.

Bob closed his eyes and could see the garbage truck careening toward the driver's side door, her door. Then she turned toward him, and he could clearly see her catlike eyes before the truck smashed into the side of the car. "No...!" he screamed.

He opened his eyes and stumbled toward the tombstone. He read the inscription and the fifty year old date of her death. Then he fell to his knees and wept.

#

Tears streamed down Cathy's face as she entered the old neighborhood. The GPS tracker indicated that Bob was still a half a mile away. He had passed by the house and was heading toward the cemetery. He must have remembered everything.

She had always been afraid of this day. That was why she had mixed feelings about his progress in school. Everything had started to come back to him. His teachers thought that he might be some kind of savant but, in fact, he had been starting to recall subjects that he had already learned. And that was when Cathy suspected that he might eventually learn the truth.

She thought again about that day three years ago. In spite of everything, she did not regret her decision. She remembered passing the pediatric ward and then entering Bob's wing. The doctor had escorted her into his room.

Cathy had stared at the pitiful old man lying propped up in his hospital bed staring blankly at a cube of green Jell-O.

She had felt the blood drain from her face. She hadn't seen him in years, and he looked nothing like his former vibrant self. He had been a brilliant, respected man, the chief technology officer of a large communications engineering firm. He had given lectures around the world, and people had paid to hear him. Today, he probably didn't know his own name.

She regretted not travelling to visit him before. She had been his only grandchild and now he was her only living relative.

Cathy recalled all the wonderful presents he had given her over the years from all the exotic places he had visited: masks from Africa, boomerangs from Australia, a stuffed Beefeater bear from London. Cathy smiled; the stuffed bear still kept guard on her bed. Even when he couldn't visit her in person, her grandfather would always send something in the mail.

But it wasn't just the presents. He had been a wonderful grandfather. When she was 12 years old, he had taken her camping for the weekend. They had slept in tents and cooked marshmallows on an open flame. Even when the thunderstorm hit and everything had gotten wet, she had been happy just being close to him. Cathy recalled that even back then she had seen some of the first signs of the disease. He couldn't remember the word "marshmallow." Cathy bit her lip, trying to keep herself from showing too much emotion in front of the doctor.

The doctor walked to her grandfather's bedside. "I would really love to help you. But his insurance runs out in five days," he said. "But you'll be happy to know that he is completely cured."

"How can he be cured? He has the mental acuity of a two-year-old." Cathy remembered saying. "What am I going to do? He can't talk. He doesn't know his name. How can you say he's cured?"

The doctor had folded his arms and looked thoughtful. "The Alzheimer's is cured, but the brain damage is already done. Once a brain cell is dead, it stays dead. It would take years to train him. Your grandfather is an old man. He has lived his life. And his insurance won't cover rehabilitation. Can you afford a nursing home?"

Cathy didn't respond, but the doctor saw the look in her eyes and smiled sympathetically. "I'm sorry. He's too old. The young kids have their whole lives in front of them. That's why they're covered. We keep them here for a year of therapy, and then we put them into public schools. But they're children. I'm sorry there's nothing I can do."

Cathy's grandfather looked at her with large puppy-dog eyes. "Mother?" he cried feebly.

Oh God, he thinks I'm his mother, Cathy thought pityingly. She enfolded him in her arms. He pulled away and stared at the lamp perched on an end table. "Look!" he yelled, pushing her away as he ducked his head. Cathy knew he was reliving the car accident that had killed her grandmother nearly 50 years earlier. *Oh, Grandpa...how can your worst nightmare be your only clear memory?*

That was when Cathy brought her grandfather home with her and decided to feed him youth pills. She had been offered stolen youth pills from Susan, one of her co-workers at StarCross Pharmaceuticals. Apparently they were the result of a research project that had been stopped after several test subjects died of organ failure.

Susan explained that the physical manifestations of aging were primarily driven by cells with damaged DNA, lipids, and proteins. The youth drug introduced a genetically engineered virus that targeted and destroyed cells with significant damage while leaving undamaged youthful cells intact. With the damaged cells removed, the remaining relatively healthy cells would receive all the nutrients and could thrive and, in some cases, divide and produce new healthy cells.

Bob's looks changed slowly over a six-month period. His skin tightened. His muscles shrank in size but their strength and definition improved. Even his hair began to grow back, colored black after undamaged cells in his hair follicles apparently reproduced. However, since his bones didn't shrink significantly, he began to look like a gawky adolescent.

Cathy parked the car in the cemetery parking lot, got out, and began walking to the grave site. Poor Bob lay fast asleep on the grave. She knelt down and gently shook his shoulder. "Honey, wake up. It's time to go home."

Bob looked back at her wearily. "Mother?" he asked weakly. She could see the dried tear tracks on his face. She hugged him tightly and then helped him up to his feet. Together, they walked silently to the car.

∞∞∞∞

Blood of the Father
by Philip Roberts

For the first ten years of Charles Mclemore's life he knew only wealth and luxury. On his tenth birthday his father pulled him from his bedroom one bright, sunny afternoon, and led young Charles down plywood steps, across dusty cement, and through an entrance hidden behind an aged, rotted cabinet.

Eyes glistening with frightened tears and the sting of dusty air, Charles struggled against his father's grip, a man he'd known as a face more than a parent. He'd always seen his father's reddened eyes from a distance, pronounced jaw and chin firmly set whenever looking upon his own son. Hired help had tended to Charles's needs, the word father itself meaning little as Charles was forced down crumbling stone steps, their only light held in his father's outstretched hand.

They ended in front of a wooden door barely able to contain the bright red shining behind it. The sight silenced Charles, mute when the door opened and his father gently pushed him into the small room.

At first Charles thought he stared at a nude man inside a wooden cage. The only light came from a metal stand with a red bulb on top of it, but Charles ignored the light to focus on the stranger hunched in the corner of the cage, his arms draped over his knees, the skin pale white.

The man's head lifted, shifted towards Charles, the movement sending ripples through the skin, bloating the flesh. The man had no face, the skin around the outside of the head pulled back into dark oblivion, and as the being pulled into a crouch, Charles could see the skin itself dripping to the hay covered floor.

Eyes pulled opened in the man's chalk white chest, ten of them in all, but melding together, turning the man's entire chest into a massive eye, his very arms being absorbed into the skin, empty face tilting upward. And then, in the middle of the eye another line formed, split it open into a toothless mouth. Charles barely heard a dry wheeze. It gave up on its attempt at speech before it could finish, pulling back into the corner instead, the more human form returned, except in the hollow face Charles saw the flesh pulling together, forming a replica of his own youthful features atop the pale, adult body of the entity.

Charles watched his father pull out a pocketknife and cut a deep gash in his own finger. He pressed the bloody tip to the glowing orb, and immediately the light shined brighter, forced the being in the cage to pull away from the glare, face returned to the void, arms pulling back over its watery flesh.

A gesture from his father led Charles out of the room. As soon as the door slammed behind them his father turned back on his flashlight and took up a seat on the bottom step.

"Dreams will start," his father said, staring at his bloody finger rather than his son. "Now it's marked you. Won't just be dreams, just where it starts, and eventually, you won't even be able to look in a mirror without seeing it standing behind you, waiting."

"What is it?" Charles asked.

"Your great, great grandfather had a thirst for something unique. Well, he did some research, and he summoned that thing in there. He learned too late he couldn't control it, couldn't make it do anything.

"When the whispers first came to him, he understood he couldn't release it, because it would get to him, and it would have vengeance. It had to stay contained, stay there forever. He made the orb, and his bloodline could keep it charged, keep the being captive, but nothing else.

"So he told his son about what he had done, and when he died, his son began coming down here as well, charging the orb with blood, and then his son, until my father brought me, and I've brought you."

His father led him back up the stairs in silence. He gently tucked his son into bed for the first time, and kissed his son's forehead. Charles fell asleep to the image of his father's dark form perched on a chair by the window. Three hours later, when Charles awoke screaming, thrashing wildly in his bed, his father had the syringe full of sedatives already in hand.

#

His father gave him ten years. Charles found the body in the bedroom, a still smoking gun clutched tightly in scarred fingers. He sent the servants away to bury his father himself in the backyard. No one saw him spit on his father's corpse.

That night he walked alone down the stone steps.

His father had confessed that he hadn't been told about the creature until he'd been in his early twenties, his own father able to bear the burden alone for far longer. The orb requires more and more blood as a person grows older, Charles had learned, and in the final year, as his father neared forty, Charles had watched his father rub a blood soaked hand on the orb in order to return its glow.

Now, standing before the hollow face, Charles needed but a drop or two, and the orb glowed so brightly the creature seemed to recoil in pain. The sight brought a smile to Charles's thin face.

He felt the creature's hatred physically wash over him as he turned to leave, and understood full well the magnitude of the thing he goaded, but having understood his damnation at such an early age, the idea of digging the hole a little deeper didn't bother him.

#

The mansion contained thirty-four rooms, including several bedrooms, two dining rooms (formal and informal), various rooms adorned with games of some kind, the majority of them outdated, three kitchens, and the portion of the house that had become the servant's quarters.

Charles stood, nude, on the balcony adjacent to his bedroom, the moon a thin sliver of light amid an ocean of glittering jewels. He could hear the sound of undisturbed sleep from the bed behind him, the woman, Rachael, unaware of the voiceless stream of noise constantly flowing through Charles's mind.

Rachael's beautiful face didn't stir as he left the bedroom. In the six years since he first began courting any woman his money attracted, Rachael was merely the third in a long parade of marriages. She had provided him exactly what he had wanted, the child he stood before, only a year old, sleeping just as peacefully as her mother.

He lifted the sleeping girl into his arms, careful not to wake her, and slipped down the basement steps. The dusty air didn't make her stir and cry until he was far from any ears to hear her. The frightened wail made him smile.

He stopped before his prisoner. The hollow face rose to meet his gaze, head tilted to the side, curious, it looked to Charles, and he hated that curiosity. He always detected a hint of amusement in the creature's body, even in the abyss of its face. He held out the screaming child, her young face wet red, tears pausing upon seeing the monstrosity crawling closer.

Every time he brought another child down here, saw the creature's skin pull forward into the face of the infant, Charles considered again whether this thing really did have thoughts, and what it thought of Charles himself. If it could feel, it never chose to have mercy on the children Charles showed it, and just as before, its face returned to nothingness, and it withdrew to its corner.

Before leaving he made sure to bite open the tip of his finger and torment his prisoner with the fierce glow.

By the time he reentered the nursery his daughter had drifted away. He pulled back, watched her intently, curious what her name was. He didn't know the name of his other children any better then he did this daughter.

An hour later he had the blankets pulled over him, Rachael's warm body beside him, his eyes closed as if asleep when the shriek echoed through the house. Only Charles didn't rush to the nursery to check on the screaming child. He returned to his balcony, unable to see the stars through the glare of so many lights turning on, everyone but him trying to console an infant forced to share the same fate as Charles. The thought made him smile.

The next day he threw Rachael and her infant from his home. A week later he filed for divorce.

#

Three jars full of dark red rested beside his feet. He opened a fourth above the glowing orb and drenched it with cold blood. In front of him the hollow face watched the thick red drip to the floor, but the orb's glow never changed.

Charles shattered the glass jar against the wall. He glanced upward briefly before hurrying from the room. Halfway up the stairs the exhaustion set in, the wariness of age in his muscles.

He knew which servant he needed. The young man was rarely on time, always stealing breaks whenever possible, and unreliable enough that no one would think anything of it if he started missing work. The boy barely had a chance to turn towards Charles's before the needle pierced his neck and dropped him to the floor.

Charles dragged more than carried the young servant down the stairs and into the prison. Sweat trickled down his forehead, through his graying hair as he lifted the boy up and took a knife to his throat over the orb. Hot red poured everywhere, down the side of the orb, pooled on the ground, a faint moan the last sound the boy would ever make. Charles threw the body against the far wall in disgust, the orb dimmer with every second.

He took the knife to his palm and pressed his hand against it. Even then the glow only slowly rekindled, his prisoner closer to the edge of the cage now, and Charles could swear he saw the glow of something within the dark abyss watching him.

"You won't have me," he shouted, hands trembling, unable to swallow.

He struggled up the steps, winded before he could reach the top.

When he reached his studies one of the maids asked him if he'd seen Julius. Charles informed her he hadn't seen the boy all day.

#

The hand caught him across the face before he could attempt to stop it. If he'd had a gun then, Charles honestly believed he would've shot Vanessa, but instead he struck her back, the sharp end of his cane cutting into her cheek.

He stepped out into the freezing February day with her voice screaming after him. Snowflakes floated around him and collected on the New York street. Just six months ago he'd never personally witnessed such poverty in his life. A homeless man on the sidewalk in front of the dilapidated apartment complex asked Charles's for money. He ignored the request and stepped into his limousine.

Before threatening to call the police Vanessa had shoved the photograph into Charles's hands, and he ran a finger over the wide-eyed boy, no more than six, in the picture, a forced smile on his face. The image reminded Charles of the few pictures he'd seen of himself during his teenage years.

The boy, Fredrick, had taken a screwdriver to his ear in an attempt to drive out the images Charles had grown accustomed to. Fredrick was the fifth Charles had searched for. All but James had committed suicide. James had been the first child, and had somehow managed the longest, nearing thirteen when he knifed to death three of his fellow students before the police shot him dead.

How many were left? Charles watched the aged city flying by his window, but saw instead the faint red glow of an orb deep within his basement, the light fading with each day.

The driver couldn't see him slump back in the corner of the seat and cry. He wept without control, reddened nose a mess of watery mucus, hands trembling, crumpling the picture, mind crying desperately for some form of escape. Forty-seven years weighed too heavily on him, and he had only three more children to seek out before his condemnation was complete.

#

In their own way, the years had been crueler to Amanda than they had Charles. Neither retained very much of the physical beauty each had once been blessed with. Years of anxiety, lack of sleep, and poor appetite could be seen in the deep sags below Charles's eyes, the thin, gray hair atop his head, and the unsteady hand he held a cup of coffee with.

A single light bulb shined beneath a gaudy cover in the corner of Amanda's living room. Two cockroaches crawled aimlessly along the floorboards. Charles had to pause when the train roared by, rattled the windows.

Amanda's slender frame had bloated considerably in the sixteen years since he'd first seen her. Her eyes marked her own lack of sleep, caused by late nights at a second job to pay the rent for the awful dwelling she inhabited. Charles hadn't been content in his youth to simply divorce those he'd been with, but to try robbing every last penny he could, imbue in them the same misery he lived with every day.

He could tell in the sharpness to the eyes Amanda held him with she had learned her lesson. He couldn't hide his eagerness towards the boy seated beside her, his only, as Charles had come to conclude, child left. Violence haunted the boy's distant eyes.

"I want it in writing," Amanda told him, fingers clasped tightly around her knees.

"You'll have it," Charles assured her, and he was more than willing to. After all, he had already intended to will his full fortune to the boy. "All in the child's name, of course," Charles added.

"That's fine."

He knew what the smile plucking at the corners of her pudgy cheeks meant, along with the shrewd gleam in her eyes. She expected him to give his money to her son, who would then shower it all upon her, the hard working mother who had raised him. She didn't know how the sight of this boy's true inheritance would change him, would force him to drive away anyone he might've once loved. The visions it offered did more than simply frighten, but deadened the very senses, the ability to feel. Charles saw hints of it already in the child's demeanor.

Charles stood from the frayed, sunken chair and grabbed his hat from the door. "I'll have my people contact you shortly. Benjamin will have to come to live with me for a time as a part of our agreement."

"I will as well," she said, her eyes unyielding.

"A nuisance, Charles thought, but one worth dealing with. "Understood."

#

From its brightest glow, to the moment of no return, the orb could last exactly twenty-three days, the elder Mclemore had written in his note generations before. Charles's own tests had shown similar results, though he'd never allowed it to go beyond nineteen days, and even then only in his youth when a few drops was enough to bring a piercing light.

Now he journeyed daily down the confined staircase, hobbling with a cane for support, his left hand a mess of deep, vicious scars. Each time he became less capable of eliciting even a bright shimmer from the orb, forced to let his blood run until his head grew fuzzy and his vision dimmed. His days were certainly near an end, a very tragic end if not for the boy he dragged along behind him.

Benjamin gave little protest, heeding almost any request Charles made with the dutifulness of a student begrudgingly doing as his teacher tells him. Charles had seen Amanda kneel down on the day the two had arrived and ordered her son to follow whatever Charles asked of him.

The boy didn't protest even as they neared the wooden door, silent and hard eyed as Charles pulled it open. Only then did Benjamin's expression change, but to one of wonderment, rather than fear, walking slowly into the room to face the monster crawling towards the cage, barely contained anymore by the soft light.

Quick fingers grabbed hold of the cane beneath Charles's right hand before he understood what was happening. Charles crashed painfully to the cement, pain arching up through his arm from his elbow. He stared up into Benjamin's cruel smile, hands tightened into fists as he snapped the cane across his knee.

Charles smiled, laughed dryly. "What, were you waiting for this then?" He shifted to lean back against the wall, the low light of the orb casting deep shadows across Benjamin's youthful features, his black hair cut long, partially obscuring his eyes. "Suffered through the dreams, the visions, but adjusted, did you? Better man then I, I guess, but if you're seeking revenge on me, trying to feed me to that creature over there, I'm afraid there isn't much you can do to get at me. I've read more than you boy, and it doesn't matter if you throw me to the wolves, you'll suffer the same as I if you don't keep it contained."

Benjamin's eyes shifted back to the creature, to the depths of its face. He pulled a piece of paper from his pocket and held it to Charles.

He had to use his flashlight to see the picture drawn in crayon. He saw his tormentor, the liquid flesh bubbling and dropping down the body, and the head overly large, nothing but blackness inside it. The image looked like it had been drawn by a four or five year old, maybe slightly older.

"It really is the same," Benjamin said with wonder.

"It's your fate," Charles said.

But Benjamin shook his head, pulled another object from his pockets. It took Charles longer to understand what the boy handed to him, even in the glare of the flashlight. "What's in it?" He asked, staring intently at the small bottle.

"My brother's blood," Benjamin said. "He filled it about a day before he leapt from our roof. The dreams told him a lot, and he told both my mother and I about his heritage, and what you had done to him. He aged fast because of you."

"You've seen it," Charles said, groped forward at the boy, but Benjamin pulled away from his grip. "It'll mark you as well."

"It might, but my brother didn't believe it would, and I trust my brother more than I ever would you. I saw what you did to him."

"It's no worse than what my father did to me," Charles whispered, feeling broken in a way he'd never felt before, just an enfeebled old man as he groped once last time for Benjamin before the boy stepped into the doorway.

"I don't know how long the vial will last you," Benjamin said.

The wooden door slammed shut, and he heard the click of the lock falling into place. By the time he dragged himself over to the door, Benjamin had left, and the door wouldn't open, not that it mattered. He fell back to the floor laughing.

He struggled to pull himself up, unscrew the bottle, and let a few drops run across the orb, fill it with a light brighter than it had held in years. He watched his prisoner remain by the edge of the cell, its flesh sizzling, but it didn't pull back, relishing the pain, Charles thought, waiting patiently for its moment to come.

He stumbled back to the wall, the vial held tightly in his grip. How long could he keep the orb lit: certainly longer than he could survive without food.

The small vial shattered against the wall across from him. The splash of blood ran slowly down the stone. Charles's gaze focused on only the orb, ignoring the entity watching him, just waiting for the glow to start diminishing.

He tried to believe he was ready for whatever fate he had ahead, but deep down understood he could never be ready for a revenge over two hundred years of imprisonment had created.

∞∞∞∞

The Taco Bell Heist
by Robb White

Odraye Maybon Dremel IV was poorer than a shithouse rat and that was the entire problem and story of his life. Out in the street he was called OD and wore his Levi's below his buttocks so that his paisley boxer shorts were exposed to every passing car on Station Avenue; he wore extra-large white T-shirts like all his boys and kept his do-rag wrapped so the two ends flopped like tiny rabbit ears over the middle of his face. He woke up late, spent his mornings watching cartoons, his Moms had the satellite dish, courtesy of his dope-slinging cousin Venard.

The front door to the house was canted at a crazy angle–also thanks to his cousin, who happened to be running full tilt when he collided with it, and it just happened there were two white boys—cops—a half-step behind him, panting, batons and titanium flashlights at the ready, hoping to be able to get close enough to Venard so they could lay a couple good licks on him. *That was some motherfucker*, he smiled. He liked telling the story, had all them ass-scratching crimeys laughing. They could laugh, too, because big, tough Venard, down on the river in the state lockup, wasn't around to do anything about it. Three weeks after busting through Odraye's front door, Venard shot a cop in the face off 38th Street because of a warrant over some stupid traffic beef. Now he had a death penalty on him. *Too bad but fuck him; what did he ever do but push weed, buy stolen satellite dishes, and make babies?*

Odraye was a father, too, and that was a big part of the problem; his baby's momma was on him all the time about money now–money for clothes, money for food, money for toys–but shit, he had to live too, didn't he?

Truth was, Odraye was worried. He had to make an appearance every day, he had to represent. Time was, you didn't see fifteen, twenty youngbloods his own age hanging out on the corners in the middle of the day like this. Money was tight. Niggers from Cleveland, niggers from Erie, even niggers from Youngstown where the goddamned dago mafia was still supposed to be in charge–it all made for one combustible lifestyle in Odraye's hood. His boy Marquis got hisself all fucked up, too. His girl Tangela having a baby, and he ain't got money either so he walks into a bank with a note and a toy gun and gets himself a fifteen-to-life bid at the state pen in Youngstown.

Odraye missed the feeling of power from his high-school days when he and his boys ruled the corridors, took money from the white punks, and had all the blonde pussy they could handle. During football season when his body, taut with muscle after those brutal two-a-days, sprinted down the sidelines, and he imagine every female in the stadium watching him with desire. Venard had been quarterback when he was a sophomore and they were both all-city, all-county. Their TD hookups always made the sports pages. Venard's momma was white, which gave him a tan complexion. Odraye mocked him one time for having black freckles splashed across his nose and cheeks like Morgan Freeman–but his cousin showed him why nobody ever messed with him over that mulatto shit. He looked slow, his eyes half-shut. Then he hit Odraye under his heart with a right uppercut that left him nauseated for an hour. While he lay there gagging on the sidewalk, he could hear laughter, someone had even called him a *bitch*.

The glory days were gone, long gone.

Odraye looked out the curtain at the street. "Slingers, bank-robbing fools and death-row bitches—all we got in this family," he whispered to himself.

He had a letter three days ago from his girlfriend's lawyer, and though he couldn't understand all that legal mumbo-jumbo, he knew what *paternity* and *putative father* meant. He had told her and her mother both–that ugly, skinny witch–that wasn't his baby. Told his

Moms, told everyone, in fact: *No, man, that bitch spreads like peanut butter. It ain't mine.* The DNA test was going to hang him by his own dick and he knew it. You just had to look at Marcellus to see that that was his, had his smile even without all its teeth in its melon head. The boy even had that exact mocha skin color as Odraye, and even had his hip-hop athlete's shuffle.

Shit, he didn't have the three hundred it would cost. "I pay you back," he mumbled over his cereal. She said she was going to have to take the money out of her savings. Then out came the biblical quotations and the Jesus hoodoo-voodoo about the forces of darkness. He lowered his face closer to the cereal bowl so he wouldn't have to hear it. He had tried to drown her preaching ways out ever since he was a kid, but it always ate like acid in his guts.

Today was the day he changed his luck. The thought warmed him right in the pit of his stomach as he walked down the front porch steps. He might be leaving the house poor, but he was coming back rich, no doubt about it. He touched the Beretta's grip lightly with his fingertips–just the thrill of having the barrel against his skin stirred his bone to life.

Everybody knew Odraye went for any good-looking white girl he could nail, which is why Shyla wouldn't let him see his own son. But nobody knew his secret. Odraye once had himself a white boy from his high-school. When Odraye was a senior, he saved him from a serious beat down after the little fool sold bags of parsley around school for weed. Odraye ordered the punk to suck him off. Just like that faggot Demesio Lee, who used to suck off guys behind the elementary school for a dollar apiece.

When the kid was caught in a stolen car with five thousand dollars' worth of stolen video equipment, he was sentenced to the county's youth facility and Odraye never saw him again— until six weeks ago when Barry Reece left a message for him with a couple slingers from 44th Street when he stopped bought a rock.

Odraye didn't connect the name at first. Then he remembered how the kids used to mock his name: *Oh boy, lookie here, we got us a Reece's Pieces* . . .

"'the fuck he want with me, Dio?"

"Fuck if I know, man. He ain't say. He say he want to talk to you about somethin'."

Odraye took the number and looked at it. He called him that night. Barry worked at a fast-food in Cleveland on Chester Avenue just off the Shoreway. Confinement had done nothing to remove his desire to take other people's property, he said, and he told Odraye he had a plan to rob the Taco Bell across the street from his place.

"The manager's in on it," he said. "We can't fuckin' miss."

Reece worked the grill on the late shift at Burger King. His Taco man insider said his place ran the drivethru until two a.m. during summer hours, but they locked the doors at midnight. "A duplicate key, a single robber with a gun—the day's receipts are bagged for deposit and kept in the middle drawer of the manager's desk inside his office—you're in, you're out. We split two ways." The take was about five, maybe seven, thousand.

"Taco manager's a stone junkie, got a monkey size of me on his back," Barry told Odraye. "The guy can't kick the heroin so he has to have money," Barry begged him. "You can't pass this by, homes."

Calling him "homes" like that, *the stupid little whigger* . . .

Odraye asked why he didn't do it himself. Barry replied, "Even with a rod, who's going to take someone my size seriously?" Odraye said he'd think about it.

"Don't think too long, bro," Barry said. "Call me by three." He handed him the digits on a piece of paper.

Odraye thought about the lawyer's letter; he knew what he had to so. "Time to step up," he thought. It wasn't going to be no 50-50 split, no matter what the white punk thought.

They met before Barry's shift at his rental place on Canal Street about three miles off the Shoreway. Odraye promised to give Dio fifty by Saturday night if he let him borrow his clapped-out Escort. Dio knew better than to ask a brother what was up.

The place was a dump. Odraye knew he wasn't going to end up like this–slinging burgers for chump change, living in a place where there was no TV, probably rats under the floorboards. His tiny fleabag apartment on Canal overlooked the Cuyahoga River and the inner-belt traffic from downtown Cleveland, which was so close it made the windows rattle.

"You should see the Bell on a weekend night," Barry said. "Makes the White Castle in the theater district look like a four-star restaurant. Place is full of crack whores and drunks. Half the night crew is on parole or zonked on speed. Customers drive up all night, they, like, tokin' right while they're ordering food and shit. It's crazy, OD."

Now he's using my street tag, Odraye thought. Damn but he was going to fix this mutt when the caper was over. Reece was still going on about all the goofs and druggies. Odraye figured he'd better him play him for a while, act like he cared about this shit. He took the blunt Reece offered.

". . . this one fiend, the guy, he's got, like, these big eyes and he's sweating up a storm and mumbling shit you can't understand."

Odraye cracked a smile, nodded. *Fuck this little cracker asshole.*

"The meth customers are the best, man, twitching and spazzing all over the place," Barry said. "The whole place is tripping on weekends."

"Can you trust your guy?" Odraye asked.

"He's cool, my man," Barry said. "No problem."

Odraye was getting a little queasy from the joint Barry passed him. It was more potent than the wet he and his boys doctored up.

"Check these out, bro," Reece said. He dumped a box of hollow points on the table in front of Odraye. Odraye held one of the black snub-nosed shells up to the north-facing window like a diamond dealer inspecting a gem.

"You just nick somebody with one of these babies," Reece said, "his fuckin' arm will fly off."

"Listen to me," Odraye said and grabbed him by the shirt. "You better be not be high tomorrow night, motherfucker, and we ain't shootin' nobody, you hear me?"

"Yeah, yeah, chill, homey," Barry said, spinning it with his fake blaccent. "We're good. It's just for show, man."

#

In fact the plan was simple enough. The manager would lock the door at midnight as he did every night of the week. Barry would give Odraye the duplicate key just before the door alarms were set. Barry, eyes glittering, acted as if it were all so obvious, how to rob a place and divert suspicion.

The money would be bagged and ready for him in the second drawer of the file cabinet on the left side of the cubicle; the safe would be left open. The manager was going to throw a few bills around to make it look like the robber was rooting around inside the office. Barry loved telling him this next part. "'Surveillance cameras inside, naturally,'" the guy says, "so you'll have to hit him to make it look real."

Barry handed him the nickel-plated .44 Magnum. "So you're just gonna hit him with this?"

"Hey, fuck you," Odraye fumed. "I ain't into no murder shit."

"He got no alibi, Odraye. Better clock him good."

Odraye rolled one of the Black Talons between his finger and thumb and thought about its terrible fragmenting power, blasting flesh and bone into pink mush.

The surveillance camera behind Burger King was Barry's alibi. At exactly five minutes to midnight until ten minutes after he would be on camera–except for the moment when he would meet Odraye and hand over the key and gun at a designated place just out of view.

"It's a blind side," Barry said. "Everybody knows that, so if we want to smoke a joint on break, we go there."

"Why not just give me the fucking key and the fucking gun right now?"

"Because when I hand you the stuff in the parking lot, I'll know you ain't pimpin' me out," Barry said.

Odraye leaned across the table and pulled Barry up close he was out of his chair. "You forget that—that *Ocean's Thirteen* shit, ya hear? Put it back in your fucked-up brain, little boy."

Odraye made a vow to close accounts with Barry Reece tomorrow night. He drove back on Route 90 at a slower-than-normal speed and prayed Dio hadn't left any gear in the car. He knew he already stank of weed from that high-octane blunt.

He seized up every time he passed a statie. They seemed to be all over the interstate; they were pulling cars over like lions picking out antelopes on the savannah. Driving While Black was still a big crime in Northeast Ohio. One of Odraye's last high-school memories was of a warm spring day his senior year in history class half-dozing while that kike history teacher droned on about Stalin's purges of the Red Army and the Politburo, whatever the fuck that meant. He was cupping Shyla's right breast from behind, feeling her nipple harden through the skimpy halter top which barely contained her mounds. Then the Jew quoted that badassed dude Stalin: "'Two can keep a secret if one is dead.'" She giggled; then she purred. The carmine tip of her tongue darted out to lick the air.

"Don't nobody say I didn't learn nothing in high school," he thought. Then his mood darkened as he thought of her lately: nagging, bitching, screaming about the money he "owed" her and Marcellus.

Be a man, he told himself. *Tomorrow night, it happens.* Before he jumped on the interstate, he had picked out a spot in the Flats down by the river where he could lie low until eleven-thirty. The Tribe was playing Boston. He passed an LCD billboard sign on Riverfront Road advertising some dyke named Melissa Etheridge in town for a concert at the arena where Number Twenty-Three, King LeBron James held court.

#

In the one ill-lit of a parking lot near Shooter's, he kept hitting the fluorescent button of his watch. His face was shiny with sweat. "Just pre-game tension," he thought.

At ten minutes to midnight he was in his spot at the Burger King–just a few cars from where he had planned to be. The checkout girl, a lumpy retard, smiled back at him. At five minutes to midnight, he felt himself get a hard-on from tension wiring him up. He wiped his hands on his baggy shirt and noticed they were trembling. At two minutes to midnight, and no Barry, he was twitching from adrenalin-charged anxiety. He pounded the shit out of the sun visor.

Then he saw Barry walking right toward him—*oh no*, the stupid shit was staggering.

"Jesus, oh Jesus," Odraye said aloud. "He all fucked up on weed."

Barry dramatically paused in front of Odraye, dangling a key from his fingers like a tiny silver fish. He leaned into the window and smiled. "Tole you not to worry, man," he said in a too-loud voice. "The fuckin' cameras can't see this far out in the lot."

Odraye felt a big drop of sweat sting him in the corner of the eye. *I'll kill this little motherfucker when it's over . . .* He snatched the key out of Reece's hand.

"Gimme the gun, motherfucker," Odraye hissed.

Reece lifted up his shirt. The black butt of the gun stuck up next to his bellybutton.

Odraye grabbed it and jammed it into his belt.

Odraye pulled into the Taco Bell lot and jammed his Escort into park; the last of the customers walked out. Reece wasn't exaggerating: middle-aged hookers, derelicts, and teenagers on the prowl. For one long, dizzy moment, Odraye thought he was going to erupt into a fit of hysterical laughter. He actually began to get out of the car before he got himself under control. *Got-damn*, he was going to enjoy double-crossing this little fool.

He firmed a band-aid across his cheek. "If they see something, let 'em see that," he thought. He wrapped a couple folds of an Ace bandage around the palms of his hands like a boxer–just in case he had to make contact with anything that could take prints. The last item was one of Shyla's nylon stockings jammed down to his collar.

He speed-walked the short distance to the doors. The key fit. He felt the deadbolt slip and he pushed open the glass doors. He knew where to go—the partition separating the food handlers from the cash register gave him plenty of room. Odraye was so pumped he just missed cracking his skull as he cleared the counter in a two-handed leapfrog that propelled him onto the slick tile floor and made him skid off balance into a stack of canned tomatoes. He went sprawling across the greasy floor. In seconds he scrambled back to his feet, racing to the back where four employees were handling drivethru duties. "Don't let anybody spot you from the window," the manager told Barry. "The whole interior is lit up like one big stage."

Odraye discovered four open-mouthed youths staring back at him. One wore a head set for taking orders. Time slowed to molasses. Odraye pointed the gun at the floor and barked them down. "Get down, motherfuckers! Move! Now!"

They all went flat simultaneously–the fat girl's eyes bugged up at him. The other girl started to whimper, so he told her to shut the fuck up. He put the gun barrel to the nape of her neck. She whimpered louder, so he jammed it into the flesh hard and said for her to shut her mouth or he'd blow her head off. Terrified, she loosed her urine. One of the males looked up at him, straining against the ties, and pleaded, "Please, man, we don't keep no money back here." Odraye stepped to him and whipped the barrel across his forehead opening a bright gash. "Shut up, nigger!"

His eyes boxed the room for the surveillance cameras. There were three covering the room including the closed-circuit TV out front.

Their eyes bored into him. When he turned, he noticed a grossly fat middle-aged black woman sitting in her car staring directly at him! Both her hands gripped the steering wheel and her mouth was a pear-shaped hole. He could almost hear through the glass the high, keening noise a decibel below dog-whistle she must be making in the parking lot. It was like in his nightmares where he was being chased by bangers with guns: he tries to run but his legs won't go—should he run outside to stop her? No, they'll scatter from the floor like cockroaches when the light's turned on. He couldn't decide what to do.

"Oh fucking God," thought Odraye. "This can't go no more wrong."

But it did.

He bolted through the door separating the two halves of the back room and crashed into the glassed-in cubicle where the manager's office was. He saw the safe—it was closed. He saw the file cabinets; they were secured shut. No Taco man. He raced to the office door and found it locked. It was one of those cheap pine jobs that blew in with a couple hard kicks. Odraye pulled at the desk drawer, forgetting he had the key in his pocket. He fumbled it out of his pants and tried it. It wouldn't turn; it didn't even fit the keyhole. He saw a fire extinguisher in the corner. He banged it savagely against the drawer until it popped open. It was empty, nothing but Ohio air in it. The rest of the drawers were unlocked but all he saw when he pulled them free and dumped them onto the floor were ordering sheets, manifests, file folders, receipts and records—all bullshit!—no damn money!

A voice in his head shrieked: *Get out—run like a motherfucker* . . .

Without a glance backward, he tore out of there as if sparks were flying from his shoes; he ran like his favorite cartoon: the Roadrunner hightailing it from Wile E. Coyote. His momentum crashed him into the Escort's side. He cranked the engine with an ear-piercing screech of metal because he had left it running (*oh fuck me*), reversed it too hard and tore a bright metal gouge out of the right front fender when he scraped the guard rail. He almost stood on the brakes as he flew into the oncoming traffic and nearly t-boned a Chevy SUV.

His eyes burned with red-hot hatred. *Oh, he would take little pieces off Reece if it took him all night.*

But the traffic on Prospect at that very moment gave him a miserable shred of luck in this nightmare. The plan was to go right out of the lot and work back toward East Ninth toward Canal Street.

Oh God, Oh God. The words rattled around in his brain like angry bees. His plaid shirt over his sweat shirt was glued to his back. He drove on automatic pilot, barely aware of traffic lights and almost clipped a pedestrian on Broadway.

By the time he swung onto Canal, he was calm. No sirens or cherry lights behind him. He was going to start by breaking all Reece's fingers one at a time, snap-snap-snap, thumbs last. Then he would use his buck knife to take off his ears and nose . . .

"Make that little cocksucker scream," he yelled into the wind blasting his face out the window listening for sirens. Odraye would never stop hurting him.

He parked on the street down from the rental house. The night sky was littered with stars, the Dog Star high overhead, and he smelled sewage from the river. Mosquitoes buzzed in tiny clouds around his head, drawn by his sweat. The two houses on the other side of the street looked abandoned. He headed for the back of Reece's house. He heard raccoons scuffling in some garbage bags near the edge of the driveway where empty lots of scrub brush and stunted bushes laced with creeper vines made them look like rows of hump-backed camels in the moonlight. Rickety steps led to a landing behind the small kitchen. He noticed both back windows were dark.

On the small landing, Odraye listened for sounds. He could see nothing through the soot-smudged window. He touched the knob. The door was open.

Odraye took out his buck knife, thought better of it when he recalled the Black Talons in the Chief Special. He pushed the door open with his fingertips. Somewhere beyond was a bedroom off the bare sitting room; except for a tiny bathroom, that was all there was to the upper floor. Barry had told him on his first visit that the downstairs was unrented since the landlord kicked out the crackheads and huffers.

His eyes adjusted. He saw light leaking out from under the door to the bedroom. He'd grab the little stoner right out of bed before he knew what was happening, pull him by his hair, stuff a rag in his mouth, cuff him with his own plastic flex ties to the radiator and then go to work on him. The night was young.

He checked the bathroom and nearly slipped on water overflowed from the shower. He nudged open the bedroom door, held the big gun sideways like the bangers in his rap videos, and inched into the room. He made out the sleeping form of the boy lying on his bed—no doubt still wasted. With his left hand he found the switch plate and swatted it but no light flooded the room.

His eyes adjusted in the pale light from the windows. He went up to the sleeping form. It wasn't Reece. It was some white guy with skinny shanks in jockey shorts. He was bleeding from a head wound. The dent in the pillow where his head lay facing away from the door was filled with a small pond of blood. Odraye stared in utter fascination at the way it had pooled around the sides where his head lay, how black it appeared in moonlight, and most of all, what was left of the dude's head. The edges had turned a crusty-looking brown. Up close, the coppery stink of blood mixed with something else: the guy had crapped himself. Odraye, a D minus student on his best day, had watched enough forensics shows to know what a bullet traveling through a man's brain in bullet-time could do to the body it left behind: the bowels evacuated and then everything stopped: no hair or fingernails continued to grow; every cell stopped permanently.

He moved around to the foot of the bed where more blood had flowed past his lifeless, outstretched hand and dripped onto the floor. The jagged remainder of his face reminded him of the time he stuck an M80 in a dead cat's mouth.

He looked down at his British Knights and saw them rimmed in blood. He backed out of the room and went across the hallway feeling his stomach revolt and barely made it to the sink before a stream of yellow vomit splashed the bowl. He thumbed the light on and this time he heard the hiss of fluorescent bulbs. The shower curtain was spattered with blood. The walls were painted with it and there was hair and brain matter, bits of bone, and chunks of gore like a barfed-up stew lying in a comet's orbit where it had circled the drain.

Odraye's knees turned to wax and he stumbled back into the hallway, staggered like a blind man feeling walls. His brain was screaming. An icy hand clutched his guts and shriveled his scrotum sac as if he'd sat on a block of ice.

He wanted to be gone—just whooshed away like the Rapture his grandma used to talk about before she fell out. He saw her in the kitchen gumming her food. He squeezed his eyes shut and cursed. Not only was his picture taken all over the Taco Bell, he had just planted his signature all over the murder scene: fingerprints, bloody shoe prints, hair, skin cells for all he knew—he could never get it all cleaned of the traces of him. He looked back at the crisscross of footprints.

"Thass why he couldn't give me no key to the file cabinets," Odraye whispered to the bare walls. There was never supposed to be a key in the first place. Taco man was a junkie, not a moron. He had to know he'd take the pinch once the cops figured a key was used. Then, again, the Taco manager was never in on any robbery in the first place because this was a calculated set-up right from the start. Reece had played him like a two-dollar whore.

Odraye groaned and pressed his hands to the sides of his head. They'd all be looking for this crazy-ass, gun-toting nigger who tried to rob the Taco Bell. They wouldn't bother with a motive for the dead guy in the sack. Felony robbery with a gun, felony murder one . . . *Sweet jumping Jesus.*

He flashed back to an image of Barry coming from behind the Burger King—Odraye never did see him actually inside the place. No one could place him there or put the two of them together. Reece, a gadget guru like he always bragged on himself, never had so much as a TV in this shitbox, no food in the fridge, no furniture, no nothing. It was just a junkie's crashpad. How had he missed all the signs of something not right? It was his need for the money that blinded him. And something else . . . a dim memory burned into the back of his brain. The day he humiliated Reece on his knees, he heard him mumbling something about "anybody can be made to wear a dress." It made no sense.

When he heard the sirens wailing their hi-lo sound down Canal and saw the lights bouncing off the walls of the houses, heard the slamming doors, he knew he didn't have all the answers yet, but he knew one thing for sure: he wasn't going to die in a gangbanger blaze of glory like those stupid Compton niggers in the tunes he loved.

Lucasville, Ohio. Southern Ohio Correctional Facility, E Block, Cell 24

Odraye called Reece's mother, only she had a different name now and lived in Indiana. She bought his story about "being great high school friends," she even accepted phone charges, to see if he could get a line on him. She said she hadn't seen Barry in months and never wanted to see him again. She said she found a loaded over-and-under shotgun hidden in the cellar of her house, which she promptly reported to his parole officer. She thought he was going to use it on her and her new husband. "Barry's real father is locked up in Lima. That's where the put the criminally insane. They did tests on Barry when he was held in the reformatory. They said he's an emotional dissociative with antisocial traits."

"What—what do that mean exactly?" Odraye inquired.

"I asked the same thing. They told me he's a sociopath," she said.

Odraye wasn't sure what that meant either, but she clarified it for him a second later: "He's a vicious, cold-blooded psychopath," she said. "I'm scared to death of him."

When the clanging of steel got on Odraye's nerves, he'd recall the smirk on Barry's face as he casually sauntered up, handing Odraye the phony key, muttering some dope-fiend gibberish, pretending to be high. Odraye was too hyper at the time to recall anything clearly but what Barry said made no sense. The more he replayed it in his mind, the more it sounded like this: *You're going to tell me someday how the dress fits.*

The Aryan Brotherhood ran D Block. Blacks were housed in A and C Blocks. The AB members had done a deal, money changed hands, and Odraye was left without protection.

After the first beatings, he begged the captain of the guards on his shift to get him reassigned, but the only place where he would be safe was in the SHU with the snitches. He spent a year there before he was returned to the general population, and it started all over again. "Blanket parties," as the guards called them. This time, however, he was gang-raped in the showers. They took turns on him, a half-hour at a time. After the stitches and the wounds healed, he saw Hykeem Doss wink at him from the chow line one day, and then he knew what was coming next.

While he was mopping down the corridor, he saw a familiar face being escorted past by two white guards. Odraye looked up and recognized his cousin Venard, just out of segregation. "Yo, cuz, what up," Odraye said, but Venard just looked at him. He thought he heard one of the guards call him a "punk."

Time went by differently once Doss made him his woman. Everybody knew better than to disrespect a man who ground a sharpened bedspring into a new fish's eye because the boy had failed to realize he owed twenty dollars for asking Doss a simple question. Hykeem laughed from deep in his chest: "Anybody axe me a question, that is my legal fee. Ain't no different from any other lawyer," Hykeem said to him at chow when Odraye asked him why he did it.

When he first had his stitches taken out, he was greeted with kissing noises and whistles as he walked by. Hykeem made that stop once they set up house. Doss was a lifer who would never leave prison except to go to the convict's graveyard down by the river, where the Rose-of-Sharon bloomed.

He cried when Doss told him he had to start wearing dresses, but he soothed him and said that was how it was in prison when you got married. Doss also asked him to wear his hair longer on one side and used mascara that the other ladies had showed him how to make with ingredients smuggled out of the kitchen. Doss took care of him. Even that hillbilly captain of guards showed Odraye respect. Hykeem promised to teach him how to deal with fear. *You ain't afraid of me, honey, is ya?*

If only he could get those words out of his head, he might sleep better, but it got into his head and wouldn't go away, those words from another life when he was free. Sometimes it stayed inside rattling around until he nearly went crazy. *Tell me someday how the dress fits . . . how the dress fits . . . how the dress fits.*

∞∞∞∞

No Alarms and No Surprises
by Brian Lyons

The first time Mickey had seen Afghanistan was as he had thundered down into its terrifyingly beautiful landscape in the belly of a great C17 Globemaster. He'd been dazzled by the form and colours of the harsh yet stunning scenery he had swept over. It seemed to him to be a land comprised of huge towering snow-topped mountains, or the swirling dunes of vast breathless desert plains with thin green stains following sparse river valleys.

As they had started to descend, his neighbours on the plane had wedged their helmets firmly under their seats. He quickly did the same; he'd seen Apocalypse Now too.

The gentle melody of *No Alarms and No Surprises*, one of the more melodious of Radiohead's tracks, rippled across his consciousness through the earphones of his MP3 player. It was a strangely appropriate soundtrack to his very first descent into this country. He took it as an omen.

Mickey loved his music and knew it could be a tool to help him through his time in this place. It could save his sanity. Now, without anything else, he clung to it, finding significance wherever he could in every line. However he was aware that his experiences, and the memories they generated, would, in the end, probably destroy the relationship he had built with those much-loved songs.

#

All around them was silent, but for the occasional moan of wind and swish of sand. Even the radio was short of its usual frantic traffic on this hot hazy day. Now and again a wayward insect crawled up the inside of a trouser leg and needed an admonishing slap, but that was about it.

"You awake?" Dook was restless. Nothing was happening and he was getting fidgety.

Mickey just grunted, he couldn't think of a sensible answer. Besides, he was enjoying the rare moment of peace they had been afforded.

"I was thinking."

Mickey groaned but held his counsel.

"You know the way these Taliban geezers, these suicide bombers, reckon they'll get hold of a load of virgins when the die?"

"Seventy two," Mickey corrected.

"Yeah, whatever." Dook paused. Mickey braced himself for whatever pearl of wisdom was, no doubt, on its way. "Well, there've been women bombers, haven't there. So what do they want?"

"What?"

"Well a bloke might want a virgin, but a woman wouldn't want one, would she?"

Judging it not worth a reply, Mickey flicked a look toward a buzzard soaring up a couple of hundred feet above the jagged ridge of rocks where they lay. He squinted at the searing sun beyond it, careful not to look directly. The sky was as big as in a John Ford western, but who were the Cowboys and who were the Indians.

He was used to pains and aches around his body, but his feet were currently giving him the most trouble. In the heat they got soft and he could feel the pads of hard skin swimming about against his boots, sore blisters forming. Blood blisters.

To Mickey, in these conditions, the joy of getting to wash his feet was almost biblical in scale. Most of the time he simmered inside the uniform and body armour in the heat and dust. When he got the chance to relax on base, stripped down to just a vest and shorts, he could feel the pleasant evening breeze caressing his skin as he inhaled the spicy scent of marijuana from the Afghan's quarters. Something to look forward to.

It was well above 40 degrees now. For some hours, since daybreak, they had been lying stationary and on the lookout for movement on the dusty track which stretched out across the bleached plain below him towards a group of small brown hills about a mile away. It seemed most unlikely to him that anything hostile would be moving at this time of the day, but what did he know. The bird up above was the only thing showing any energy and it was just floating on the thermals swirling up from the baked earth.

"Bollocks," he cursed quietly to himself as a large drop of sweat slid down from the tip of his eye-lash and plinked into his eye. Without thought, he twisted his hand up from the pistol grip below the rifle where he rested his cheek and wiped at the salty solution in his eye. "Shit," he swore again, with more venom this time, as a few grains of sand found their way into his eye. He blinked rapidly to dislodge them, reluctant to show any more movement than necessary.

"Whassup bitch?" queried Dook. "Can't you keep still?" Like most of us to some extent, Dook's speech showed sharp signs of the transatlantic cultural influence.

Rich coming from you, thought Mickey. "Sand in my eye, you dick."

"Dipedy-fucking-do, man. Sand in your dick, my eye."

"Twat."

Dust devils appeared out of nowhere, skipped across the dry sand and disappeared just as quickly. All was quiet again and fat flies played around them as Dook busied himself wiping the sand from his rifle barrel.

A celestial pencil marked the vapour trail of a high flying jet on the lapis lazuli sky. Mickey wondered what sort of plane it might be; it was far too high to discern whether its purpose was to deliver tourism or death.

Porteus, their platoon commander, leopard-crawled through the rocks to them with Muldoon, the long-suffering platoon sergeant, in tow. Mickey and Dook exchanged a private look which Muldoon must have seen. "Enjoying yourselves lads?"

They grunted their monosyllabic replies.

"Nice day for it, eh?" He looked in vain for enthusiastic responses. "You'll be delighted to know we've just ordered up a little lunchtime entertainment for our ragheaded friends over there."

On queue, a Harrier jet screeched overhead. It performed a first pass - presumably to check what it was supposed to be attacking - executed a long sweeping turn and came back around to unload both of its rocket pods into one of the hills they had been watching all morning. It erupted in a series of explosions, the sound rippling across to them moments after the vision.

"Those bastards'll be back in the bar for a beer and a blowjob before you can blink," alliterated Porteus.

He seemed to be expecting more action so they all dutifully watched and waited until it became clear that no more Harriers were coming to the party after all. Dook thought aloud: "What if they hit the wrong hill?"

Porteus's matey smile disappeared as fast as a banker's conscience. "OK boys, let's go and clear up that mess." He scuttled off, Muldoon frowning behind him.

"Miserable tosser," commented Dook when he judged him to be out of earshot.

#

After hiking the mile across the desert, Mickey and Dook found themselves in the smoking ruins of the demolished hill. They picked their way through the remains of what had turned out to be a relic of a previous conflict. There were a series of badly battered trenches and shallow bunkers, not very extensive, and they were carefully checking them for any occupation. So far there was a striking absence of any sign of insurgents. The Stereophonics' *Just Looking* was playing in his head.

Dook prodded at something in the debris with the end of his rifle. It was half of a broken wooden sign, black Cyrillic script painted on a faded white background.

"This must have been a Russian position," Mickey reflected.

"What do you think it says?" pondered Dook.

"Beware of Harriers?"

Mickey caught the slightest movement at the very edge of his vision, behind Dook"s back, and turned his head in time to see a head and shoulders appear from a hole in the side of a pile of earth and stones. A wiry, feral little man, with a bloody head bandage and a stained loin cloth, burst out of the hole and flew towards Dook waving a rusty old scimitar and shouting "Allahu Akbar".

In the same moment he both screamed out Dook's name and fired at the man, hitting him in the thigh and the stomach. The man's legs gave way under him and he fell face-down into the dirt. He frothed at the mouth and with a muttering growl kept repeating his mantra, over and over again. His arm, with the sword in it, thrashed about until Dook fired several more rounds into him. It had happened so quickly - then all was quiet again.

"Jesus, that was so weird," Dook was genuinely shocked.

"The odd thing was if he had stayed put we probably would have missed him."

The man had curled up into a foetal position at the end. Mickey didn't say anything, but he really didn't feel bad about ending this man's life – the critical fact for him was that he had protected his mate.

"It"s like he wanted to die."

"Maybe the sign means *look out, fucking nutters about.*"

#

Now they had moved on to the outskirts of a small town, a dusty little place built of mud brick on the edge of the eternal desert which had switched back and forth several times between British and Taliban control. Mickey watched as Porteus, described colourfully by Dook as "a two-faced prick, as useful as a worm's hole to an elephant", hovered while Muldoon studied a map with the Khadamdar, or platoon sergeant, of the Afghani unit they were working with.

The Section was strung along the bottom side of a dusty little square which the main road cut straight through. On the opposite side, about twenty metres away, was the village bazaar. Metal-shuttered shops behind them were set up in a row of mud-brick buildings. The more security conscious local businessmen set up their businesses in shipping containers nearby. Bloody skinned carcasses, presumably of sheep and cows, hung in the open on filthy hooks. Black clouds of flies swarmed about them. Mickey wondered if this marketing ploy could work anywhere else.

After reaching some decision of vital strategic importance Muldoon and the Khadamdar moved off down the main drag between mud-brick compound walls and across a battered bridge over a dusty nullah about fifty metres away. Porteus jogged after them leaving Mickey and the others sitting and waiting for orders, and feeling vulnerable.

While they were waiting for orders Mickey was having a little rest in the shadow of a decaying wall which, like every other structure in the whole sorry country, could have been there for ten years or a thousand. On the radio someone was moaning that half the locals in the unit they were working with were doped out of their heads again and more of a danger to Mickey's mob than to the Taliban.

Mickey watched the busy to-ing and fro-ing of daily life keenly as he sat on the ground with his back against the wall, resting his aching feet. He laid his rifle across his knees and risked slipping off his helmet and scratching his scalp. A pair of women swathed in grey burkas washed clothes and rugs outside a house further down the road. One of them was particularly young and moved like an athlete, her step as light as a cat. Most of the local men were off working at Coalition bases; he wondered what temptations there were for pretty young girls here in their absence.

The problem for Mickey and the others was that they were sitting targets. Any lunatic with a rifle could be drawing a bead on them at any moment and the longer this waiting went on, the twitchier they got. Every village or town had its "dickers", the ones who watched and recorded their movements, passing them on to the insurgents who could then prime their rockets and lay their ambushes. Sometimes they sat there brazenly with a mobile phone, watching them.

Everyone moving through the little square kept their distance and traveled slowly. With the omnipresent threat of suicide bombers, and too many soldiers with itchy trigger fingers, the locals were eager not to make any mistakes.

Dook arrived just then and sat down next to him, kicking up a small cloud of dust with his customary puppy-like energy.

A tall, thin young Pushtun rode by on a sad looking donkey pulling a small cart which bumped along behind it on a pair of car tires. He had a dun-coloured pakol hat perched on his head and wore the ubiquitous white dish-dash with a black waistcoat. His sandaled feet skimmed the stony road and he looked completely out of proportion to the little beast which bore him. His straggling black hair and face put Mickey in mind of Grace Jones sucking a wasp.

Dook spat in the direction of the Pushtun and smiled. "Wonder if he plays football like Drogba too."

Dook was a positive, forward-looking lad and had decided in his wisdom that they would go on to do something together in the real world after they had both survived this thing. He always said Mickey should be the brains and he would be the brawn, the energy. Together they would rule the world.

"I *was* thinkin' of bein' a porn star."

Mickey could only smile. Although it was fair to say, if you wished to maintain your self-esteem, Dook was not the man to stand next to in the shower. "I remember."

Dook's ideas for life after Afghanistan had been many and varied. "But I was thinkin' the shaggin's alright, but having to do it hour after hour, day after day with them slags? Nah, it'd end up puttin' you off. Might catch AIDS off 'em."

"True."

"Nah, imagine old slappers like Jordan wavin' their growlers at you all day long."

"So that's it. No jig-a-jig for a living?"

He paused. "Nah, music, that's the game for me."

"Music?"

"Yeah. You've inspired me. You and all the music you listen to. I'm thinkin' I'll be a DJ."

Mickey shook his head bewilderedly; what next, politics?

"I'm going to put together a demo, Progressive House. Chilled-out stuff, you should take a listen. It's gonna' be a one hour long mix compilation. I'll stick it on the net. Got a mate back home with contacts who can get us a good venue an' all."

These ideas always sounded plausible to begin with. Mickey let him think on it and quietness settled between them.

Digweed, a baby-faced 18-year-old with a soft West Country accent when Mickey had met him back in England at the Depot, walked past with the regular tread of an automaton. He had aged at least five years in the few months they'd been in-country. Mickey had noticed this effect with many of the kids after their first taste of real combat. They become thinner, like winter-skinny deer, and quiet with the dull stare of people who have been to a lot of very dark places in too short a period of time. Digweed didn't smile any more, or speak unless he had to. Mickey pulled his knees up in front of him, and watched him pass.

"Oi, Shitseed, how's it swingin'?" Dook called out in Digweed's direction.

Digweed stopped and looked over at them briefly. Despite the heat of the sun his face was pale as a ghost and he made no comment. He simply turned and moved off with his rifle slung over his shoulder, plodding down between the high dirty walls of the compounds towards the bridge.

"There goes one mad motherfucker."

Mickey said nothing in reply and once more they drifted off into their own thoughts.

Suddenly he was thrown onto the floor as reality was tested violently with the quivering, body-shocking rage of a huge explosion. It hit them after some single storey buildings on the other side of the bridge dissolved into a wall of dust. It took several seconds for Mickey's brain to re-engage and begin to make sense of what had just happened to him. The blast wave had hit first, stunning him and throwing him back against the soft brick of the wall. Then a cloud of debris had boiled up the lane from the bridge like a pyroclastic flow from a volcano. Somewhere in the jumble of sensory impressions the concussion of the explosion had rattled his inner ear into numbness. He tasted the metallic tang of blood and smelled the damp cement-like odour of building dust and burning plastic. Consumed by the cloud he curled into a foetal ball, the barrel of his rifle clutched in his fist. He coughed and spluttered, dirt filling his eyes, mouth and ears.

He came to his senses and remembered he had been sitting next to Dook seconds before. He looked back to where he thought they had been and all he could see was rubble covered with a thick layer of dust. Then one of the piles moved, rolled clear of the others and started to shake itself off like a dog.

Bits of building and twisted metal were raining down and they both dived back against the wall for cover. They waited until there was just dust coming down.

"Shit, that was a big one."

"Bloody hell, look at your lid Dook." His helmet had a piece of shrapnel embedded in its top, about the size of a fifty penny piece.

Dook took it off and examined it, running his finger along the edge of the metal. "Felt like a slap round the ear by my Ma." One of the few things Mickey knew for certain about Dook was that he was an orphan. His mother had died when he was quite young.

"Maybe it's her way of telling you to be careful."

For once Dook had nothing to say. He put it back on, declining to remove the metal fragment. It looked like a tiny satellite dish to Mickey and he smiled.

"Was it one of them suicide fuckers?" Dook had his voice back.

"Does it matter?"

People were shouting at each other over the radio.

Mickey turned back to look at what was left of the bridge. Dook started growling like a wolf and popping off shots at apparently random targets. "What the fuck are you doing?"

Dook stopped firing. He stood breathless looking at Mickey, his eyes slowly focusing back on him from some distant la-la land. "Come on, Mickey, let's go see what's left down there."

Witnessing the effects that an explosion can have on the human body was not an enticing thought, but Mickey braced himself for it yet again. Dook leapt up and scampered off down the left-hand-side of the lane scanning ahead and to his right. Psycho-bunny was back. Mickey took to the right side and covered the left and behind them.

He soon became aware his mind was playing a soundtrack as he moved along; anachronistically it was *One Day Like This* by Elbow.

When they got to the bridge a hyperactive Porteus appeared from nowhere with barely a scratch on him – Mickey knew somehow, wherever he went, he was always going to manage that trick.

They found enough of Muldoon and the Khadamdar to fill a small bag, but they never saw Digweed again, any of him.

#

That night in their compound, Mickey whiled away the hours after sunset, as the odours of local cooking dispersing on the breeze. Nearby his mates amused themselves gambling on mortal combat between scorpions and camel spiders, or lit their own farts.

"Here, have you heard this? Listen to this shit." Dook had arrived waving a mobile phone at Mickey.

"What?"

"There's a recording on it. Got it off the corporal attached to Intel. They've got scanners listening to all the radio and phone traffic for a hundred miles."

The quality wasn't brilliant on the recording; there was a fizzling background and bad reception. Two or three voices were conversing by radio, speaking one of the local languages. Mickey guessed Pustun as it was the one they seemed to hear the most, but he was no expert.

The voices were excited, hurried. Suddenly, the middle of the stream of foreign jabber, a phrase leapt out at him in a broad Brummie accent: "*Salim, Salim, where are you.*"

There was a crackling pause, followed by the same voice again: "*This jihad game's tough, man.*"

There were sharp exhalations of breath as they looked at each other, the implications sinking in. There had been rumours about this, but that is the first time they'd actually heard it.

"Did you know any Asian kids back home?"

Dook shrugged. "I suppose."

"Did you get to know any of 'em, you know, play football over the park with them?"

"Suppose."

"Get on OK with them?"

Dook screwed up his nose. "Maybe."

"So what would you do if you met a Talib out here that you recognised from back home?"

"Might buy him a drink."

"What if he had done something terrible, like killed a mate of yours, and you had the bead on him and he begged you for mercy?"

Dook grinned. "Well, if he'd topped Porteus I'd offer 'im a fag and beer."

"Seriously though, if he'd killed one of us."

His eyes narrowed and darkened. "No problem, I'd fucking gut 'im."

#

As Mickey ran, there was the sound of boots scuffing and thudding hurriedly into the dust and a dull metallic clink as an errant piece of metal inevitably – no matter how carefully bound - found some other metal to clank against.

They were clearing a mud brick compound, everything dull brown and dusty. Like dozens of other villages and compounds they had been through many times before. Sometimes they came under fire, sometimes they didn't. In this case they received some small arms fire and a rocket propelled grenade or two from a few hundred yards away as they passed; nothing out of the ordinary and not particularly accurate. This compound was about one hundred metres square with most of the buildings up one end away from the main gate. A few huts and lean-tos were dotted about the rest of it.

Porteus, affecting a stern look and a clenched-fisted salute based on fictional film and TV references, was now being followed around like a puppy by Savage, a nervous young sergeant who was the official replacement for the sorely missed Muldoon. Savage, skipping along behind Porteus and seeking to ingratiate, had rather irritatingly taken to aping this salute. It was Dook who first coined the phrase 'Porteus and Savage out fisting together' to describe the phenomenon, but before long the whole company was in on the joke. Having such a sergeant didn't bode well for their future well being.

Dook was convinced that if Mickey's and Porteus's schools had been reversed, Mickey would have been the officer and Porteus would have been the squaddie: "A very dangerous accident of birth," as he put it.

Porteus had told them an RPG attack had come from this area and so they were making their way through it, first grenades into each room and then firing past each other into the dark interiors. Muldoon used to call it ratting, and he had often wished aloud he had his little Jack Russell with him.

Mickey was having a breather, squatting down with his pack leaning back against the mud wall of the compound. The rest of the section were working through some rooms further on, he would join them in a moment. Holding his rifle with his right index-finger on the trigger, always careful, laid it across his legs. He took off his helmet with his left hand and, releasing the rifle to lie across his lap, wiped the thick film of sweat off the inside edge of it. Flicking the liquid away into the dust he then stared upwards into the beautiful clear blue sky. The sun was intense as usual and the air dry as a bone. He guessed the temperature must be well above 40C degrees, possibly as high as 50C. Great things helmets, although he always felt they restricted your hearing. He rubbed his hand through his sweat drenched crop and listened, now unimpeded, as the section shot-up something in the main house.

In the middle of the compound a wind-blasted tree stood stark black, decorated with just a few bird droppings to brighten it up. It was left with just a few papery-looking leaves, clinging to it like lost prayers.

A small lizard with black and white stripes along its body sat on a pile of sandy debris a couple of yards away from him and they stared at each other, the lizard loving the heat and the soldier grudgingly putting up with it. Mickey wondered what the big issues were in the creature's world today.

Then the lizard shivered and turned its head to face a corner of the inner wall beyond which the remainder of Mickey's section was working. Its little feet twitched and in a blur of movement it scampered off its pile and disappeared.

A second later Dook darted around the same corner and slid down into the dirt to a sitting position, like a Premiership goal scorer, with his rifle held out in front of him. "So this is where you are, Porteus wondered where the fuck you had got to."

Mickey smiled; he would have to keep a closer eye on the local fauna. "On another day Dook, in another land, we would pay good money to be sitting watching the wildlife in a place with weather like this."

Dook looked around him at the dirty little compound and screwed his nose up skeptically.

"Bit of a shit hole really. I'd prefer to be a long way away in a pair of shorts and a tee shirt."

Mickey picked at the stiff edge of his front body armour plate. It didn't take long for the rubber edging strips of the modular plates to get worn and for the edge to get a little frayed. In time, with the heat of the day and with the damp waves of sweat, his skin had become rubbed raw.

Dook sat down beside him and for a moment they both gazed into an imagined future. "…and flip-flops, of course."

A sudden gust of air rattled the rotting door of a small hut about 10 yards away against its frame. It startled them both and they instinctively trained their weapons on it.

"What do you think?" Dook asked, the moment of light relief had vanished and they were sharp again.

Mickey said nothing but sprang up and quickly covered the ground to the wall of the hut. He stood with his back to the wall to the right of the door and Dook sprinted to the left. Mickey checked his rifle was cocked and ready. Neither of them had any grenades left so Mickey used hand signals to say that he would go in first and Dook would support.

After taking a deep breath Mickey, deciding on a whim not to kick the door, gently pushed it in with the barrel of his rifle.

There was a slight creak as it opened and, since the room had no windows, he peered carefully inside and waited until his eyes grew accustomed to the contrast between the stark brightness of the sun outside and the dim interior. He was using the sight on his rifle and could see something in the far corner, a heap of rags perhaps.

He couldn't see any obvious wiring anywhere for a booby trap so he decided to chance a move. He slipped across the doorway and crouched down inside against the wall and scanned the room through the rifle-sight.

The image resolved itself as his eyes became accustomed to the darkness and he realised that he was actually looking at a man lying still on some primitive kind of trestle. He was clearly badly wounded, there were blood stains on the torn white shirt and baggy trousers, and his left hand was draped over his chest. His right dangled down in the shadows below him.

On the floor near the man lay an AK47 and an old fragmentation grenade – pin intact, next to it. Mickey quickly moved close enough to kick them away well out of reach, all the while keeping his rifle trained on the man. Then he backed away again.

It didn't take him long to realise the man was either asleep or unconscious and senseless to the sounds of him and his rampaging section outside – given the noise the rest of the section were making, it was probably the latter. Black hair, rags and blood, mates of his had been shot or blown up in similar circumstances – Mickey would not take chances.

As he watched he saw the man twitch in the gloom, his dark Asian eyes blinked open and seemed to take an age to focus on him. The right hand lifted gently up from the shadows holding something up towards Mickey. It was a small rectangular black thing with a wire snaking back from it into the darkness near the man's neck. His thumb was on top of it and he cradled it in the rest if his hand. He held it like a TV remote control towards Mickey. Was he about to trigger a bomb?

He looked a little like a certain middle-eastern gent, laid out after a hard day on a cross; the appalling innocence behind those dark assassin's eyes. Being who he was he certainly wouldn't have thanked Mickey for such an observation.

Something was stopping Mickey from pressing the trigger of the rifle which he aimed at the chest of the man. It was as if he was showing Mickey something, like an offer of redemption. It was that thought which Mickey couldn't get past and it stopped him from shooting.

"I'm on a roll this time. I feel my luck could change..." Radiohead were haunting him again, *Lucky* this time.

Then there was a crash as Dook finally lost patience and burst through the door, and a fraction of a second delay as his eyes become acclimatised to the poor light.

Dook was a man driven by instinct, not by thought, and his decision was made before he realised it himself. He had seen the thing in the man's hand and he fired two quick shots into the breast of the dying man.

A low gasp escaped the Asian's throat and it reminded Mickey of his own father's death. Mickey saw the puncture holes in the chest and saw the blood flush gently across what was left of the torn white shirt, slowing now he was dead. For the first time he noticed the room smelled strongly of faeces.

Dook looked down at the dead man and pointed to the thing in his hand, "Is that what I think it is?"

Mickey prodded it with the barrel of his rifle. "Depends what you think it is."

"Could be a booby trap, be careful Mickey." Dook involuntarily moved backwards towards the door.

Mickey reached down and lifted it up gingerly, examining it carefully. In the poor light it took him a moment to recognise that he was looking at a small black MP3 player. There was a dull glow from the little LCD screen on the side of it and he saw it was still working. There was even a track playing. He looked at the earphone dangling from the dead man's ear but it was daubed with blood and he didn't fancy it.

He pulled his own earphones out of a pocket and plugged them into the player. He was expecting some sort of Asian music, like the stuff they used to play in Indian restaurants before they shipped out all the flock wallpaper. Or perhaps a recording of one of those gents who sits at the top of the minaret and calls the boys to prayer.

When he realised what he was listening to, Mickey looked at the little thing in surprise. The last track the man had chosen to listen to was really not what he was expecting. Thom Yorke's tortured tones urged on gentle melody of *No Alarms and No surprises*.

The man's eyes were now blank, the face slack, any idealism, religious energy or hatred had evaporated.

∞∞∞∞

The Nine Lives of Chairman Mao
by Craig Gehring

Chairman Mao sat at the command table. Truil brushed past a woman making her exit and took his seat.

Mao was in the nude. The sight was uncommon enough to make Truil raise an eyebrow.

"Nothing," said Mao.

"You expected nothing," said Truil. "Perhaps a pill."

"I wasn't talking about the woman. Nothing on either count, though," said Mao.

Mao looked at the projector table.

"You needed my council?" asked Truil.

"Watch," said Mao. He tapped his console.

A holo video of the last conflict with the Outsiders played. Jupiter loomed brightly behind the United Nations of Earth Fleet. Hundreds of their tiny fighters swarmed to the Outsiders. The huge Outsider ships were pulling gas from Jupiter with their gravity. They grew even larger as the fighters approached. Then a dozen U.N.E. fighters smashed into one another. A dozen more. They made compact balls of white light. The holovid reached its end.

"I've seen it, Chairman," said Truil. He'd seen it thousands of times.

"Everyone's seen it."

"Yes."

"They made a hologame out of it," said Mao.

"Yes."

"What's your emotional response?" asked Mao.

Truil opened his mouth, then closed it. He smiled.

"If you were our run-of-the-mill citizen of the U.N.E.," said Mao, "survey says you wouldn't have one."

"Hmm?" asked Truil.

"Computer says the Outsiders will kill us, 99% chance. The whole population knows this. And 99% think we should enjoy the eighty years that we have. They aren't worried. There's no response. Nothing." said Mao.

"How do you feel about it, Chairman?" asked Truil.

"I agree. Worry is useless, and could spoil our last years. The odds are impossible. But Computer points out that, comparing this data with wars in its memory banks, this is a highly irregular response, even with the odds."

"Man hasn't had war in 700 years, since the Luna conflicts."

"I keep thinking about it. Computer's there to do my job, and all I'm left to do is think. I think there's a way to change the odds, but…"

Truil nodded. "Computer includes in the odds the possibility of the odds changing…" he said.

Mao nodded back. "You're the oldest of my councilors, Truil. You come from a time where the response may have been different."

Truil sighed. "Not in my time," said Truil. "I am only three hundred, not that old. But my forefathers, yes."

"What made it different?" asked Mao.

Truil thought it over. "There were philosophers, a couple hundred years after Atlas, that said that mankind was changing, evolving. As we went without need, without producing to survive, without pain or war, we evolved culturally into..." Truil struggled with the word.

"Impotence?" suggested Mao.

Truil smiled again. "At least, our will to survive has evolved to a will to...just...exist. That was what the philosophers said. I heard some disagreed with the pain-proofing."

"What do you think?"

"I think...well, I think...just a bunch of clichés pop to mind, really," Truil answered.

"What do you mean?"

"I don't know what I mean. I'm an old man. I could say that without pain, pleasure loses its contours. Without something to lose...Well, maybe both pain and pleasure are necessary to drive mankind to survival. But I'm just saying bumper slogans. I haven't felt pain since I was twenty-three, and I have two backup bods."

"Do you miss it? The pain?" asked Mao.

"No. No one misses it that can remember it. No one misses the fear of dying, either. Except the drones."

"Hmm," said Mao.

"But to answer your question, if I understand your question: You've studied that pain was a survival mechanism to keep one away from contra-survival factors," said Truil.

"Yes."

"Well, what happens in our society when one of our children touches a hot stove and burns his hand?" Truil asked.

"The nanites rebuild the dead cells from within the body. The child's tutor cautions him about stoves. There's no need for pain, if that's what you're asking."

"What happens when one of our youth incautiously kills himself in a car wreck?"

"He's revivified in his backup bod. Maybe he's missing a few weeks of memories. He's cautioned. No need for pain to learn that lesson, either," said Mao.

"Even the pilots who fought the Outsiders came back. They couldn't have learned their lesson, otherwise. But what happens when the Outsiders heat the atmosphere of Earth by a few hundred degrees?"

Mao imagined fire sweeping his planet. "We die," said Mao. *No need for pain there, either,* he thought. He felt he was missing Truil's point.

"I don't think any of us know what that means - to die," said Truil. "And I don't think any of us want to find out."

"I don't think anyone thinks he could find out..." said Mao. He understood. He decided to just say it. "Truil, there's a part of me that wants to fight it."

Truil didn't say anything. He did not agree or disagree.

"Maybe it's just my own uselessness, trying to find a purpose for my existence - the genetically perfected ruler with a Computer to rule for him."

"What do you think, Chairman?"

"I think I've thought enough."

#

Mao thought more, though. He did want to fight the Outsiders.

He thought about what Truil had said. He'd heard the words before, the clichés as he'd called them, in old books in the archives that didn't make any sense.

Something Truil said did make sense.

Mao thought he'd figured out why he needed a pill. He had an inkling as to why just about every male on Earth needed a pill. He would solve it.

He disguised himself as a drone, slipped his bodyguards. He had nothing to fear on Earth. And he had seven bods.

He went to the slums, the drone fields.

He saw her working in the orchard. She was clothed from knees to neck; all the drones wore homespun. The mystery of her body allured him. He watched her picking the apples. After a while he joined her.

"I'll help you pick the apples," he said.

She sized him up. She seemed to like what she saw. "Don't you have your own work?" she asked.

"Finished it," he said. It was true. It had been finished for him by Mao V and his great Computer. And he was Mao VII.

She was cautious but let him pick. She showed him how to do it. The apples felt good in his hands as he twisted them off, hundreds to the branch. She had to take a break.

"If I finish this barrel for you, can I take you to dinner?" asked Mao.

"Yes," she said. "Sure. What's your name?"

"Mao," he said.

"Like the Chairman?" she asked.

"Yeah, just like the Chairman," he said.

The sun fell before he finished the barrel.

"Are you cold?" he asked her.

"No, I've got a heater. Aren't you?" she asked.

He looked down at his body. It was shivering under the homespun. It felt…pleasant. He knew the nanites would protect his body from real harm. "No, I'm fine."

She walked closer to him.

They reached the pub. It was warm.

He ordered their dinner. They shared it. They laughed. He liked her; she seemed to like him.

He asked her, "Can I take you home?"

She splashed her drink in his face and stormed off.

It felt…pleasant.

#

Two weeks later Mao visited the orchard again. He'd reversed his pain-proofing. He'd had to transport a special doctor from North America. It hadn't actually been done to a human in two centuries.

The Computer, his advisors, even Truil disagreed. "Pain clouds the ruler's judgment."

To which he'd answered: "None of you know what pain is."

The drones knew. They hurt. They refused to let machines provide for them, refused the pain-proofing, refused the bod backups the U.N.E. freely supplied. They did backbreaking work in the field, like robot drones. They felt they were the only ones that *lived*.

She hurt. She saw him in the orchard and he knew she hurt. But she did not leave. She just sighed. He asked her if he could help her pick the apples. She nodded.

He picked for hours. After a little while his arms burned. It felt wonderful. He kept at it. Eventually he had to take a break.

She giggled at him slumped panting against a tree. "Last time you were like a robot."

"This robot is out of batteries," he said.

The sun fell. He felt nervous. He felt like his stomach was in his feet, and his feet were in his stomach. He didn't like it.

"I'm sorry," he said.

She nodded.

"Can I take you to dinner?" he asked.

She nodded again.

He didn't get splashed in his face at the pub. He told her goodbye at the door.

It hurt. It felt good.

#

Mao started reading. He read the old books that were down in the archives that didn't make any sense. They weren't even in Computer.

Someone called Shakespeare, someone called Dickens. Histories that seemed to be fantasies, although he knew they were real: Alexander, Napoleon, Hitler; American presidents, Gandhi, King. There were even books on Atlas that he'd tried to make sense out of in his youth and finally put away. He read them all now.

He understood more, now that he'd felt what they felt.

He understood their drive, too. He'd never experienced it, except with her, now.

#

He picked apples with her for five weeks. Every night was finished at the pub.

She knew he wasn't a drone. She knew he felt pain, though, like she did. She never asked about any of it.

One night she asked him quietly, "Will you come home with me?"

They made love at her place. He was sore by the end of it. It felt wonderful. He lay with her, her breasts soft against the side of his chest, her legs warmly enmeshed around his leg, their homespun on the floor. He could not catch his breath or stop smiling. He was very sore.

He woke up and no one was in the bed.

He felt a pang of fear and loss. It was so intense he felt like retching.

He realized she had gone to work. She'd left a note.

It said, "I love you."

#

After three weeks of nights, he could not watch the vid of the Outsiders. It infuriated him. Twice he broke the vid table with a chair. He yelled at Truil and the rest of his staff. He physically assaulted three aids.

He bypassed Computer and clumsily started a recruitment campaign for the fleet. Computer said it was futile but could not override him.

He diverted much of the U.N.E.'s wealth to the military labs.

"All we're getting is hologamers for pilots and idiots for researchers! Not a single discovery to date! They're still reading their goddamn texts!" shouted Mao in a conference. "Why don't the drones help? They could help. They've at least got something to lose. They'd do *something*!"

The Panelists looked at each other. No one understood what he meant.

"The drones, Chairman?" asked Computer. It had a screen at all meetings of the Panel. "The drones are uneducated and lead simple lives. Not only would they be even more useless as soldiers or scientists, they are unreachable. Not one will follow U.N.E. They believe U.N.E. to be an abomination."

"We *are* abomination if we let Earth die. It's in our goddamn title. United Nations of *EARTH*!" bellowed Mao.

He couldn't get a rise out of any of them. The whole Panel of fourteen men and women looked at him pleasantly without the slightest sign of disturbance.

Truil said, "Chairman, I believe I speak for us all when I say that not one of us wants to see the end of Earth."

Mao checked himself. A few of the Panelists were thinking. He could see them thinking in their chairs.

"No," Mao said. "Of course not." He fiddled with the back of his chair. "Listen, I appreciate everything that you're doing. I know you're doing what you can. Carry on," he said.

He walked out.

#

On Sunday, the drones' day of rest, Mao walked with her in the orchard.

He walked barefoot with her. The grass's cool tendrils snaked between his toes. Every now and then a briar poked him.

They walked between two rows of trees that framed a white-capped mountain. The air tasted crisp and energized him.

He loved the Earth for giving him her.

He loved her for giving him the Earth.

#

One day she was not in the orchard. He found her still at her place. She was crying into her pillow. Her aunt had died.

He comforted her.

"I'll miss her. I'll never get her back," she said.

Aunt didn't have a bod backup. Aunt was a drone like her.

She cried all day and talked about the disease. There was a sickness spreading. Mao held her the whole time.

He was happy that no matter how many times he died, she would always have him.

He started figuring out how to get her a bod.

He wouldn't. She wouldn't want a bod, no matter what he said. She'd never forgive him if she woke up in one.

#

Mao stopped talking to the Panel.

The more he talked to them, the worse the rift. They were at a total disconnect. He sounded like one of those ancient books.

A year passed. They were no more ready than the day their whole fleet was smashed to bits over Jupiter.

Humankind was willing to be eaten by the Outsiders.

Mao had nightmares of the Earth melting into a butterball of light, just like the fighters.

The grass would disappear from between his toes. She would disappear from their bed.

There would be no note that said, "I love you."

#

The idea came to him while he lay in her bed.

She had said she had a headache that night. He was looking at her bare shoulder in the dark room and wondering if she really had a headache.

If he were Chairman Mao, he could order her to take a headache pill and do as he willed. She would be reimbursed for her services by the State.

He was just Mao. He was wondering if she really loved him and had a headache, or if she was sick of him. He loved her.

Love was not a pleasant emotion usually.

He took a walk. It was winter. His body shivered and hurt down to the bone. He grew hungry. The nanites could rebuild cells, but they couldn't feed him. The sun rose behind the mountain.

He reached the foot of the mountain. He was still cold, but mainly starving.

He climbed the mountain. He got halfway. He couldn't breathe well anymore. The air was thinner and he was exhausted. It was freezing even with the sun high in the air.

Wet snow.

He sat down. He slept.

#

He woke up in his backup bod. He just slammed into it. One moment he was asleep and the next he was awake in the bod. It was just the same as the old bod. It wasn't even pain-proofed.

He remembered everything. As Chairman, he was only one of a dozen people walking the Earth that had a continuous perception dump to his backups. Everyone else had to do a memory dupe every few months. Where the awareness goes, so must the memory.

He had seven backup bods scattered all over the Earth. He would end this one quickly.

He stepped out of the bod tube. He felt the connections slide out. He took the gun of the nearest guard and fired it into his own head.

#

The last time Mao woke up, Truil was in the room. Truil had been waiting at bod number 7.

He had a gun gripped in his bony hand.

Mao waited for Truil to speak. Truil did not lower the gun.

"Computer estimates a 98% chance you're insane," said Truil.

"It doesn't matter if I'm insane. I'm Chairman for life."

"You're Chairman until dead. If you don't end your own life, Computer says I should end it."

Mao looked at the gun. Truil was a practical old man. He would not risk Earth to the rule of a crazy man. This was reality. Mao knew that in a very few seconds, the muzzle of Truil's gun would flash, and his own eighth and final life would end on the steely floor.

Mao despaired. He hadn't expected this. This body was to *live* in, not to die in. Not now, anyway.

Arguments swarmed like a tornado through Mao's facile mind. With the gun leveled at his eyes, though, Mao could not grasp a single one.

An emotion burst past the stoicism he'd been trained into since birth. He could not grasp the emotion, either; rather, it grasped him.

Mao could no longer look at Truil and his gun. He collapsed and trembled. The floor was hard and cold against his face.

Truil continued, "Mao VIII is already growing in a tube."

Truil did not kill him.

Mao could not saying anything. His crying had turned into shrieking, however. His reason had turned into cornered terror. He blubbered, "Please don't kill me," and tried to hold his hand up for mercy, only to collapse again. He begged for God's mercy, for him and his Earth. He shouted the girl's name.

Truil watched him for fifteen minutes.

Mao did not understand why he was still alive, but could not think further than that. He could not bear to look up. He knew he'd convinced Truil he was crazy. There would be no way out.

Mao heard the click of the gun's safety.

Truil had lowered his gun.

"Chairman Mao," said his advisor, quietly…pleasantly, almost to himself, "you've attained the necessary emotional response."

Truil left the room, securing the door behind him.

#

THOU SHALT NOT PROOF FROM PAIN.
THOU SHALT NOT CREATE A BODY IN THE LIKENESS OF A MAN.
THOU SHALT NOT DUPLICATE A MEMORY.

Chairman Mao read his dictates one hour later at the emergency Panel. He felt like the Moses he'd read of in the archives. He let the networks broadcast live, so there could be no discussion.

He finished by saying, "The penalty for any violation is total death. All U.N.E. citizens have 365 days to comply, effective now, this 19th day of the twelfth month, in the 802nd year of the Atlian Era."

Truil, most respected, calmed the Panel and garnered compliance.

#

She did have a headache. She was having a boy.

Seven months into her pregnancy, she caught the disease.

She died in Mao's arms.

#

Mao saved the boy. He was the first child ever born to a Chairman, genetically imperfect in all ways and never pain-proofed. The boy looked like his mother in the wintertime, when the cold sky caught his eyes.

Forty years later, that same boy advanced Atlas's graviton field theories to workable weapons technology.

He was heralded as "the Atlas of our times."

Chairman Mao called him his ninth life.

Earth, human Earth, might yet survive.

#

Mao took his boy to the orchard. The boy was a man, but still in the orchard he was Mao's boy.

They picked the apples until their arms ached and they were laughing hysterically.

They pelted one another with apples. They burst to bits when they hit the tree trunks. Mao was getting too old for this, but getting too old not to. They could not stop laughing.

They collapsed on the grass.

"Dad," said the boy, "what was mom like?"

"Like this," Mao answered.

An hour later, they got up from the grass.

"I wanted to talk to you," said the boy. "They're taking my guns up, and my shields. It's really happening."

"Yes," said Mao.

"I'm scared," said the boy.

Mao nodded. He clapped his son on the shoulder. "Me, too," he said.

The boy studied his father's eyes. The Chairman gave no comfort, no empty words to soothe the wrenching in the boy's stomach.

"Me, too," said the Chairman again, quietly, almost to himself.

It was all the reassurance the boy needed.

∞∞∞

The Bull Riding Witch
by Jamie Marchant

I remember little of my life before I woke up with a raging hangover and inside a body I knew wasn't mine. But you try explaining to people that you're a woman trapped in a man's body. See how far that gets you, especially when you're a bull rider.

I have a rodeo in Lafayette tonight, so I'm trying to get ready. Not an easy feat if you've ever seen my trailer. I find my western shirt and jeans easily enough, but my belt is buried somewhere in the god awful mess. You'd think with its huge buckle I could find it, but everything that isn't covered by frozen pizza boxes and empty beer cans is stacked two feet to three feet high with books—Jim Butcher, Barbara Hamby, Mercedes Lackey, *Parallel Universes, Guide to the Supernatural for Dummies.* Unfortunately, the books have proven about as useful as the pizza boxes in explaining what happened to me. But somebody, somewhere has to be able to tell me how I got stuck in Josh Killenyen's body and, more importantly, how to get back into my own.

There is a knock on my trailer door, and I open it. Mr. McGillihan is standing there. In exchange for odd jobs, Uncle Gilly—as everyone calls him, although to my knowledge he's nobody's uncle—lets me keep my trailer on his land and pays me a pittance. About enough to keep the insurance current on my truck. Insurance for myself is impossibly expensive since my profession tends to include a lot of injuries.

"Horse. Colic." Uncle Gilly nods toward the barn. He rarely speaks an entire sentence.

I follow Uncle Gilly into the nearby barn. When I enter, I feel a crushing pain in my gut. Wild Girl is rolling her eyes, snorting and groaning. Her gut feels just like mine, and let me tell you, it isn't pleasant. Colic is one of the most painful and dangerous things that can happen to a horse. I approach carefully because a colicky horse doesn't pay much attention to its surroundings and can step on you without even realizing you're there.

I touch her, and she instantly calms. I kneel next to her and put my hands on her gut. Then I close my eyes and reach inside Wild Girl's intestines with my magic. They're blocked all right. Uncle Gilly must have bought a finer grade of grain because it's packed her insides up tight. I work on loosening it up and moving it along the intestines. Wild Girl lets out an immense fart and then poops out a huge pile of . . . well, you know.

I straighten, both my guts and Wild Girl's feeling a ton better. "She's fine now, Boss," I tell Uncle Gilly.

"Good." He nods and walks away. Neither of us has ever said the word aloud, but Uncle Gilly knows about my magic. He figured it out about a year ago when one of the barn cats got hit by his truck. Nothing human could've saved the poor thing, but I did. Ever since then, he comes to me every time one of his animals has a problem. With all I save him in vet bills, you'd think he could pay me a little more.

It's probably because of my magic that someone didn't want me around, and they could hardly have picked a bigger loser to put me inside. At twenty-three Josh has never had a job, except occasional farm work and bull riding. Good thing he was decent at it, and I'm better than he was.

As I clean up after Wild Girl, I try for the thousandth time to think who might have done this to me, but I can't even remember my own name. I do remember that things are different where I come from. There are no trucks or computers or electric can openers. But magic and magical creatures—like dragons and trolls—are common. I think it's one of these parallel realms things that Hamby and some of the others write about, except they got it wrong. According to their theories, my magic shouldn't work in this world, but it does. I got the skills of my own body and Josh's as well. I didn't need to learn how to drive a truck or read, write, and speak English. Most of Josh's memories came with his body, too, but few of my own. Does Josh have my magic in my body? Have my enemies completely eliminated him, and I have no body to go back to? Being stuck inside Josh Killenyen forever isn't a pleasant thought.

I go back to my trailer and finally find my belt under *Dragon Riders of Pern* and *Spells for the Clueless and Inept*. I grab my new hat, which I bought with last week's prize money. Cost me pretty near all of it, but a proper cowboy needs a proper hat. Sometimes I find myself thinking like Josh Killenyen, and it scares me.

I get in my truck with its camper shell on back and start the three-hour drive from Hamilton on the west side of Alabama to Lafayette on the east. I'll sleep in the back tonight like I usually do for the two-day rodeos; I can't afford the price of a motel.

At the rodeo grounds in Lafayette, I drink in the scents of roasting corn, chicken-on-a-stick, and cotton candy. It's exhilarating because it means shortly I'll be having a brief, but wild ride. Nothing compares to the adrenaline rush of being on the back of a bucking bull. I wonder if in my other body I was addicted to adrenaline or if that came with Josh's body as well. On my way to the arena, I pass a booth that sells T-shirts. I spot one that says, "Cowboys make bad lovers. They think 8-seconds is a long ride." I laugh. Whoever wrote that has never been on the back of a bucking bull. Eight seconds *is* a long ride.

When I get to the staging area, I check what bull Josh has drawn—Man Killer. I smile; Man Killer is about the fiercest bucker on the circuit, and if I'm going to win tonight, I need a good bull. After all, half my score is based on just how hard a time the bull gives me.

From the staging area, I watch the rodeo. Fortunately, I came late enough that I missed the girls riding around with their flags to the sound of patriotic music while the announcer talks about God, America, and Dodge trucks. Rodeo people seem to worship all three with equal reverence. While I watch, I attune myself to my magic so I can be ready to ride.

Finally, it's time for the bull riding. I climb onto the launch chute, then onto Man Killer's back. He snorts, and I don't try to calm him. That was the mistake I made when I first became Josh. Instead, I reach into him until I become one with the bull, making it possible for me to match all the bull's movements like I was born on the back of a bucking bull.

I nod, and the chute opens. Man Killer roars into the arena. We're giving them quite a show when something hits my hand and I suddenly let go. I fly off and hit the ground, knocking the wind out of me. The bull's hoofs crash down inches from my head before the rodeo clowns are able to distract the beast. I run for the fence, vault over it, and stand there panting.

"What happened, man?" Dan, the closest thing to a friend Josh has, asks.

"I don't know." I shake my head, but I do know. Someone just used magic to try and kill me. I turn every which way looking for the magic user, but of course, there's no one wearing a pointy wizard hat. I close my eyes and reach out with my magic, and I feel something, across the arena in the third set of bleachers. I tear off. Halfway there I come to my senses and stop. Charging down an unknown magician wouldn't be the brightest thing Josh ever did. Before I can decide what to do, I lose the magician's scent. I close my eyes to try to pick it up again, but I feel nothing. Still, I wait, and I only go into the back of my truck when the lights have been turned off and nobody's wandering around.

When I curl up in my sleeping bag, I start shaking. I see again the bull's hoofs coming down inches from my head. I feel the ground tremble underneath with the impact. I'm damned lucky to be alive. I don't know if I dare ride tomorrow, but if I don't, I'll barely have gas money to get back to Hamilton. I'll have to beg Uncle Gilly for an advance on my wages to buy groceries.

What little sleep I get that night is full of dreams that nearly make me vomit. You picture the effect an 1800-pound bull would have on the human head. Not pretty, is it?

I spend all the next day prowling the rodeo grounds. I haven't a clue what I'm searching for, and I don't find any neon sign that says, "Magician will sit here tonight." When the gates open, I stand near them with my eyes closed, trying to sense everyone who comes in. The sensations of that many minds about causes me to lose what few marbles the fall yesterday didn't knock out of me, but I don't sense any magic.

When it's time for the bull riding, I decide to chance it. I really need the money, but tonight I've drawn a bull named He-man—you know, from that stupid Masters of the Universe cartoon—but he should probably be named Daisy-Muncher. I haven't a chance to win on that bull unless everybody else falls off. Dan Foster scores an eighty-three, and Ben Walker, a man I can't stand, scores an eighty-five and ends up with top prize money of eight hundred and seventy-five dollars. Nothing weird happens when I ride, but I score a whooping sixty-five and end with a whole sixty-six dollars in prize money. I guess I'll live on beans and rice for the next week. You can survive on that, but a man ought to have meat.

I freeze. I just thought of myself as a man again. Am I completely losing touch with who I am? I almost want to cry, but then I remember men don't cry.

After a week on rice and beans, I'm so mad I want to beat the living you-know-what out of the magician who made me lose. You might think that nearly dying should have aggravated me more than eating rice and beans, and yes, I still have nightmares about that bull's hoofs. But I'm hungry for something different to eat. I'm nervous as hell about the upcoming rodeo in Robertsdale, down by Mobile, and that makes me mad, too. I nurse the anger all during the five-and-a-half hour drive, fantasizing about what I'll do to her when I find her. I'm not sure why I decide my enemy is a woman, but I'm convinced the magic had a feminine feel to it. You might be wondering just how feminine magic feels different than masculine magic, but you're just going to have to go on wondering. I can't explain it.

I win the bull riding in Friday night's rodeo for a whopping $615. Robertsdale's purse has always been a little on the small side. More importantly, nothing funny happens. Dan and me and some of the others go to celebrate at a sleazy bar called Hole in the Wall. The bar owner knows me and cashes my prize check. I open my fool mouth and say the first round's on me.

I pack away more than a couple of beers, then in walks Ben Walker—did I mention I can't stand him?—with a blonde wearing a ponytail, a short skirt, and a low-cut blouse. She's hanging all over Ben. The skirt and blouse don't catch my attention—although they do catch the attention of every man in the place—but what comes with her does—the distinctive odor of magic. It was her. The magician who tried to kill me.

Mad and drunk, I storm right up to the blonde, grab her arm, and shout, "Why in the hell did you try to kill me?"

Ben tells me to get my filthy hands off his woman, and I tell him where he can stuff it and his mother. He punches me in the gut. Now,

Josh is big, but he must never have learned how to fight worth a hill of beans.

When I can't get up any more, Ben grabs the magician's hand. "Come on, Eileen. They let any old trash drink in this place."

I have no idea how I end up back at the rodeo grounds in the back of my truck, but I hope I didn't drive. I have a whole $75 in my pocket and a note that the bar owner took the rest to pay for damages. Why should I have to pay for damages? It isn't like I wanted my head to break the bar stool.

The next day I'm in no condition to ride, and Ben wins the top prize money again, which pisses me off even more. Eileen isn't in the staging area like some riders' women, and I can't sense her anywhere else in the arena. But the pain in my gut is taking most of my attention, and she could be ten feet from me and I might not feel her.

Because of my magic, I heal fast, so by Tuesday I'm feeling mostly alive. I'm more than determined to find this Eileen and get the truth out of her by any means necessary. Ben is from Auburn. Thinks he's all high and mighty because he goes to the university there, and I figure Eileen is some sorority chick. So I go to the Hamilton public library where they've got computers, and I google Ben to get his address. Then I borrow Uncle Gilly's truck because Ben knows mine, and no, I don't ask, but I leave a note and the extra key to my truck. That should be enough for any reasonable person, especially considering how much I save him in vet bills.

I get to Ben's apartment complex at about three in the afternoon. He comes home about four with one of those university-student book bags, wearing khakis and a polo shirt. He isn't even wearing boots. Some cowboy.

About an hour later he comes back out and gets in his truck. At least he has a truck and not some fancy-assed BMW. I follow him, and as I hope, he drives over to another apartment complex and picks up Eileen. Now that I know where she lives, I lean back in Uncle Gilly's truck and wait.

About two hours later Ben's truck squeals into the lot. Eileen flings the door open almost before the truck has a chance to stop. She jumps out and screams, "I hope I never see you again," then slams the door and stalks off to her apartment. Ben squeals out of the parking lot. I can't help smiling. Anything that makes Ben unhappy is mighty fine with me.

I give Eileen a minute to get settled. Then I knock, and she opens the door. Before she can recognize me, I push my way in and grab her arm. I'm about to ask her again why she tried to kill me when I'm hit with what feels like a sledge hammer.

When I wake up, I'm on the floor with my hands and feet tied. Eileen's sitting on the couch across from me. I'm starting not to like Eileen. Now, you might be wondering why I don't magic my way out of the rope. My magic only affects living things, and even with living things, I have to be touching them, so I'm pretty much stuck. You might also be wondering why I didn't use magic on Ben the other night. Well, I was so mad and drunk I didn't think about it.

I try to stall Eileen while I work at untying the ropes. "You have me where you want me. Before you kill me could you at least tell me why?"

She snorts. "What witch would ever dare kill? Don't you know that whatever magic of ill-intent we do comes back on us four-fold? A death curse is suicide for a witch."

I have to keep her talking because I'm not having any luck with the ropes. "You expect me to believe there is another magic user around here?"

She rolls her eyes like I'm the stupidest dumb ass she's ever had the misfortune to meet. "Of course there are other magic users. My coven has five members, but I promise you it wasn't one of them. If it was a witch, she would need something of yours—hair, fingernail clippings, blood—to work any magic against you. A wizard or sorcerer wouldn't though. They're more powerful."

"Huh?" I know, brilliant comeback, but my head is reeling. Of course, I've read about witches, wizards, and sorcerers, but the words mean different things in almost every book. "If you have a whole coven along with wizards and sorcerers, how come I've never run into any of you?"

Eileen rolls her eyes again. "We don't exactly advertise. Alabama isn't friendly to witches. You know, Exodus 22:18: 'Thou shalt not suffer a witch to live.'"

I have to admit she has a point. I don't "exactly advertise" my skills either. "Well, how many magic users are there around here?"

She shrugs. "Probably less than a dozen, but there might be more. The more powerful ones can shield themselves so I can't feel them. I can feel you though, but I don't know what you are."

Maybe I'm stupid, but I believe her when she says she didn't try to kill me. Mostly because if she wanted me dead, I'd be dead by now, so I decide to tell her the truth. "I'm a healer."

"A what?"

"A healer. You know, I heal things, make them better." Well, truth be told, I can make them worse, too.

"A healer?" she says like I'm speaking Chinese. "Witches do some healing, but I've never known a man with any talent for healing."

"I'm not a man. I'm a woman trapped in a man's body." She looks at me like I'm crazy. "Look, can you untie me? I'll tell you everything." I've just about given up getting the ropes off.

"I'm waiting for the rest of my coven. When they get here, you'll tell us everything, then we'll decide whether to untie you or kill you."

"I thought you said witches don't kill."

"If we do it as a coven, the feedback is diffused enough that we can handle it. It isn't pleasant though."

I gulp, wondering just how many times her coven has killed people, and start working harder on the ropes. Eileen just sits there with her arms and legs crossed, swinging her foot and not looking at me. "You mad at me or Ben?" I ask, hoping her fight with Ben doesn't get me killed.

"Don't mention that jerk to me!" She snorts. "Can you believe he thinks I'm a liar? He doesn't believe I'm a witch."

"You told him?"

She glares at me. "Long story. None of your business."

She looks away from me and doesn't say another word until her coven shows up. The first to arrive is a pretty black woman with her hair shaved to a fine buzz. Eileen introduces her as Kinyisha. The other three eventually arrive. Sandy, Nadeen, and Susan are white, but only Eileen has that sorority chick look.

My hands are numb, and I wonder how I'm going to talk them out of killing me. I tell them about the attack and everything I know about my situation, which isn't much. I think I'm a princess from some parallel realm. Then one day I wake up in Josh Killenyen's body. I don't know how I got here or how to get back where I belong.

When I finish, the witches sit there and look at each other for awhile and then down at me and then back at each other. "I think he may be crazy," Kinyisha says. "But I don't think he's dangerous to us."

They debate my sanity for what feels like forever, and when I try to hurry them up, they threaten to gag me. Apparently, they don't have a leader, so they have to come to a consensus before they do anything. Eventually, they reach the consensus that I'm either insane or a—I won't say the word they use, but it's foul—liar. I can't convince them otherwise, especially since I can provide so few details and merely say, "I don't remember" to most of their questions.

Finally, they decide I'm probably not dangerous and untie me, but they make me stay out of touching distance. Then they debate whether or not to help me. Kinyisha—I'm starting to like her—is all for helping me. "Isn't that the purpose of a coven? To help those in need?"

"But he's nuts!" says Nadeen. "He claims he's a princess from a parallel universe. You ever hear of any parallel universes? Does he look like a princess?" I'm starting not to like Nadeen.

Still, they eventually decide that if there is some unknown magic user working hostile magic in their territory, they need to know more about it. They agree that one of them should stick with me at every rodeo. Eileen doesn't want any part of it because she's mad at Ben and doesn't want to be anywhere near him. When the other women ask her why, she won't tell them anything. I figure she probably isn't supposed to tell people she's a witch. The other four agree to take turns, but Nadeen is far from happy.

Kinyisha comes with me to the next rodeo in Poplarville, Mississippi. She weaves some of my hair into a ring and charms it. She says it will block any curse aimed at my hand unless it's thrown by a really powerful wizard or sorcerer. I'm still not quite sure what the difference between a wizard and a sorcerer is, but Kinyisha tells me in no uncertain terms that a wizard is not a male witch. There's no such thing as a male witch.

After making my ring, Kinyisha sits in the stands to try to feel for the presence of any magic users. Nothing funny happens, and I score an eighty-five, which means that unless somebody gets real lucky tomorrow, I'll walk off with the top prize money.

I offer to let Kinyisha sleep in the back of my truck with me.

She's reluctant, but doesn't want to pay for a motel room, and I don't have the money for one. "If you try anything, I'll curse your genitals"—she used a different word here—"and make them fall off."

"Hey, I may look like a man, but I'm a woman. I'm not interested in you that way."

She snorts, still thinking I'm crazy, but she climbs in the back with me and seems disappointed in the morning that I didn't at least *try* to molest her.

Nobody uses magic against me on Saturday either, and nobody tops my score. I end up with $852 in prize money.

Nothing happens over the next few weeks, and I continue to win. The witches are starting to get tired of me, and frankly, I'm tired of them, especially Nadeen who always looks at me like some garbage she just stepped in. Meanwhile, Eileen makes up with Ben—apparently he apologized and bought her flowers and chocolates and who knows what else. She talks about how wonderful he is, and I just about lose my lunch on her sorority girl shoes. She comes with me—well, with Ben—to the rodeo in Millbrook, Alabama, just up the road from Montgomery. She makes me a ring like all of the other witches have done, and I get on my bull. It's Man Killer again. We barely get out of the chute when something hits my hand, and I go flying off into the wall, breaking my arm. I'm in so much pain I can't concentrate enough to look for magic users. To my humiliation, I have to be taken away in the ambulance, and, of course, with me out of it, Ben wins the top prize money.

On Saturday I drive to Auburn to meet with the witches. Eileen says she didn't feel anything, which scares the witches because only someone powerful could hide from them. Besides, Eileen's ring should have stopped anything done by a less powerful magic user. They wonder if they're in over their heads and should take it to someone more powerful. They decide not to because they don't trust the local wizards and sorcerers and because it could be one of them behind it. Instead, the witches decide they're all going to go to the next rodeo I'm fit to ride in.

I haven't a clue how I'm going to pay the hospital bill, especially since my broken arm keeps me out of bull riding for a week, but as I said, I heal a lot faster than normal, so I'm ready to ride the week after that down in Panama City, Florida. The witches are excited because they can go to the beach between rodeos. At the rodeo ground, the witches spread out throughout the crowd to feel for magic users. Nothing happens on Friday night, but I draw He-man again and only score in the sixties. Ben scores an eighty-two, which will be hard to beat on Saturday night.

Eileen goes off with Ben the next day, but I go with the rest of the witches to the beach. Nadeen seems disappointed that I don't react to her in a bikini.

On Saturday I draw Kracken—he's not quite as tough as Man Killer, but mighty close, and with all of the witches spread through the crowd I figure I'm safe enough. I'm not about to let Ben beat me again. I ride first, and for the first few seconds, I think everything's going to be fine. Then the curse hits my hand, and I go flying off. This time when I hit the ground, I'm so mad that I don't go over the closest fence like I'm supposed to. Instead, I ignore the danger of the bull and charge across the arena to the stands where I felt the curse coming from.

I gape in disbelief. Right in the middle of the stands sits Eileen. Kinyisha and the other three witches run up to me, and they gape at Eileen, too. When the crowd clears out, Eileen claims she didn't do anything, and there must have been some other magic user near her. The other witches don't believe her, and I don't either. They decide to take her off to a coven thing. I insist on coming with them, but the witches won't have any outsider involved.

"Just try and stop me from coming," I say, and Kinyisha hits me with one of those sledgehammers.

When I wake up, the witches are nowhere in sight. I go wait at my truck.

I fall asleep waiting, and about three in the morning, Kinyisha crawls in the back with me. From the sound of her voice, I can tell she's been crying. "She finally admitted it. Breaking all our codes, she sent the curse against you. Ben provided her a few strands of your hair the first time. And you gave her plenty to use the other two times. If it helps any, she wasn't trying to kill you, just make you fall off so Ben could win. She said you were using magic to win, and that wasn't fair."

"Well . . ." I start to defend myself, but I think she might have a point. I'm not about to admit it, though. Instead, I say, "So Ben believes she's a witch."

"She broke our vow of secrecy and told him. He didn't believe her at first and just gave her your hair as a joke. He made fun of her when she told him that she made you fall of the bull. That's why she was mad at him, but when you started winning again, he made up with her. She told him it was too dangerous for her to do it tonight with the rest of us here, but he bullied her into it, saying he needed the prize money for tuition."

"Whether she meant to kill me or not, she came damn close. Just what do you plan to do about that?"

"She'll be taken care of. You won't have to worry about her again."

"Taken care of? Just what does that mean?"

Kinyisha shakes her head, and no matter how many times I ask her, she won't tell me. She does offer to introduce me to the more powerful magic users she knows to see if any of them can help me with my body switching problem, even though I think she still believes I'm crazy.

I take her up on her offer. Maybe something good will come out of nearly having my head smashed open like a watermelon.

∞∞∞

Silent Partner
by Henry Gaudet

As dream jobs go, private eye doesn't rate in the top ten, or the top hundred for that matter. It's not the sort of job you aspire to. It's the job you're left with when life closes all the other doors. Ask any ten dicks how they got their start, and you'll get ten tales of ten falls from grace.

My story's no different. Not so long ago, I was doing alright. I was an ordained Sheppard, a Knight of the Golden Shield, charged by Mother Church and the Divine Trinity to defend the public from dark magic and heathen witchcraft. Not an easy job, not a fun job, but it wasn't all bad. That little gold badge comes with a lot of fringe benefits. Even so, for all the window dressing, it's still the same old story.

Loyal readers of the Herald may remember that dust-up about three years back involving the Cult of the Slumbering Eye and a few bored socialites looking for the next big thrill. Turns out the next big thrill involved a sacrificial troll calf and at least three dead pagan gods. One botched séance later, and we're up to our collective neck in tourists from beyond the grave.

The poor little rich kids were, of course, the first to go, but they made a splash before they checked out. Lowside Park was all but swallowed whole, and gates popped as far away as Battersbridge and Grifton. Kept us busy for a week solid, and I'm convinced we never plugged all the holes. Two months later, we were still finding a corpse or two every day.

My partner Frank and I pulled the short straw and Father Cussler tapped us to look for strays. Not a lot of detective work, just a straight bug hunt. Personally, I'd rather be chasing down the puppet masters, the ones in this world and the next. Instead, we had to settle for breaking their toys.

At least Frank was happy. "No pulse, no problem," he'd say. "Let the cops deal with warrants and due process. I'll stick with the deaders. No one sues when you shoot."

We were on the way back to the station after an especially nasty bit of work on the South Side. Sure, we looked rough, but just you try looking daisy fresh on the two-hours-past-the-finish-line side of a twelve hour shift. Even so, we can take only so much credit for the stench. In our line of work, spatter is an occupational hazard.

The shambler was ripe, dead at least a month. It moved in with a bricklayer and his family a couple days earlier and stayed for dinner. Landlord went to the cops about the smell. Cops came to the door, got one whiff and called us.

There was a uniform waiting for us on the front stoop. He was a skinny kid, about 18, so pale I made him for a corpse and went for my badge. I was set to drop him when he spotted us and started acting like a breather.

He did his best to fill us in, stammering through the shock and hysteria like any teenage boy. Said he'd gone round back earlier and gotten a good look in the kitchen window. Stuck around long enough to lose his lunch across the screen door before figuring he might be better off waiting out front. You ask me, he should be proud he didn't wet himself.

Sure enough, the shambler was there in the kitchen. It sat at the table, fumbling a fork across the days-old breakfast. A broken coffee cup crunched in the brown stain underfoot, most likely from an earlier effort.

Usually, it's only the new dead that try to remember their rituals. Once, I rested a body sitting on the crapper. Seriously, sat through the whole rite trying to pinch a phantom loaf. But you don't see this so often with the older corpses. Botched or no, the rites that got this thing moving again had some serious juice.

The bricky's wife and their eldest were still alive, but both were missing too many pieces and too much blood. They weren't going to make it. Thankfully, they were both too messed up to know just how messed up they were. Everyone else, the dog included, was picked clean. Never mind what you see in the papers. Brain-eaters may make for good headlines, but shamblers aren't big on reading.

We didn't waste time with protective rites. We pulled weapons and on three, Frank kicked in the door. We opened up, blasting chunks away until the thing started acting dead. Then we sent it on. It didn't go easy. Even as hamburger, it still took all seven greater circles and a solid hour of chanting to rest the damned thing. Like I said, serious juice.

By the time we were finished, the cops had sent over a couple of squad cars. The kid was gone. We stuck around long enough for the meat wagon boys to show and left clean up to them. Privileges of the gold badge.

Anyway, I was in a hurry to get back to the station. Alice from the lunch counter finally agreed to go out with me and I really, really needed a shower.

But traffic stopped cold in the Barrows with about a mile to go. Rush hour. Over fifteen minutes or so, we crawled past half a block of tenements and Glo-Writ signs declaring "Checks Cashed Here" and "Tattoo Tattoo Tattoo".

Frank stared absently out the window at a pack of goblins hanging out in front of the grocer on the corner. There were eight of them, slouching in a loose circle with a casual menace that drove foot traffic into the street.

"Damn duskies," Frank muttered. "Ought to run 'em in."

"On what, Frank?"

"Aw, don't give me that. They're trouble. You know it and I know it." Sometimes, I think Frank missed the war. The good old days when you could blow away a couple dozen goblins and they'd give you a medal. Back then, the grays were the Enemy. They were these hideous creatures swarming up from their rat holes to rape our mothers and eat our babies. After V Day, after the Accord, they were suddenly people, and for some reason, killing them wasn't okay anymore.

"They're not doing anything."

"Sure, Joe. Maybe they're just waiting for a lift to choir practice." Frank's snarl reflected back at me in the window.

"They're breathers. Not our problem. Leave it for the cops."

One of the punks spotted Frank and they made us. Insults and cat calls carried over the dull grumble of motionless traffic. Wide mouths stretched into predatory smiles filled with too many teeth. Fingers stood erect with that confident ease that only comes from hours of practice in the bathroom mirror. Frank's face turned seven shades of red, his jaw clenching so tight his teeth squeaked. I looked away. "Let it go, Frank."

The truck in front, an old Booker oil-burner, pulled ahead six inches and I nudged forward, close enough for the black exhaust to roll over the hood. Frank was growling now, eyes locked on the punks on the corner. I decided to play it safe and kept my eyes forward, so I never saw what set Frank off.

"Aw, that's it!" he said, door already open. "I don't have to take this crap!" Then he was out of the car, hand reaching for the cannon under his meat spattered jacket.

By the time I had my seatbelt off, Frank was in a shoving match with the beefiest, a squat mastiff of a punk with a face covered in labyrinthine gang tattoos. At least the gun was still holstered. The others were circling, hooting and cheering and shoving. Most of the pedestrians had already crossed the road, but the drivers started to get nervous.

One of the little guys came in close, giggling. "Hey, Father!" He struggled to hold back the laughter long enough for his one-liner. "You got a limmmf . . ." Without taking his eyes off the big one, Frank palmed the kid's head and shoved.

Only the kid was charmed, some sort of ward. There was a crack and a flash, and Frank spun face first into the side of a bus. The scrawny kid never budged. The gang exploded into that freaky goblin laugh, all wet and hissy. I was still on the wrong side of the car, watching through the Booker's oily exhaust.

Frank staggered to his feet, his nose broken and bleeding. He steadied himself against the bus, dragging a muddy palm print down the side. The goblins staggered with laughter, hissing and hooting, their too-white milk teeth and luminescent eyes stark in the growing shadow.

Then Frank pulled his cannon and blew a hole in the kid the size of a beer can, and the crew stopped laughing.

For one second, one magical moment, nothing happened. We all just froze, everyone staring at the dead goblin kid crumpled up next to the fruit display by the window.

It didn't last.

Engines revved and horns blared and cars jumped the curb, trying to get the hell out of there. Everyone panicked, running and ducking and screaming. Everyone but the goblins. They didn't run; they crouched.

They weren't screaming either. Instead, they growled some sort of tribal chant, low and slow, the kind of deep buzzing you feel in your molars. With everyone else screaming and running and diving, Frank and the goblins were completely still.

I pulled my own piece and my badge. "Trinity!" I screamed, too high and shrill. "Everyone, on the ground!" They ignored me. Frank too. This wasn't my dance. "On the ground!" I shouted again.

Frank never turned. "I got this, partner." Somehow, I heard him. His voice was low, monotone, dead. But somehow, I heard him over the engines and the horns and the panicked screams.

"Yes, partner." A raspy hiss of a voice, thick with Sub-continental accent. Tattoo-boy. "The Good Sheppard has everything under control." He took a step forward and his gang fanned out. "Isn't that right, Father?" Another step. The chant was getting quicker, rising an octave. The punk's hand dropped casually behind his back. "Say a prayer for us, won't you, Father? Save us from our blasphemies and pagan heresies."

Another boom and Tattoo-boy's knee disappeared. Frank didn't budge. Tattoo-boy tipped over howling something ethnic, before the chant rose to a crescendo.

The others made their move. Half a dozen goblins hopped up on what I hoped was just adrenaline lunged for Frank, leaping at least eight feet in the air. Another boom and Frank caught the next one in the face.

In the face.

The kid spun away as the rest came down on my partner. Hard.

Frank toppled under the wave of grays, a mass of teeth and talons and I thought I saw the flash of a switchblade. Still, Frank was a big man, six feet with some change left over, and he was giving as good as he got.

At last, I got close enough to do some good. I couldn't take a shot, but I pulled one kid off and slapped a binding on him. The thin chain whipped round, tying his legs together, pinning his arms to his chest. His snarl turned to shock as the chain constricted and he fell over, arms lashed painfully across his torso.

In that time, Frank had bloodied two more, leaving them writhing on the sidewalk, but one of the others bit into his arm and the cannon went skittering. Frank and the remaining three scrambled after it in a tangle of bodies, but it was Tattoo-boy got there first. I have to admit, he moved pretty quick for someone down half a leg. He hefted the gun and swung it around on us.

He was kneeling, balanced on a blackened stump, bleeding from his nose and a nasty gash over a swollen eye. He looked like hell, but the kid leveled the gun like a pro. Like a killer. I turned my own gun on him, nowhere near as steady. We weren't going to win a stand-off. The others were already circling, closing in. So I pulled the trigger.

It was just a brass caster, not like Frank's cannon, but it put a neat steaming hole in the kid's forehead, punctuating the runes across his face. His head snapped back, his face a perfect portrait of goblin grace. He was like that for ages, kneeling in front of the grocer, eyes upturned. Then he tipped to the side and stopped breathing and just like that the kid was dead.

There were still three goblins off to my left, but they never made their move. I guess they didn't like the odds. Frank groaned as he bent down and reached for his cannon.

"Don't move, Frank." I couldn't recognize the voice as my own. It was dead, just like Frank's earlier. Just like the meat on the sidewalk that used to be three kids.

Frank looked up at me, chuckling. "What are you going to do, Joe? You going to stop me? You going to put me down?"

His bloodied hand was on the butt of his gun now. Somewhere behind me, the last goblin legged it around the corner.

"Leave it. The cops will be here soon. Don't make it worse." The shake was gone from my hand now. Frank was square in my sights.

"The cops?" Frank laughed. "The cops will thank us and buy us a round when their shift's over. You're really going to stand there and tell me that you'll turn on your own partner over this pack of duskie shit bags?!" The gun was in his hand now.

"We don't have to do this. Put the gun down."

I'm pretty sure his next words were going to be "Fuck you, Joe," but he was bringing the gun up, so I pulled the trigger and killed for the second time in my life.

The cops showed up later, and the reporters. I just sat in the car, badge on the dash. They had lots of questions, sure, but they'd think twice before asking.

Privileges of the gold badge.

I just sat in the car, stinking of rotten meat, until Father Cussler and the boys came to pick me up.

Frank and I gave Mother Church a public relations nightmare. Lucky for me there were so many witnesses. Frank got the blame. Frank got the condemnation. All I got was fired.

Well, that and the ghost.

Frank didn't waste much time before he started haunting me, but his heart was never in it. He said he just couldn't stay mad at me. I have a feeling it may have more to do with the fact that, gold badge or no, I can still rest him.

Instead, we struck a truce, and when I went private, he came along. I even put his name on the door, just under mine. When clients ask, I tell them he's a silent partner.

∞∞∞

Favours
by Richard Keane

In Brad's world, money could only get you so far, but do a favour for the right person and doors would open you never even knew existed. Do a favour for the manager of the Langham hotel in London – say a nuisance broad who didn't know when to keep her mouth shut needed to disappear – and you could get an all expenses paid weekend in the penthouse. Whilst a favour for a detective at the local precinct could ensure an unfortunate event in the near future would go largely unnoticed.

Favours were the thinking man's currency.

But, as with anything, too much of a good thing is bound to come crashing down sooner or later. Get on the wrong side of the wrong person, and then things got real complicated...

The favour was for an anonymous client – that was how things worked most of the time. You do a favour for me, I do a favour for you, but that doesn't mean I need to know if you work for the government – hell! You could be doing a favour for the Prime Minister and be none the wiser.

The favour had been passed on by an intermediary. Not that there was a call centre where favours were handled all day long. In this line of work it was best not to know who you were doing business with. The job was simple. A warehouse on Dart Street, down by the docks, needed to accidentally catch fire and burn down to the ground. Not one of his most discreet favours, but he wasn't complaining.

He had the gear in the trunk of his Sedan, the car a rental under a different name. Hey, that was just good business sense. It was the early hours, at least another hour or two before the sun would show its face. The streets were empty, and his foot was firmly down on the gas pedal.

He pulled up a street over from the warehouse.

He knew the area well enough. They used to build cars in the warehouses around here before the contracts went overseas, along with the livelihoods of countless workers and future generations. At least someone was going to get a payout from one of the abandoned buildings when he was done.

He got out of the car and collected the gear from the trunk: fireproof gloves, three cans of petrol and a box of matches. What could be simpler? He walked down the street, with the equipment in tow. What would the cops say if they happened to see him now, carrying the gear for his bonfire to be? He would probably find he had done a favour for one of the guys in the past, or their boss, and everything would be cool. That was the thing with favours, what made them such a unique currency. The guys with good business sense didn't just do a favour for somebody, and then get one in return. No, you had to put some in the bank for a rainy day, when something bad went down and you needed a get out clause.

The warehouse came into view.

The doors were boarded up, most of the windows broken, and those that were not were as black as the night sky. When he came to the door, he heaved his gear to the ground. Then, from behind his back, hid securely by the elasticity of his trousers, he grasped his trusty crowbar. All it took was a few jolts, and the door was open.

He stepped into the building.

His footsteps echoed loudly, as if the building were groaning at his admittance. The smell of damp was ripe in the air, and other smells he didn't care to think about. Through holes in the ceiling crept strands of moonlight, which flickered and danced on machines that had been left behind to become little more than rusting gravestones.

He got to work, placing the cans at strategic points as planned, and created a trail of gas to make sure things got going quickly. Though, now he saw the state of the place he doubted he needed so much petrol. There was more than enough flammable ware left in the place. He got the box of matches from his pocket, and held a match ready to light…

The building was thrown into blinding radiance.

He threw his hands up before his face, almost losing his footing at his surprise. The light was coming from outside, his mind already formulating an exit strategy. It wasn't looking good. The next moment, as if by some trick of the light, he was at the window as he wiped the dirt from the glass.

A flash of red.

He felt his skin crawl. It couldn't be. Not now. Not tonight. He looked again. There was a person dressed in red leather from head to toe, a woman, one of three to be precise. She opened her mouth…

He darted away from the widow, and at that moment a piercing scream battered his eardrums. The window frames shook on their hinges, already weak from age and disrepair, until they exploded into the warehouse. The fragments of glass came down like snow drops, snow drops that could cut skin and blind eyes. He held his jacket over his head for protection, and crouched under a rusting machine.

The sound stopped, and the blinding light went with it.

He could hear his heart beating fiercely in his ears. He looked to the entrance of the building, but no one entered. His gaze lingered there for a second nonetheless. He rose to his feet and began pacing. The glass scrunched under his feet. Why were they here? He had heard they were on the warpath after some untouchable guy was killed, but he had had nothing to do with that. And a job like this was too small time for them.

Outside he could hear voices now, but he paid them no attention. He needed to think, needed to throw a curve ball that would mix things up and somehow get him out of this.

"Damn it", he said aloud, as he stopped in his tracks.

There was no other option. He didn't like it, but this was why you always kept a favour or two in your wallet should things get screwed up. But still, he'd rather big favours like that remain in his wallet.

He took the phone from his pocket, and began to dial. He watched the door closely. Why had no one come in yet? It took only one ring of the phone for the man to answer.

"I was wondering when this day would come." The man's voice was gravely, but by no means sounded like someone who had been awoken unexpectedly in the early hours.

Brad didn't say a word.

"So, what'll it be? Something big I'm guessing." He hated the cheerfulness of the man's voice.

His eyes remained fixed on the door. "I need a get out clause, Bob." He had to force the words from his mouth.

"You? Never thought I'd see the day." Neither had he.

He could hear footsteps approaching. "Look, you're going to need to make this happen quickly."

"You've got one go at this, Brad. A slight mistake or miss-shot, and you're toast."

"I know," he said begrudgingly. He moved further away from the door.

Bob only had a few skills, but they had their advantages. Even impossible situations like this became possible when you had that kind of talent. Still, the guy wasn't an energiser bunny and a skill like that was only good every week or so.

"Right," Bob said, and the phone went dead

He put the phone in his pocket.

A flicker of red appeared at the door, and then again and again. The Three Sisters. They wore red to mirror the blood of their victims, and to send a wave of fear into their enemies. And hell, it worked well. They were the police of the Other Side, only they didn't stop to ask questions.

All of a sudden, there was a flash of light, but it was not a blinding one. He turned. On the wall had appeared a large hole, which looked out onto a setting that was not the mess of the factory. It looked like a field of wavy grass, cloaked in darkness. His head turned at a flicker of red metres away from where he stood. He needed to move.

Bob's words reverberated in his head.

A slight mistake or miss-shot, and you're toast.

Taking a deep breath, he jumped through the hole.

He was falling…

He didn't know why he was falling. Maybe something had gone wrong. But then, there was a residing splash when he fell into the river.

Son of a bitch, he thought.

He resurfaced, and gulped in the cold night air. He looked up. The hole remained open above him, like a void into another universe. The colour of crimson appeared at its mouth, deadly in pursuit. There was no face, only blood red that covered the pursuer's body from head to toe.

The hole closed, and he breathed a sigh of relief.

After a moment, as his adrenaline faded and violent shivering took hold of his body, he realised the water was freezing and that if he didn't get out and into a change of clothing soon he would likely catch hyperthermia.

He couldn't have made the hole open onto a grass field? Even a pig sty would have been better.

He swam to the river's edge, and shivered violently when the chill of early morning collided with the river's water that soaked his body.

The sun was beginning to dawn. Soon there would be people. He needed to get out of the open, and he desperately needed a change of clothes.

There was only one option.

He ran.

He ran faster than any man or woman could. That was his skill. He was like a shadow, there one moment and gone the next, a mere blink in your peripheral vision. Yet, it seemed now that no matter how fast you ran you couldn't always outrun your problems. He was in trouble. Someone had set him up, but who and why? He was uncertain if he was more annoyed because someone had had the cheek to set him up, or because one of his most precious favours had been used.

A get out clause gone down the drain.

And the Three Sisters.

He had heard stories about them, like everybody else on the Other Side, but to actually have them on his tail was a different story all together. They weren't even sisters as far as he knew, but who could tell when they dressed like red demons? He had seen them once before, and he had seen the damage they could wreak. Them being there tonight meant this was big. The Three Sisters didn't deal with small time jobs like the warehouse. That was kid's play to them.

Whoever set him up must have had friends in high places.

He dashed along the river bank like the road runner, a glimmer of light in the morning dawn. The sound of birds' singing was a constant whistle to his ears, unable to settle into any meaningful tune. But he was growing tired, and he was still shivering in an alarming fashion. Every skill had its limitations, and it had been a long night.

He wasn't going to the city though. Not yet. Soon he would ask questions, but not yet. He needed to visit one of his hideouts, out in the woods. Living on the Other Side, and the way he did, you needed to be prepared for anything, needed to have a place to go when things got too hot. The Three Sisters' arrival had been unexpected, but he was a pro and had learnt early on that you had to be ready no matter how unexpected things got.

He slowed his pace. The sound of the birds' singing became harmonious.

He stopped, and his hand was already turning the key in the lock. It was an old disused barn. No one came out here. Not families who thought it a nice place to escape the city for a day, or kids looking for a hideout while they got stoned and reached second base. The place was protected by invisible barriers – just another one of his past favours put to good use. But it wouldn't provide protection against the Three Sisters.

He needed to move fast.

He opened the door. There was nothing homely about the barn. There were no colour-matched furnishings, or any other sign that somebody lived there in comfort. It had the bare essentials, for when things got uncomfortable. He removed his sodden clothes, which weighed a tonne and smelt more like sewer than river, and put on some clean clothes he had found and wrapped a blanket around his shoulders.

There was some wood kindling already on the fire ready to be burned. He got a new box of matches from a drawer – the other ones were wet – and lit the fire. He stood before it, rubbing his chest, until the warmth of the fire grew and eventually seeped into his bones, taking away the misery of the night's events. No one would see the smoke from the chimney; another facet of the invisible barrier.

He found a can of chicken soup in a cupboard, in what could barely be classed as a kitchen. He put it in a pan and rested it above the fire, but only waited until it was lukewarm before devouring it. He ate in front of the fire on a stool, until the shivers that had teased him so greatly began to subside. When he was warmed up and well fed, he lay down before the fire. Sleep didn't come easy and when it finally did he dreamt of gaping holes in the sky that peered out onto other worlds, where red demons with only darkness for faces stared back at him

He awoke with a start.

His eyes surveyed the barn. There was no one there. He had been dreaming, a bad sign as ever there were. He never dreamed. Dreams were for schmucks who yearned for something better than what they had, a common ailment amongst the nine to five workers. But still, it was a bad sign. This mess must have gotten to him worse than he thought.

He looked down at his watch. Five p.m. He had been asleep for over ten hours. Bob's skill sure had its drawbacks. But it didn't matter. It would be dark in little over an hour, and then the city's own unique sewage would come flowing out of the gutters, ready to talk. The darkness had a funny way of making people talk.

He left the barn when the light began to fade. He didn't run. It would take him half an hour to reach a place where there were people, and he didn't want that to happen until his old friend the darkness was by his side. He felt rejuvenated after his rest. It wasn't so much what had happened at the factory that had tired him out before, however unexpected it was, but more because of Bob's skills. Travelling like that was never meant for the human body, it was too weak. Any lesser man would have crumpled like an old man on ice, but Brad wasn't just any guy.

Moss and wood crumpled under his feet, as he filtered through the trees like a spectre. All was quiet otherwise. He tried to think back to the phone call for the job at the factory, any sign that may enlighten him to who was behind it. But he couldn't recall anything suspicious, and the safety measures they put in place would prevent him from tracing back to the contact directly. The job had sounded easy. He should have known better.

The darkness settled, like a cloak around his shoulders. He felt comforted by its shadow.

When he came to the river he continued along the embankment, before turning onto a public pathway. It was surrounded by shrubbery on each side, which steadily gave way to fences and tarmac, until only glimpses of foliage could be seen. There were faces in the darkness now: couples holding hands; shopkeepers locking up; drug dealers standing on street corners; police sat in cruisers looking the other way; and children who had been allowed out to play amongst the city's vermin.

The neon lights of the restaurants and bars surrounded him, accompanied by raucous chatter and laughter.

Finally, he came to his destination. He would have his answers soon. He looked up at the flashing sign, the words *Sandra's bar* overlapping a pair of barely covered neon breasts.

He walked in.

The stench of smoke greeted him, repulsive itself, but he could smell the sweat and cheap cologne undercurrent. He went to the bar. The bartender double-checked when he saw who was standing at his bar. He had been in the middle of serving another customer, but the patron was forgotten in an instant and left to whisper to himself irritably.

"Hey, Brad." The bartender could barely meet his gaze, his voice as frail as a schoolgirl. He cleaned a glass with a dish cloth, a little too vigorously.

"Long time, no see."

"Yeah." The bartender forced a grin. "What can I do for you?"

"I'll take a glass of bourbon, if that's not too much trouble." He peered around the bar, but there were few faces to note.

"Sure thing." The bartender grabbed a bottle from behind the bar, and poured its brown liquid into a glass.

Brad took a sip when the glass was handed to him. He savoured the feel of warmth it ignited in his throat, the coldness he had felt after his near drowning in the river gradually becoming a distant memory.

"Is he here?"

The bartender seemed to recoil at his question. His gaze flickered to a row of tables at the far side of the bar.

Brad nodded. He collected his glass and walked over.

The old man sat alone reading a newspaper and smoking a cigarette. An empty glass stood on the table, next to an ashtray crammed with cigarette butts. The old guy didn't look up when he approached, but Brad knew how good the guy's hearing was. Looks are deceiving – the phrase must have been created for guys like him. Most people didn't learn that until it was too late.

He sat down and placed his glass on the table, but the man continued to read his newspaper. The man's hair was cropped, tinges of grey beginning to take over what had previously been dark hair. His face was also showing signs of age, sagging skin and frown lines the result of an eventful life.

He scanned the bar for anyone that may deserve his attention. He was feeling a little more skittish than normal, unsurprising after the past day's events.

"So, you made it?"

He took a sip of bourbon, and noticed the newspaper had been set down on the table. The old man watched him intently.

"Thanks to you, Bob." He leaned back into his chair. "But I can't say I appreciate the soaking. A little unnecessary, I thought."

Bob laughed. "You young guys, you always expect things to be done yesterday. You don't understand the finer details. And let's not forget, you did call me at five in the morning. Portals aren't tools I have in abundant supply, no matter what you may think."

He waved a hand dismissively.

"So, what happened?"

He rubbed his temples. "I was set up." The words tasted sour. He took a sip of bourbon, to ease his rising temperature.

"Who the hell would set you up?"

His lips twitched into a faint smile. "That's why I've come to see you."

"Not enough that I saved your ass, now you want information? It's always the same with you, Brad, always wanting more."

"The Three Sisters were there."

Bob paused for a moment, taken aback. He ran his hands through his hair, the occasional flicker of brown still visible amongst his greying hair.

"What is it you want to know?"

"I need a name. Something to get me started." He downed the rest of the bourbon, and wiped at the corners of his mouth with the sleeve of his shirt. "I wouldn't ask but–"

"Don't give me that crap," Bob interrupted him. His tone wasn't stern, but nor was it gentle. "We're old friends. I mean come on." He shook his head. "I'm the one who got you into this game. You know I won't let you down." His expression became thoughtful. "But I can only give you a step in the right direction."

"Thanks."

Bob tore a strip from the newspaper, and wrote on it with a pen from his pocket. After folding the piece of paper up, Bob handed him the note. He nodded his thanks, and rose from his seat. He nodded curtly to the barman on his way out, but the wave he got in return held not an ounce of believability. He was thankful to leave the stench of the place.

He came out into the darkness of night again. But it was not truly dark.

Life, if that's what it could be called around this place, overcame the shadows. The people feared what the darkness would reveal, and so they hung around bars and strip joints, or under street lamps huddled together, not to keep the cold at bay but to feel the protection that came from being with other people. He eyed them like a vicious animal, his anger after what had happened at the factory suddenly flowing through his veins.

He shook his head.

There was no point wasting his energy on one of these dregs of society, not even the drug dealer at the street corner currently selling drugs to some schoolgirl, while the police sat idly by supping on joe and scoffing doughnuts.

He retrieved the strip of newspaper Bob had given him from his pocket, and unrolled it. When he saw the name, he stopped abruptly in the street. A person bumped into him and began to mouth off, until they realised who it was they were talking to and carried on walking with their head down. He stared back at the name on the piece of paper. He had thought things were complicated enough

Charlie.

He knew the name. He knew where she lived - hell! He had been living with her at her place for two years, before things had gone off the rails. How was she involved? The thought was a troubling one. He could only hope Bob had made a mistake, heard wrong from somebody, and that Charlie was no way involved. But he had to find out.

She owned a strip joint on what he liked to call *bourgeois alley*, courtesy of the rich scum who left their wives and kids at home while they went to watch girls who were barely older than their own daughters take their clothes off. Or more if the price was right.

He came to the entrance.

Two bouncers the size of tree trunks tensed up when they saw him. He squeezed his hands into fists. They may be as big as houses, but no one could move as fast as he could. Before he reached them, a woman with dark skin arrived at their side. She placed a cautionary hand on each of their shoulders, and whispered something into their ears. They then stepped aside like good guard dogs. When he walked past them he gave them a wry smile.

He joined the stride of the dark skinned woman. *Charlie.* She was beautiful as he remembered; her shape, her slim but strong cheekbones, and her devilish eyes that could eat away at any man's soul. He had forgotten how perfect she was. They had broken up over a year ago, but you never forgot a woman like Charlie.

She turned, and saw him staring. A knowing smile graced her lips.

"The day Brad Chambers walks through my door is a bad day for all of us. A storm must be coming."

He remained quiet, as he allowed her to lead him through the throng of the strip joint. The music was loud, but barely resonated over the jeers and cheers of old men who stood ogling at bare skin swinging from poles. His eyes remained fixed on Charlie. Not one of the girls in the place could match her beauty.

She led him through a door at the rear of the club, and up some steps that led to a large office. The décor was a stark contrast to the dark and dank setting below, her little safe haven. Charlie took a seat on the edge of a desk, at the far side of the room. He remained standing by the door. When they broke up it had been on good terms, or as good terms as you could hope for after a break up. But, he didn't know what to think after Bob had given him the note with her name on it.

He watched her take a cigarette from a box on the desk, and place it elegantly between her lips. She lit it and took a drag. He had always hated to be with a woman who smoked, but with Charlie he couldn't help but make allowances.

"So," she said to him, "there are whispers on street corners of strange things going on, and lo and behold you appear." She smiled. "Coincidence?"

He took a step closer into the room. The smell of her fragrance was intoxicating. It overshadowed the smoke filtering through the room. "Things have been a bit crazy. I wouldn't be here otherwise."

"I'll say," she said, and tapped cigarette ash into the ashtray on the table. "And why would you come to see me, then? After all this time, having not seen me since we broke up, why would you come back?"

He shuffled on his feet uncomfortably. "I saw Bob downtown."

"Good old Bob. He still going?" She placed the finished cigarette into the ashtray, and lit another one. "Whose name did he give you?"

He felt the hairs on the back of his neck stand on end, as he walked over and handed her the note. He watched her face when she opened it, and wondered what thoughts were running through her head. Whatever they were, she displayed no sign of them in her expression or body language. Maybe Bob had got it wrong?

She glanced up from the note. Her unwavering eyes met his. "You came all the way here to give me a note given to you by some old fart? A note with my name on it? You shouldn't have bothered."

She thrust the note into his hands, and stormed past him.

"Charlie," he said weakly.

She stopped, and looked back at him. Her lips twitched into a faint smile, and then she turned and walked out of the room.

He stood there for a moment, his mind trying to figure out the next step. He couldn't believe Charlie was a part of this. Wouldn't believe it. Bob must have heard wrong. Just looking into her eyes was enough for him to know that she could no way be involved.

He didn't see Charlie as he left the strip joint, and was thankful for that. He didn't think he could stand to see her wounded expression again.

The night air felt colder now. Everything did. He could still see the look of sadness on Charlie's face, when she handed him back the note. The notion that she would set him up was absurd, and yet he had taken the time to contemplate it. Who would be next on his list? Who else would be tainted by his accusations, before he got any answers?

A beggar was sat by a cash point on the street. A blanket covered most of him, or her. Brad threw a coin down by the person's side, unaware of the flicker of red that appeared for a second when the blanket got caught in the breeze. He continued onward, not knowing where he would next go. Charlie was a dead end, in more ways than one. He turned down an alleyway. He couldn't stand to be amongst the crowds of people.

Should he go back to Bob? He had already tried his luck in getting Charlie's name, but then why would Bob give him Charlie's name if he didn't think her somehow involved?

What if…

He heard footsteps behind him. Damn! How had he not noticed he was being followed? The next moment, something struck him on the back of his head. His feet buckled from under him, and he felt something warm trickle down his scalp.

Everything went dark…

His head was banging. What happened?

He opened his eyes, but was met only by darkness. They had put a blindfold over his eyes, and a gag in his mouth for good measure. He could hear footsteps, slow and deliberate. There was more than one of them, whoever they were. There was a strange scrunching sound to the footsteps though, somehow recent in his memory, and the smell of chemicals that was all too familiar.

The blindfold was removed from his eyes, and he instantly knew why the smell was so familiar, and why the footsteps had sounded so strange. He was back in the warehouse, the chemical stench that of the petrol he had planned to use to set the place alight and the scrunching sound of shards of glass now resting on the ground like a carpet of snow.

The light was faint, but this only made the three shapes in red stand out all the more. He felt a chill run down his spine. The Three Sisters. But he didn't moan or show any indication of the fear he felt. He wouldn't give them the satisfaction. If they had wanted to kill him they would have done it by now. But what could they want from him?

One of the Three Sisters stepped closer to him. Which one was it? It was impossible to tell. In their red, skin tight, leather outfits who knew where one began and another one ended.

He grimaced when the gag was removed from his mouth.

He didn't speak. But neither did they, and that was what filled him with cold dread. He chuckled in his head at what someone would think if they were to walk in on such a strange scene - him tied up, and three females dressed all in red leather. They could be forgiven for thinking it some kind of freaky sex game.

He tried to meet their gazes, to show them he wasn't scared. But he was scared, a sensation he had felt on rare occasions in recent times. He couldn't stand to have their piercing eyes on him any longer.

"Whatever it is you want from me, I don't have it."

A loud cackle of laughter escaped the throat of one of the Three Sisters. It echoed around the warehouse.

"Who said we wanted anything from you?" It was the one stood before him that spoke, an undeniable level of sternness to her voice.

He grappled with the rope that held his hands. *The last act of a desperate man*, he thought.

"If you don't want anything from me then why am I here?" He could feel his anger rising with each word he spoke. "Why the hell did you hit me on the head and bring me here?"

The Sister who had spoken walked up to him, and punched him in the face. His head bobbed backwards and forwards, only for another hit to connect with his nose. He felt blood gush down his mouth.

He laughed, and it seemed to take The Three Sisters by surprise for a moment. He didn't know why he was laughing. It wasn't a funny situation by any means. But he felt it was either that, or allowing the terror he felt to take control of him.

Better to laugh in the face of danger.

Or so he thought, until a right hook connected.

His vision blurred, by what he thought must be blood coming from a cut above his eye. With his head slumped backwards, he noticed one of the other Three Sisters to the side removing a cloth from a table, to reveal an assortment of knives and other tools.

He felt his blood slowly turn cold. The Three Sisters watched him, as each tool was examined to determine which one would be first on the list.

And we have a winner, he thought dryly.

The Sister approached him, a sharp-edged saw in her hand, while the one who had punched him stepped aside.

"We don't require any information from you, Brad." Her voice was like nails being scraped on a blackboard. "We are not doing this because you hold some insight that will enlighten us. Far from it." The Sister ran the saw sensually across her thigh, the sound of friction against leather. "You've done one too many favours, Brad. Got under the shoes of the wrong people." The Sister exchanged glances with the other two. "Killed the wrong person, and now people in high places are taking notice."

He wrestled with the ropes that held him. "I never killed anybody," he shouted.

The Sister faltered at his words.

It was true. He had never killed anybody. He had allowed people to think he had taken people's lives, but who hadn't gone to lengths to allow certain beliefs to manifest. It was part of the job.

"Whoever it is you're after, you've got the wrong person."

"I can assure you, Brad, we are never wrong."

The Sister brought the saw down on his thigh violently. He yelled in pain, and then again when the saw was brought down for a second time. It was a piercing sensation that reverberated throughout his body.

He tried to move away from another strike, and as he did so he noticed one of the dominant red shapes in the muted light fall to the ground, closely followed by a second. The Sister who had struck him with the saw had also noticed. He saw a familiar shape coming toward the remaining sister.

Charlie.

Charlie's skill - against an unsuspecting Sister it was all well and good, but when a Sister had you in her sights no amount of close proximity teleportation could save your ass.

Charlie advanced on the remaining sister, who held the saw aloft ready for its next taste of blood.

She had come to save him. He had doubted her, and yet here she was trying to save his skin, and putting her own skin at risk at the same time. He had to do something.

The remaining Sister stood a yard to the side of him. He could see a mad glint in her eyes, and a touch of doubt in Charlie's. He wrestled with the bindings on his hands, but they held strong. Desperation made him rock the chair from side to side, slowly at first until he gathered momentum. The moment Charlie came before the remaining Sister, his chair toppled over and he collided with the Sister. Charlie took the opportunity to tackle the unbalanced Sister to the ground, and the saw escaped the Sister's grasp.

The Sister fell down next to him. Her cold stare met his, and he felt as if he was staring into the depths of hell.

Charlie retrieved the saw. Her gaze held no hint of doubt any longer. She moved to finish the Sister off, and the words that escaped him were more a shock to him than anyone else.

"Stop!"

Charlie faltered

"What are you talking about?" She said in disbelief. She placed the saw at the throat of the Sister.

"Something's wrong," he said. "Don't kill her."

Charlie pursed her lips. "But they'll kill you, and then they'll kill me."

"No," he said. He knew the rules, knew how to play the game. "Killing them won't get me any closer to finding out who set me up, and who really needs to pay for this."

Charlie seemed to battle with the notion for a time, before begrudgingly removing the saw from the Sister's throat. She then brought her foot down on the Sister's face, and three figures dressed in red lay unconscious on the warehouse floor.

He looked up at her in puzzlement.

"Hey, I'm not taking any chances."

He laughed. "Think you could untie me?"

"Haven't I done enough?"

She untied him, and they stood silent for a second. He looked down at the Three Sisters. "I wonder if anyone has seen what they look like?" He met Charlie's gaze, and added, "Probably not the best idea."

When they left the warehouse it was still dark, perhaps a few hours before dawn. Brad was surprised. He had thought he had been knocked out for longer. He limped by Charlie's side, as they walked to the place where he had left his car the night before. He used the sleeve of his shirt to wipe some of the blood from his face. He could only imagine how much of a mess he must look.

They didn't speak a word to one another, but having her there by his side was a comfort. He had not realised how much he had missed her until now.

"What made you come back for me?"

The flicker of a smile appeared on her face. "Memories, I guess."

He nodded. "We did have some good times."

She met his gaze, but then looked away. "What will you do now? They're just going to keep coming for you."

He looked up at the opaque moon. It had been one of the strangest nights of his life, but it wasn't over yet. "I don't think they'll come after me again." She paused at his expression. "But I know where I'm going next, and you're more than welcome to join me."

Her eyes narrowed.

The bar was empty. Only the barman Brad remembered from earlier that night was there. He wore the same anxious expression, and was quick to direct them to the far side of the bar. Brad told Charlie to grab a drink and wait at the bar. She protested at first, but stopped when she saw he meant it. He walked over to the table where Bob was sat. His face was nestled in a newspaper, his stance relaxed despite Brad's arrival.

To think he had once admired the man.

He sat down at the table, and waited for Bob to protest his innocence. Of course, any pleas of remorse never came. He should have known the old guy would be too stubborn for that.

"You made it, then?" Bob said, his face hidden behind the newspaper.

Brad waved his hand over to the barman, who arrived seconds later with two glasses of bourbon. He took a sip, enjoying the way it burnt his throat, and then surveyed the man before him. He found it hard to believe this was someone he had once counted as a friend. In his line of work you couldn't afford to have many friends, and he had lost one tonight. He looked over to Charlie at the bar. But he had also regained one.

"You taught me well."

Bob smiled crookedly "You were always too good for your own good. I should have known I couldn't play you false."

He leaned back into his chair. "Why did you do it?" He was surprised at the calmness in his voice.

Bob waved his hand dismissively. "Why do any of us do it?" His face seemed to suddenly become haggard, as if the years had caught up on him in one foul swoop. "I ran out of favours. I'm too old for this shit. I can't keep up with all the young guns going about these days." He wrinkled his brow. "But I couldn't let you go without repaying your favour."

He gave a bitter laugh. "That's why you helped me escape at the factory?"

"A favour unpaid will only come back to bite you in the ass."

Brad took another sip from his drink. "A good rule to live by," he said, but he couldn't shake a nagging thought. "Why me?"

"Convenience," Bob answered in a flat tone. "I killed someone I shouldn't have, and then the Three Sisters were on my ass. They took little persuading in thinking it was you though," he said, and drank down his bourbon in one go. "In fact," he said, "here they come now."

Brad's head spun to the bar. The Three Sisters were approaching them. He saw Charlie was safe at the bar, and was thankful for that. He felt the wound on his leg. He had used a spare t-shirt from his car to cover the wound. The Sisters' clothing had tasted little blood this night, but things were about to get messy.

He turned to face his old friend, who seemed to be in good spirits at The Three Sisters' arrival. Brad's expression became grim at the knowledge of what it was he had to do.

The Three Sisters stopped before their table. He was glad for the faint lighting in the bar. He didn't want to see more of them than he had to.

"Looks like time has run out for you, Brad," Bob said with a glint in his eye. He picked up the newspaper from the table, and began reading. Brad's gaze flickered from the Three Sisters to his old friend.

He still couldn't help but wonder how it had come to this.

When he spoke, his words carried no hint of pleasure. "I believe you owe me a favour."

It was only a second before a violent rustling began from where Bob was sitting. The newspaper he held shook vigorously in his grip.

"No," Bob said, breathlessly. He didn't lower the newspaper.

Brad took a last swig from his glass, and then rose to his feet. "I'm going to miss you, old friend," he said, and then gave a faint nod to the Three Sisters.

He went to the bar to get Charlie, and they began to leave. He didn't turn back when the screams began, or when the man who had once been his friend began screaming his name.

That bridge was long since broken.

He and Charlie walked out into the first light of a new day. He regarded her out of the corner of his eye. They had been up all night, but she looked as good as ever.

"What next?" she said.

His lips twitched into a smile. "There's a guy at the Empress hotel who owes me a favour. Penthouse sound okay to you?"

∞∞∞

Zombies Have No Respect for Plumbing
by Tony Southcotte

Zombies have no respect for plumbing. They don't teach you that when you fill out the paperwork for your apprentice license.

Since the plague slowed down, people didn't see the need to finish off their family members. You just pay a wrangler to tie them up, slap a rubber ball in the mouth, and send them home. They may want to tussle with you every once in a while, but for the most part they just sit there. People hold on to some hope for a cure, but I know better. Christ could raise Lazarus, but Lord knows he wouldn't try to bring a pork chop back to life.

I used to just pull hair out of drains. Use a snake or some other such tool to drag natted balls of bath grime and shaving leave-ins out of bathtubs.

This brings me to my current predicament. Standing in the shower of some blue haired granny who just couldn't say goodbye to her oaf of a husband. I saw him walkin' in, that festering pile of meat. The red ball in his mouth would have made him look like a pig on a spit, that is, if he still had any natural color left in him.

She called to tell me her drain was backing up; that a horrible smell and rusty colored substance was coming through. I figured it was a sewage back up. Not my favorite call, but you can gouge these people and they have to pay it.

Unfortunately for me, it wasn't sewage.

When I start pullin' the snake back, the white chunks start dropping off the cable, little flaps of raw skin. At this stage, it starts to fall off like a bad sunburn, only meatier. The smell hits me and I want to double over. At least if the worst happens I am in a bathroom and can easily find the can.

"Ma'am, do you know anything about this?" I ask, pointing at the muck, retching under the stench. I'm pretty sure more than a couple teeth are in the mess now.

"Oh dear. Why don't you plumbers make these drains good enough?"

"Well, we don't expect you to push the cherished remains of your dead husband down the drain."

"But he needs his shower, his hygiene was never in order, even before his accident. I just pushed it down with my toes."

Now, I normally don't take kindly to this sort of viscera, or the type of person who puts up with it, but something struck me in that moment. Its brilliance was so simple, but I had the idea that would revolutionize the in home zombie phenomenon and plumbing as we know it. "Miss, would you like me to install a garbage disposal in here?"

"Can you do that?"

"Yes. Yes I can."

∞∞∞∞

Throw Him Away and Get a New One
by Patrick Whittaker

"Mr. Highsmith! Open up, please. I assure you I only have your best interests at heart."

"What's wrong with you? I told you to go away!" Angus Highsmith gave up his struggle with the childproof top and threw the bottle of drain cleaner at the wall. Unbroken, it rolled along the faded lino and snuggled up to a nest of empty whisky bottles.

The banging on the door continued. It played havoc with Angus's hangover.

"I know what you're doing, Mr. Highsmith. Or rather what you're trying to do."

Angus sat heavily on the bed and placed his head in his hands. "Go away, go away, go away!"

"Very well. You leave me no choice." There was a sound of metal on metal and then the click of shifting lock tumblers.

The door opened. A man in a business suit and round glasses put away the hair grip he'd used to spring the lock. "Good afternoon," he said. "My name is Winthrop. May I come in?"

"No!"

Winthrop came in. Closing the door, he gave the hotel room a cursory scan. "Well, I've seen worse. Do you mind if I open a window? Damp plays havoc with my lungs."

"Do what you like." Angus flopped back onto the bed with its uneven mattress, nearly-white bed sheets and strange aroma. Not for the first time, he noticed that one of the stains on the ceiling looked like a map of Africa.

After opening the window, Winthrop picked up the bottle of drain cleaner and read the label. He shook his head and tutted. "I can't believe you chose this," he chided, placing the bottle on the window sill. "You've no idea how unpleasant an overdose can be. You'd have died in screaming agony."

"I don't care."

"Yes, I know. That's why I'm here."

Angus sat up. "What are you? A cop?"

"Oh gracious me, no."

"So my wife sent you. Well, go on. Serve your papers and get out."

"You're under a misapprehension, Mr Highsmith." Winthrop reached into his inside pocket and pulled out a business card. Angus took it with ill grace and read the copperplate lettering:

Mason Winthrop
Life Consultant

Angus flipped the card over but the reverse was blank. "What," he asked, "is a life consultant?"

"I help people like you, Mr. Highsmith. People whose lives have fallen apart. People who are sad, desperate and lonely. People who seriously contemplate drinking drain cleaner."

"You're wasting your time, Winthrop. I've no money. So you may as well clear off and find someone else to scam. You snake oil salesman! I want nothing from you. Do you hear? Nothing!"

"Really, Mr. Highsmith?" From his jacket pocket, Winthrop produced a small bottle of whisky. If he didn't have Angus's complete attention before, he did now. "I think you'll find this tastes much nicer than drain cleaner."

Angus wanted the whisky. If he wasn't weak with hunger, he'd have attacked Winthrop to get it.

Winthrop's smile said *now I've got you*. "You can have this one now and the one in my other pocket when you've told me how you've come to be sitting in a cheap hotel planning to dissolve your innards with caustic soda."

"Why do you care?"

"What does it matter, Mr. Highsmith? So long as you get your whisky?"

Winthrop placed the bottle on the mattress. He picked up three empty whisky bottles from the room's only chair and crammed them into the waste bin with the two empties already in there. Then he sat down and straightened the seams of his trousers. "Tell me your story, Mr Highsmith. Delineate, if you will, your descent from middle class respectability to insolvent ruination."

Angus took the bottle. He opened it and sniffed the contents. It was whisky all right. The glue that had held him together these past few weeks.

He took a swig. And then another. "I haven't always been a bum," he said, sitting on the bed.

Winthrop nodded. "I know, Mr. Highsmith. I know."

"I used to have a nice house, a great family and a job with prospects. If ever a man was living the English middle class dream, it was me. I was doing very nicely, thank you. And then, about a month ago, without warning, it all went horribly wrong.

"It was a Wednesday. As soon as I woke up I had a feeling it was not going to be a good day. But if I'd known how bad it was going to get, I would have stayed in bed.

"I smelt bacon. That was my first intimation that something was wrong. It was only 7 o'clock and Hilary, my wife, was seldom awake before 8, let alone up and cooking breakfast."

#

Angus got out of bed and put on a dressing gown. He slipped into worn, grey slippers and went downstairs. From the kitchen came the sounds of breakfast. The clatter of crockery and plates. The hiss of a frying pan. The mechanical pop of a toaster. The happy gurgling of the coffee percolator.

A feeling of dread came upon him as he gripped the handle of the kitchen door. He had a notion his life was about to take a regrettable turn.

Don't be silly, he told himself. *This is your house, your kitchen. What on Earth can there be to worry about?*

Nervously, he entered the kitchen. Hilary was frying an egg. His children – Andrew and Jessica – were at the table, looking smart and freshly scrubbed in their school uniforms. They, along with a stranger, were tucking into substantial breakfasts.

The stranger was about Angus's age and well-dressed. His build was average as were his looks. In a crowd, he would not have stood out. At Angus's kitchen table at 7 in the morning, he was an anomaly that refused to be ignored.

Angus refrained from interrogating his guest. Refrained too from pointing out that the chap was in his seat. A guest, after all, is a guest.

"Good morning," said Angus.

"Good morning," said the children.

The stranger rose. "You must be Angus. I'm Tony."

Angus shook the proffered hand. "How do you do?"

"Very well, thank you." Tony sat back down. "Lovely house you have."

Hilary turned off the gas cooker and brought the frying pan to the table. With a deft flip of her spatula, she deposited an egg onto Tony's plate. It settled like a sudden snowfall on a landscape of bacon, sausages and beans.

"Marvellous cook, your wife," said Tony.

"Thank you," said Hilary. She turned to Angus. "You'll have to make your own breakfast. The house needs tidying and I don't suppose I can rely on any help from you."

Angus was baffled. "It's a bit early for housework, isn't it?"

"In case you hadn't noticed, we do have a guest."

"Oh please," said Tony. "Don't go to any trouble on my behalf."

"It's no trouble at all." Hilary smiled sweetly at Tony and then scowled at Angus. "You could at least get dressed before coming down. Whatever must our guest think?"

Perplexed and wounded, Angus sloped back upstairs. When he got to the landing, he heard Jessica say, "Mummy says you were in the army, Uncle Tony. Did you kill anyone?"

Angus showered, shaved and cleaned his teeth. He entered the bedroom to find Hilary in front of the full length mirror touching up her make-up. She was stripped down to the waist with her best top on the chair next to her.

Folding her arms over her breasts, she turned her back on Angus. "Do you mind? I'd quite like some privacy."

After hastily dressing, Angus took refuge in his study where he leafed through sales reports without reading them. He knew manners dictated he should be entertaining his guest but Hilary had made it clear she'd rather he kept out of the way - perhaps for fear he'd embarrass her.

Finally it was time to drop the kids off at school and head into work. But when he came downstairs, Hilary was already ushering Andrew and Jessica out the front door. Tony stood by the hatstand jangling his car keys.

"What's going on?" asked Angus.

Hilary barely glanced at him. "Tony's very kindly offered to take the kids to school."

"I'm quite capable of doing that myself."

"You're always complaining it makes you late for work."

"No I'm not."

"Let's not argue in front of our guest."

"I'm not arguing."

"Good. It's settled then."

Tony stepped forward and patted Angus on the shoulder. "Pleasure meeting you, old chap. And may I say what an utterly charming family you have?" On his way out, he kissed Hilary on the cheek. "I'll be back soon."

With a glazed look, Hilary closed the door after him.

"Do you mind telling me what's going on?" asked Angus.

Hilary picked up the post. "Tony's staying for a while. Did you see how the kids adore him?"

"But who is he?"

"He's Tony."

"I can't say I like the chap."

"No, you wouldn't, would you? He's funny, warm and attentive. Not your sort of person at all. Now why don't you get to work and out of my hair? I have things to do."

"He is not staying in my house."

"It's *our* house and I can invite who I like to stay with us. And I'd thank you not to raise your voice at me."

"I was not raising my voice."

"Just go, Angus! Before you make me lose my rag."

Angus went. Perhaps when he came home, Hilary would be in a more reasonable mood and they could talk things through like adults.

Perhaps.

#

As was his habit when domestic matters troubled him, Angus threw himself into his work. He sat in his office going through reports he'd never meant to read and chasing orders that needed no chasing. It was just after midday when Mrs. Gladstone, his secretary, rang through to say there were two gentlemen to see him.

"Who are they?" He glanced at his appointment book and saw only blank spaces.

Before Mrs Gladstone could answer, the two gentlemen in question entered. They wore raincoats, Trilby hats and an air of menace.

"Angus Highsmith?" said one.

"Yes," said Angus.

"Of 3 Acacia Avenue?"

"Yes."

"We have a court order."

The other man dropped an envelope in Angus's lap. "You are to stay at least one mile from your house, your wife and children at all times. And you are not to contact any of them except through your wife's solicitor. Any breach of this order could lead to your imprisonment. Good day to you."

The men trooped out, leaving Angus moving his lips like a goldfish as he struggled to articulate his dismay.

Mrs. Gladstone hurried into the room. "I'm sorry, Mr. Highsmith. They just barged in."

"Not your fault," said Angus distantly. With trembling hands he opened the envelope and took out three sheets of paper, each looking more official than the last. "Would you happen to know if Charles Warren is in?"

"The company lawyer? I saw him not ten minutes ago."

"Could you arrange an appointment for me, please, Mrs. Gladstone? Tell him it's urgent."

"I'll get on to it right away, Mr. Highsmith."

#

Charles Warren saw himself as a lovable rogue. His slicked-back hair and pencil moustache were inspired by Errol Flynn, a man he believed to have been cast from the same mould as himself.

Feet on desk, he finished reading the papers and placed the pages back in their envelope. "Someone's really done a job on you, my friend," he told Angus who was sitting opposite him. "I've never seen such a draconian exclusion order in all my life. What on earth have you done to your poor wife?"

"Nothing," said Angus.

"You've not hit her?"

"Certainly not."

"Threatened her?"

"I'm not a monster, Charles. I'm a perfectly ordinary husband who loves his wife and kids."

"I see." Warren didn't sound convinced. "Have you by any chance heard of an organisation called Elixir?"

"No. Should I have?"

"Probably not."

"Who are they?"

"An urban legend. Forget I even mentioned them."

"What do you advise me to do about the court order?"

"Obey it to the letter. Stay away from your family and get yourself a good lawyer. There are about a hundred ways you can breach this order and any one of them will land you in prison."

#

To the surprise of many, Angus left work early. It was almost unheard of for him to depart before 7 let alone the middle of the afternoon. In doing so, he was jeopardising the promotion he'd been fighting long and hard for.

As he walked across the company car park, he sensed his rivals gazing down on him, marking his early departure as some small victory. He considered flipping them a finger but decided now was not the time for petty gestures.

Besides which, the two men who'd served him the papers were hanging around his car. The shorter one was peering through the back window and scribbling in a notebook.

"Get away from there!" Angus broke into a half-run. "What the hell do you think you're doing?"

The taller man answered. "Merely taking an inventory, sir. The court requires a list of your assets."

"This is a private car park. You've no right to be here and you've no right to be snooping."

"I think you'll find otherwise."

"We'll see about that. I'm on my way to consult a solicitor."

"A very wise move, if I may say so, sir. Very wise."

#

Marcus Canning of Canning, Canning, Canning and Dunstan barely looked at the papers before handing them back to Angus with a sad shake of his balding head. "There's not much I can do for you, Mr. Highsmith. Except advise you to comply."

Angus had expected more from such a renowned lawyer. "Can't I appeal against this?"

"You couldn't afford to."

"I have money."

"Not any more."

"What do you mean?"

Canning got up from behind his fine mahogany desk and walked to the window. "Is that your car down there, Mr. Highsmith? The blue saloon?"

With a sinking feeling, Angus joined Canning at the window. He was not altogether surprised to see his car being lifted on to the back of a truck while the two men from the court looked on. "They can't do that!" he protested.

"I'm afraid they can," said Canning. "I see they've assigned Bateman and Redmond to your case. That's a very bad sign."

"Which one's which?"

"Bateman's the shorter one. You don't want to be messing with him. He's had four convictions for GBH. Come to that, don't go upsetting Redmond either. It's never been proven, but there's every indication he murdered his own brother."

#

Marcus Canning did not charge Angus for his time. On the contrary, he thrust a £20 note into Angus's hand. "You're going to need it, old chap," he insisted. "From now on, take every scrap of kindness that comes your way."

Angus went straight from the offices of Canning, Canning, Canning and Dunstan to his bank. He inserted his bank card in the ATM and typed in his PIN. After what seemed an unreasonable length of time, a message popped up on the screen: "Insufficient funds. Your card has been retained. Ask at your branch for details. Thank you for using this machine."

He turned to find Bateman and Redmond standing by the bank's main entrance. Defiantly, he marched into the lobby.

They were still there when he came out of a hastily-arranged meeting from which he'd learnt two things: his wife had withdrawn the £30,000 in their joint savings account and his assets were frozen.

And to add salt to his wounds, he'd been forced to hand over his credit cards.

Angus started off down the road. A quick glance over his shoulder confirmed he was being followed. He ducked into a supermarket and hid behind a rack of magazines. Bateman and Redmond weren't far behind. Having lost sight of their quarry, they split up and disappeared down the aisles.

As soon as they were out of sight, Angus slipped out of the supermarket, ran down the road and took a couple of random turnings.

Satisfied he'd shaken his tail, he stood in the doorway of a fish shop, caught his breath and took out his phone. He rang home.

The phone was answered after three rings. "Yes?" It was Tony's voice.

Through gritted teeth, Angus said, "I'd like to talk to Hilary."

"She's not here at the moment. May I ask who's calling?"

"Her husband."

"You know you're not meant to phone here, don't you? I won't report you this time, but you really mustn't do it again."

"All I want is to collect my things."

"I've arranged for them to be sent on to you. Goodbye, Mr. Highsmith."

Tony hung up.

There was a wheelie bin outside the fish shop. Angus kicked it. Then kicked it again. And then he punched it several times and kicked it once more.

"Damn you!" he cried. "Damn you all!"

A dog began to bark.

#

Angus spent the night in a YMCA where he was shown to a room with four rudimentary beds. Because the hostel wasn't busy, he had the room to himself but was warned he might have to share if there were last minute bookings.

As he lay on his bed drinking cheap cider, he thought what a great idea it would be to kill Tony. Not only would it rid him of a great vexation, it would deter Hilary from hitting him with court orders. He'd show her he wasn't a man to be trifled with.

Yes, he thought. *I'll fight for what's mine and bad luck on Tony if he gets in my way.*

Who was Tony anyway? This mediocrity who had pushed him out of his own nest? Had Hilary been having an affair with him?

No, he told himself. *I would have noticed.*

But was she having an affair with him now? He pictured Hilary and Tony together, in Angus's bed in Angus's home with Angus's children asleep in adjacent rooms. And then he pictured Tony with a bullet in his head and Angus standing over him, smoking gun in hand.

Tomorrow he would take action. He'd somehow get together enough money to buy a revolver and then – court order or no court order – he was going home to Acacia Avenue to take back what was his.

And if he couldn't afford a gun, he'd use the axe in the garden shed. Or the club hammer. Or his bare hands...

Eventually the cider numbed his mind enough to allow him to fall asleep. When he woke up, the light was on and a man was pacing the floor.

"It's a crock!" spat the man. "A total and utter crock!"

His suit was crumpled; his tie was at half mast. He had the look of someone who had seen terrible things.

"Do you mind?" said Angus, propping himself up on his elbows. His stomach churned from the effects of the cider. "I'm trying to sleep."

"Yeah, yeah, yeah," said the man. He sat on the bed and hauled out a small bottle of brandy. "So you sleep with your clothes and shoes on, do you?"

"I don't see that's any concern of yours."

"It's just an observation. I ain't criticising. Between you and me, I've been wearing these clothes the best part of three days. Slept in them too. And you want to know why?"

"No," said Angus. "I do not."

The man opened his brandy bottle and tossed aside the top. He took a heavy draft and sighed like a great weight had been dissipated. "I've lost everything. My wife, my kids, my house, my job. All gone!"

"I know the feeling. Now will you shut up and let me sleep?"

A great wracking sob was the answer. The man started blubbered shamelessly. "Everything was great. I was paying my mortgage, playing squash, vying for promotion, getting my children's teeth straight and going on holiday twice a year. I was living the middle class dream. Doing everything right. And then one morning I came downstairs and there was a stranger at my table.

"His name was Gordon. I'd never seen him before but my wife treated him like an old friend. She got angry when I asked him who he was and what he was doing in my house. Said I shouldn't interrogate guests that way.

"Later that day, two men came to my office and handed me a court order. It said I was to keep away from my wife and kids. Did you ever hear of such a thing?"

"No," said Angus. He lay back down and closed his eyes. "I didn't."

#

In the morning, Angus had a shower and noted with disgust that his roommate declined to do the same. He found the thought of going to work in yesterday's shirt, socks and underpants abhorrent but he had no choice. What little money he'd had on him – including the gift from Marcus Canning – had been reduced to a handful of change. And there was still the question of how he was going to get to the office.

In the dining room, he piled his plate with bread, ham and cheese, poured a himself mug of coffee and sat at an empty table.

Angus surreptitiously slipped a few items of food into his jacket pocket. Then he built himself a sandwich with several layers of ham and cheese. He was halfway through demolishing it when a voice said, "Mind if I join you?"

It was his roommate sporting a plate even more crammed with food than Angus's had been. He sat down, picked up a slice of processed chicken and crammed it in his mouth. "Hmm, delicious" he said. "Name's Bunbury, by the way. Felix Bunbury."

"Angus Highsmith," said Angus in a tone he hoped conveyed he was interested in neither company nor conversation.

"It only occurred to me a few minutes ago that you must be one of us."

"*Us?*"

"The Dispossessed. Your suit's a dead giveaway. I mean you and I aren't typical hostel fodder, are we? There was another chap here the first night I stayed. Name of Miller." Bunbury threw a slice of cheese onto a slice of bread, rolled it up and took a huge mouthful. He chewed six times before washing the food down with a slurp of tea. "He used to own a used car business. Did very well for himself. So well he was thinking of selling up and retiring to Spain. And then – well you can guess the rest. He came down one morning and there was a stranger at his table."

"I don't understand how this can happen," said Angus. "It goes against every tenet of natural justice and British fair play."

Bunbury leaned forward and whispered, "Elixir."

Recalling his conversation with Charles Warren, a chill ran down Angus's spine. "Elixir?"

"A secret organisation that uses obscure laws to rid housewives of their husbands."

"You mean they really exist?"

"Some say they're as powerful as the Mafia or even the Freemasons."

"And all they do is wreck marriages?"

"That's not how they see it. As far as they're concerned, they're making discontented wives happy. Bringing magic back into their lives."

"But my wife wasn't discontented!"

"Sure she wasn't. That's why she threw you away and got a new one."

It was a low blow that struck home. Angus decided to have no more to do with Felix Bunbury except to ask him one final question. "How much do they charge for their services?"

"To get rid of a husband: 20 grand. To get rid of a husband and bring in a replacement: 30 grand."

Exactly the amount in our joint savings account, Angus reminded himself.

Angus was about to tell Bunbury to go to Hell when two officious looking men strode up to the table. One placed a hand on Bunbury's shoulder.

"Felix Bunbury," he said, "I am arresting for being in breach of a court order. Namely that you are injuncted to keep a distance of at least one mile between yourself and your spouse, Mrs. Anthea Bunbury, and have failed to do so."

Bunbury paled. "But I haven't been anywhere near her!"

"Au contraire," said the second man. "With our own eyes we saw her drive past this very building not two minutes ago."

"Well, I can hardly be blamed for that."

"Come along now, sir. Best you don't make a fuss."

"No! I won't do it. Do you hear?"

"You're only making things worse for yourself."

"Worse? How can they be worse?" Bunbury leapt to his feet, knocking his chair over. He pushed aside the two men and ran out the door.

They made no attempt to stop him. Just stood shaking their heads sadly.

"He's really done it now," said the first man.

"Silly person," said the second. "Silly, silly person."

\#

Angus walked to work. Along the way, he thought about his children and wondered how they were coping with the sudden upheaval in their lives. He hoped they were missing him as much as he missed them. Perhaps they'd be the ones to bring Hilary to her senses. Make her realise that children need a real father, not someone who's just walked in off the street.

Not Tony. Whoever he was.

Arriving half an hour late, Angus said good morning to Mrs. Gladstone and went straight to his office where four suitcases stood in a row. Mrs. Gladstone hurried in after him.

"They were delivered this morning," she said. "There's no indication who they're from or what's in them."

"It's all right, Mrs. Gladstone. I know what this is about. Will you see I'm not disturbed for the next half hour?"

"You're due to have a meeting with Willis from Manufacturing in five minutes."

"Cancel it."

"It's very important."

"Rebook it for this afternoon."

"Mr. Willis won't like it."

"I don't give a rat's arse, Mrs. Gladstone. Now, if you'll excuse me, I'd like to be left alone."

"Right," said Mrs. Gladstone with a note of hurt in her voice. "I'll leave you to it then."

As Angus had suspected, the four suitcases contained his clothes and toiletries. Nothing else. Everything that had once been his and Hilary's was now Hilary's alone.

He took out some clean clothes and his electric shaver. However bad things got, he was determined not to let standards slip and end up like Felix Bunbury. In fact, he was going to let Bunbury stand as a warning to him.

"I can fight this," he said aloud. "They are not going to beat me!"

#

And now here he was in the crummiest hotel in town. No job, no money, no prospects. Nobody on his side. Feeling like a shell of a man. Pouring his heart out to a stranger.

"I sold the contents of my suitcases and then the suitcases," he said. "I kept my electric razor until I had nothing else to sell. All I got for it was enough to buy me a scotch egg and a bottle of drain cleaner.

"I've managed to get a bit of money out of the social services but that goes straight to the owner of this rat hole. I haven't eaten properly in days and I smell."

"It can't be easy for you," said Mason Winthrop solicitously. "You had it all, didn't you? And you blew it."

"I said I'd never end up like Felix Bunbury and I have."

"Not quite, Mr. Highsmith. Although you're probably not aware of it, Mr. Bunbury was until yesterday evening staying in the room above yours. You may recall there was a power cut."

"Yeah. I spilled some whisky because of it."

"That was Mr. Bunbury stepping into the bath with an electric heater."

"Dear Lord," said Angus. "The poor man."

"I tried to help him, but he wouldn't have it." Mason Winthrop stood up and advanced upon Angus. "Why do you think your wife wanted rid of you, Mr. Highsmith?"

"None of your damned business!" Angus emptied the last dregs of whisky and let the bottle fall from his grasp. It bounced on the lino with a loud thump. "And you owe me another bottle of scotch."

Winthrop produced the promised bottle and allowed it to be snatched from his grasp. Without asking if he might, he sat next to Angus on the bed. "You feel better for telling me your story, don't you?"

Angus opened the bottle and took a bracing swig before answering. "Nobody would listen to me. No sooner had my work colleagues heard about my misfortune than a rumour went around that I'd been involved in domestic violence. At the YMCA they asked me not to come back. Said they didn't want my type.

"My boss sacked me for the most spurious of reasons. Then the Jobcentre told me I'd engineered my own dismissal and turned me down for benefit.

"Even at church, I was treated as a pariah. There was me in one set of pews and everybody else in the other. Father Knowles, who's known me since I was a boy, refused to take my confession unless I owned up to being a wife-beater.

"I bet if I phoned the Samaritans they'd advise me to kill myself."

Mason Winthrop chuckled.

"What's so funny?" Angus snapped at him.

"Your little joke about the Samaritans. It's most amusing."

Angus thought about it. And then he smiled. "I suppose it is."

For the first time in a long while, Angus could see a break in the dark clouds hanging over his life. It was no more than a chink but it was enough to allow through a thin, watery ray of hope. He'd promised himself he wouldn't go the way of Felix Bunbury; now was his last chance to make sure he didn't.

"You know," he said, "I've thought long and hard about why Hilary discarded me. At first, it made no sense. I was a good husband and father. There was always food on the table. My kids were the first on the street to get the latest Playstation. I never even came close to committing adultery.

"I was everything any woman could reasonably hope for."

"Except?"

"Except I was dull. Dependable, loving, faithful – but dull. Dull, dull, deeply and desperately dull."

"Now we're making progress," said Mason Walters. "Admitting a problem is the first step towards curing it. Drink your whisky, Mr.

Highsmith. and get some sleep. On the morrow we'll see about unfreezing your assets and getting you a new job. So long as you do as I tell you, you'll be back on your feet in no time."

"Can I ask a question?" said Angus.

"Of course you can."

"Do you know anything about Elixir?"

Mason Walters smiled enigmatically. "I can't say that I do, Mr. Highsmith. I can't say that I do."

#

Jeremy Ashworth felt good. After a deep and refreshing sleep, he'd woken to find sunshine pouring through his window like liquid gold.

He slipped out of bed and noticed with satisfaction how crisp the bed linen was, how fragrant the room smelt and how neatly his clothes were laid out.

Perfection, he thought. *Absolute perfection.*

The smell of frying bacon and fresh coffee stimulated his senses. It was unusual for Mildred, his beloved wife, to be up so early. She must have decided to surprise him with a cooked breakfast before he dropped the kids off at school.

Donning dressing gown and slippers, he all but skipped down the stairs and into the kitchen.

Tarquin and Mathilda, his adorable children, were tucking into a hearty breakfast. Mildred – God bless her – threw a couple of rashers into the frying pain as she hummed a merry tune.

"Good morning!" chirruped Jeremy.

Mildred was startled. "You made me jump!" she complained, placing a hand over her heart. "If you want breakfast, you can make your own. I don't have time to fetch and carry after you today."

Jeremy noted a place setting at the top of the table where he usually sat. The plate there was filled with sausages, baked beans and a fried egg.

He was about to ask who the third breakfast was for when a stranger in a business suit walked in.

"Hello," said the stranger, sitting at the head of the table and picking up a knife and fork. "You must be Jeremy. My name's Angus. I'll be staying a while."

∞∞∞

Damaged Goods
by Dinesh Pulandram

There I was again, at the Hive Mind, scratching my tusk against the bar. Was like a recurring nightmare. Here to see the Marx again. Here to beg him for work again.

It'd been a real shit week too. I'd got shot by stone soldiers, thrown off a 10,000 foot drop by a razor tank, and barely escaped. To boot I'd used up all my medibots. Ahh, the ice cold feeling of medibots going through my veins. Them medibots were almost like biocrack. I couldn't do a job without 'em.

I was sick of it. Sick of doing it all myself, sick of the cycle. Even a rhino has limits, you know.

I tapped my hoof to the pulse-punk and ordered my favorite. A liter bottle cognac and synth-meat satay skewers with peanut sauce. I'm a vegan, don't eat real meat. Yeah, everyone's surprised when I tells them. You can be big and strong without eating meat, ya know. Just look at the diplodocus. Herbivore.

"Where the Marx?" I shouted at the bartender, Limei. Limei was one of the Marx's dunces. Half her face was tattooed--one of 'em a dragon that kept blinking at me. She had long arms covered with bangles. I never seen bangles look so hot before. I stared at her arms--she could leave them bangles on--as she passed the cognac and synth-meat. I slurped on the cognac and eyed her boobs.

She said, "Hey, the Marx is in a trawling session. He'll be envirtua for about a week. Strictly not to be disturbed."

"Taik!" I yelled. I thought maybe I should barge his sanctuary, rip him out of his jack. But fuck it, there was no point moping.

I hit the dance floor and joined a quad'ette: a redhead, a brunette, a blonde, and a raven-head. My colors of the rainbow. Hive Mind brang everybody together: hybrids, physicals, rhinos, software-selves, and aethers--some call 'em ghosts, but they're just holos after all.

My dancing hooves didn't last long, and soon I dizzied out from stim-darts, uber-caffe, and too many liters of Louis XIV. I left the floor, pretended I was fine. Rhinos have reps to maintain.

I crashed to this airseat and fumbled in my pocket for Wilson's Chocolate-Orange snuff. How I take it, I put the chops on a hooftip, inhale, and savor that sweet hit. Then quick take a drag from the cigar I grip on the same hooftip.

I was tired, so I knocked off. When I blinked awake, I saw her.

She moved like a military mech, choppy, as if her legs and arms swung on hinges. Anything that moved like a machine, I'd been trained to zoom in on. She was on Velvet Delight, the level above where the guests went for a tumble. I followed her reflection on the LED mirrors. She walked backwards. Strawberry-fluro cocktail in one hand, the other held out. Three human males crowded her in. They herded her to one of the private booths and pushed her behind the drapes. That didn't seem right.

I got off my arse and ran through the sweaty bodies on the dance floor. I jumped, grunted as I hit my chin against the ledge, grabbed it, and vaulted over the rails. I landed with a boom. (Rhino's ain't made for elegance.) It was much quieter and darker there in the passageway.

I burst into the booth. One of the men was squeezing her jaw. Two others held her arms apart. They turned maggot white when they saw me.

I said, "Get out."

One. Two. Three. Poof. Them was gone.

I started to ask, "What was they--" but she said, "Got a light?" pretending it was every day a rhino saved her ass. I scented her fear--it came thick and strong.

She was cross-legged on the velvet sofa. My eyes traveled down her body, and my cigar went tumbling out.

She had no real arms or legs. The only parts of her that was human was her torso, neck, and head. Her neck jacked in to a squarish frame that covered her tiny chest. Her entire exo looked like it was assembled from Coke cans.

Embarrassment--a sour scent--mixed with her fear. She didn't look away, though. She stared right at me. Daring me to say something.

"Light me up," she said.

I snorted, flicked the burner. Her lips trembled.

Her eyebrows were surrounded by red and white dots that curved down to her cheeks. Jawline sprinkled with glitter. A nose ring twinkled bright against her black skin. She was breathing hard, and sweat beaded up on her collarbone. I wanted to lick it.

I tried to do the human intro thing. Hand shaking. Rhinos just sniff each other.

"Amalric," I said and put out my hoofhand. She ducked. My hoofhand was half the size of her face.

Stratos high as I was, I tried not to stare at her artificial limbs. I been stared at all my life. Fuck if I'll do that to somebody else.

"I guess them three ain't part of a bondage act," I said.

"Huh. Anything but." She took a long drag, flicked at the hair that fell over them dark eyes, and said, "Thanks for dropping by."

"Always keen for a fight."

"So it's true what they say about rhinos, then?"

"What? Them say lots of things."

The edges of her lips curled. "Seat? My neck hurts looking up at you."

"Curry-laksa," I said, seating next to her.

"Huh?"

"That's what Malaysia is famous for. You know, tasty red coconut curry mixed with 'em noodles. It's delish. They got it here. I get it with extra tofu. Hungry?"

She looked at me and then laughed.

"What?" I said.

"You eating tofu," she said. "Go ahead, I'm starving. It's been ages since I had a laksa."

See, I warmed her up. My rhino charm works on all the ladies.

While we ate, she talked about Jesus, Mohammed, Krishna, and Buddha. I heard the names before but had no idea who they was, 'cept for Mohammed. He was a boxer.

By nature I'm a crap listener. Most people seem to spout shit, so I switch off. But when she talked…I never been that enthusiastic since I led a charge with the Rumble-Pack, even if I didn't understand much.

She said, "I'm interlacing my points of view with rationalism and romanticism."

Romanticism I liked the sound of. I told her I only knew about rhino-ism, and she laughed.

"Where you get all that info from?" I said.

"Books."

"You read books?"

She said, "I've lots of antique fetishes."

Outside, the music had slowed down from pulse-punk to L&S-Goth. Love music makes me sick, no matter how the DJ tries to mash it. I knew we must be coming to the end of the night, but I felt as if I'd swallowed a dose of medibots. I didn't want to leave.

I edged closer to her.

Her purple lips blew smoke-rings. I snatched at one, and it broke apart.

"Ha ha," she laughed.

I blundered it, then. Asked her, "So how you end up like that?"

Her lips smooched left and right. She turned away.

Then she said, "I remember the signage in the Water Wars. It was always a giant-sized rhino in magmite armor. Did wonders for the recruitment campaign. Where did you all go?"

Normally I don't like answering questions like that. Ain't nobody's business. But she was curious. The gov'ment left us untagged, so it's hard to find rhino details these days, even on the neuralnet.

"Few left go abouts here and there. We don't travel together, though, always by ourselves."

"Don't you get lonely?"

"Nah," I lied, "them's no trouble. Main trouble is feelin' like, like maybe there ain't no purpose for being here now them Water Wars is over."

Whoops. Couldn't believe I admitted that. This girl was having a strange effect on me, opening me up like a rhino ration pack.

She looked in my eyes the longest time, then nodded, took a last drag.

"So where you live?" I asked.

She stumped her cigar butt on a steel ankle. "Come see for yourself."

#

She lived in the povo part of town. So stupid. She couldn't even look after herself in a nightclub. We was in an alley with critters in the shadows. They perked up when they saw her, but when they saw me they pissed off.

"This is it," she said.

The place was white with black windows. A drain that stunk real bad gushed next to the building.

Inside her apartment, it was different. First thing I noticed--she lived alone. I know cause her place was as empty as mine. Her walls were digiprinted with black-and-white pebbles. Her kitchen had this little waterfall that fell between two plants. Them plants looked so delicious that I took a bite out of one. I chewed, only it wasn't as green as it looked, more crunchy than I expected.

She looked at me all strange.

"What?" I said.

"I can't believe...That's an authentic bonsai you've just...Oh never mind. Come this way."

She grabbed me like she was in a hurry. Her rusty exo-fingers got a decent grip. In the living room there was an oversized neuralnet recliner. Multi-pronged. It was the only thing worth money in her place. I kind of guessed it would be the center of her world. I mean, where else would you go if you had no arms and legs? Swimming?

"You want to try the hook?" she said.

I said that I did.

"Go ahead," she said.

I jacked myself in. The apartment faded as her virtual dashboard came online. There was mixed-up colors (too weird to say what they was), and music--religious chants with a dash of pulse-punk. A giant worm, transparent bats, and the scent of pineapple. Ahead, rainbows and lollipops floated on foam. A thousand AIs spoke.

Humans are crazy. It was starting to give me a tuskache.

Anyways, in the middle all that, I saw a black island. My fighter instincts got me prickly. I only spotted it cause I ran a scan. I learned that when I started trawling. If you don't run scans in the neuralnet, you get burnt by Inquisitors.

The island led to an inky corridor. It was ambush-quiet in there. My hearts started to beat quicker. On the black slab a scroll melted out. I read it.

I logged off. I was shaking. I ripped the jack out, said, "You got a Gene-Vault's blueprint stored on your root drive? You insane?"

"I lifted it three days ago. It was a silent copy. The Inquisitors have no idea."

"It's a fucken Gene-Vault!"

She arched an eyebrow. "I've got blueprints for all *seven* Gene-Vaults."

"No way," I said. She had to be boasting. Not even the Marx could trawl the net that good, and he had unlimited processing power.

I said, "How...*What* you plan to do with this?"

"Rob it."

"What?"

"Look at me." She knuckled her exo. It made a hollow ting. "I can use the inventory in the Gene-Vault to make me normal. Give me legs and arms like a real girl, so I don't have to plant myself into this chassis every morning. Do you know how long that takes?"

Her black hair swung down as she stared at a rusty toe. "I'm sick of people looking at me like I'm a freak."

I said, "The freak thing we got in common." I raised her chin. Shit, for a sec I was shaking bad. Something about touching her fuzzed me up.

Her eyebrows lifted, and her lips opened. She said, "We do? But you're a rhino. Invincible. Invulnerable." She laid a hand on my chest.

I thought what she had to do each morning. She would wake up, maybe wriggle around to slot herself in that chassis. I was born strong, with all my limbs intact. Never thought *that* was special. Until I seen her.

The holoprint rotated above my hoofpalm. "Why this one?" I said.

Her hand was still on my chest. I shifted closer and put my hoofhand around her waist. She felt so teeny, like she'd break if I hugged her.

She said, "It's taken me eight years. I started looking when I was twelve. That particular Gene-Vault"--she nodded at the blueprint--"holds the highest-grade gene-ampoules. I'm talking yoctobot-synthetics."

I raised my brow ridge.

She said, "It's stolen. Governments stealing from governments. I believe the Australians lifted it from the Chindian government."

"Yoctobots," I said, "we only got nanotech. They what, ten generations ahead?"

A single yoctobot gene-ampoule was worth squadjillions. If I got in on this, I would never have to beg the Marx for work again.

"It's stealing what's stolen. So it's not *really* stealing," she said.

I said, "That don't worry me. Unique sigs, that's the problem. That type of tech is going to have 'em."

I'd tried and failed to rob a Gene-Vault before. Since then, I'd thought a few things out. I knew I needed someone with smarts.

"I can wipe the signatures," she said.

"Shit, yeah? Even if you escape somehow, you'd have to go off-planet."

She said, "I'm not particularly attached to where I live. Neither are you."

I huffed. "What's your name?"

"Manjulali Chekitana. Lali for shorts."

I told her she was a cheeky girl and she smiled. What a smile! It punched your heart.

I rubbed my snout against her nose--the rhino handshake. Lali smelled of pleasant surprise. Right then, it wasn't about a shitload of cash.

People is only ever interested in rhinos cause they want to use us for toughs, but there was something else with Lali. She trusted me. She knew I'd be there to catch her.

#

I watched the last of my golden liquid fall on the Sydney Harbour Bridge.

"Charming," Lali said. "Do you always urinate on national monuments?"

"Just glad to be back in Australia." I tapped on the steel beams and grinned. "You think that's bad, eh? You should have seen this big load I did on the Statue of Liberty." I winked at her.

"Sounds like you've got some deep-seated psychological issues with authority."

"I did piss on the Great Wall once."

She shook her head.

"Here, a present." She bent down and unzipped a large bag.

"Fifty-medibot slim-packs! Now *them* is the key to my heart." The slim-packs were disc shaped, made out of steelcrete. They must have cost a fortune. The armor on my thighs was fitted with sockets that hooked up to slim-packs. I stowed 'em away on my back webbing, made sure they was tied snug.

"We're going to need those," she said seriously.

"Hey, check out my back-strapped scabbard." I twisted to show her.

"Triple-headed missile launcher," she said. Her fingers made a "ting" against one of the heads. "Nice belt, too." She nodded at my socketed belt filled with grenades.

She said, "My turn. Have a look at this." Lali unhitched a bolt-rifle.

"Nice." Her rifle was heavily modified: extra large LED on the sights and a mesh of red micro-circuitry. I checked out its sights and whistled. It had alternate-fire mode, so it could lob grenades. A real evil gun. I liked it, a lot.

I handed it back to her, said, "It's small but powerful, just like you."

I think she blushed, but she turned away real quick.

We double-checked everything. Then I checked again. My motto: check, check, and recheck. The escape plan involved a boat. I used a GPS scan to check the boat was still tethered to the pier.

Lali had a bunch of portable comps to tap into systems. She also had the set bombs. She was supporting artillery and intelligence. I was the siege engine.

"Did you check the hover-boards charges?" I asked.

She nodded. "Yep, they're full. I even brought extra battery packs."

I said, "C'mon, then. Let's go."

I floored the hoverbike and we tore through them streets. The Gene-Vault was right in the middle of the Sydney Opera House Crater. My wikinet search said the SOHC was consecrated ground. You couldn't normally place buildings in those zones. How the heck these people manage to place a Gene-Vault there?

Lali's grip tightened on me as we drove the streets. When I felt her boobs press against my back, I lost focus and almost cleaned up a biocrack addict. Shit! Them peoples was more dangerous than radiation potholes. The addict stumbled behind us. As we turned a long corner, he approached a group of cybes. They dangled a packet of blue powder in front of him and prodded his groin. He stared at them, eyes waxy.

"He's dead," I said. I knew what them cybes would do to him.

"Damn biocrack. He can't be more than eight," Lali said.

When we passed the Sydney harborside, Lali made all these sad noises. Said she visited there ages ago. Said the water was blue before. I kept quiet, but as far as I can see, there's nothing wrong with glowy green water. Mutant fish look like sliced tendons, but they actually pretty tasty. I ate them in the war.

I parked the hoverbike in a secluded area, and we got off.

The opera house looked like cracked eggshells. Wall chunks all over the wet ground. Lali said the walls was called sails 'cause the opera house was designed to look like a big ship sailing into the ocean.

Sticking out from the middle of this mess, like a tooth that had bit through, was the Gene-Vault. Its slopey sides disappeared into the water. Six rhinos in white masks guarded the entrance, armored and magazined to the brim. In front of them, burning bins gave off a black smoke. Them bins was filled with tar-fuel to keep the rhinos warm. Normal fire won't warm through our skin. On the roof was two large cameras, their lenses stretched out.

"I thought you said that the Gene-Vault was lightly guarded?" I said. It was looking like my failed job for the Marx all over again.

"Compared to the others," Lali said. "Actually, what we're seeing here is the rear entrance. The front entrance is underground, and that's where our egress point is."

"Timings check, please." I synched the clocks on our comps. "Deal is fifteen minutes. That's it. If we there longer, I'm pulling us out. Got it?"

Lali nodded.

I hawked up and spat a goober.

"Today is a good day to die!" Lali laughed. "Hey,"--she walked to me, stood on tippy-toe, and smooched my tusk--"be careful." Then she jumped on her hover-board and headed to the Gene-Vault.

"You coming?" she says.

My three thumbs traced the spot she kissed. I cursed and shot after her.

When we reached the entrance, them rhinos opened fire.

I slammed my board against a bunch of rocks and ducked the lase-fire. I didn't even get a chance to peek over. I blind-threw all six grenades, and they whistled through the air, zeroed in on their targets. There was a "clunk" as they stickered themselves to the bins.

"Get down!" I shouted

The grenades exploded. Black smoke poofed in the air, and I saw them turrets come alive. Necks whizzed like they was infected with viralware. The cams couldn't spot us cause we was still ducked under. But soon as we stepped out, they would.

Lali took out something like a briefcase.

"What you doin'?" I said.

She said, "Distracting those turrets." She popped her case open, and n-moths fluttered up, millions of them. They clouded them turrets in blue wings.

"Now!" I shouted. I jammed on my oxyfilter and sprinted to the entrance. My hooves crunched on the debris. Turret fire thundered in my ears. Lali had gone in already. The girl was fast. She had this strange move: she'd run two large steps, do a small step, then take another two large.

Inside, it was dark and wet. The sprinklers spat water. I slipped a few times and then smashed the crap out of 'em. The red emergency lights were low, but finally I found the passageway.

Damn. Twin clanium doors barred our way.

I retreated, then charged head first. I slammed the doors. They shuddered. I had to do it two more times before them doors gave in. Then I crashed through.

It took me a second to realize I was on stairs, and they was vibrating. Lali passed by in a blur. Then them stairs collapsed. Lali had detonated our set-bombs. I was thrown, hit a steelcrete pole and rolled to a stop. Everything was dusty. My left ankle took a bad twist. It sent sharp bites into my feet, all the way up my calves.

"Lali?"

Gunshots came from the corridor. I ran and found Lali laying behind a pillar.

"Shit," I said. Lali's frame was shot. Purple liquid oozed out her artificial legs. "That okay?"

"I feel great. You want to help kill those?" Lali nodded in front of her. She ducked shrapnel as another salvo of lase-beams blasted.

"Okay." I rolled next to her, unclipped my gauss-cannon, and fired. The grenade blasted out, detonated at the far end of the corridor. The backdraft singed my skin. I knelt and covered Lali. Her silver-pink hair smelled of circuit-boards and mech-lube.

"I'm alright, Mr. Muscles." She fit so nice in the crook of my arms, but she slipped out of them, pointed behind me. "The vault is right here."

Lali knelt before the vault. The doors had two yellow bars across 'em. Thousands of network ports was embedded on the door. Just looking at it confused the crap out of me. Lali took out a data cable from her navel-receptacle and jerked on it. When it had enough slack, she jacked into a port. The display on her forearm blinked with scrolling code.

"Quickly, three seconds left!" I said. I covered her and aimed down the hall. I heard footsteps.

Damn, but those was the tensest two minutes of the entire mission. The Klaxons stopped blaring, and the lights flickered off. I switched on the four LEDs on me shoulders. The yellow beams narrowed my vision, so I had to keep turning to catch everything.

"Found it. There." Slowly, Lali pumped code down the wire. She thumbs-upped me. "Double done."

The vault door swung open, and there it was. Rows and rows of gene-ampoules hovered along them walls. Lali's fingers brushed each one, searching for her yoctobot-synthetics. I had never seen so many gene-ampoules in my life.

"Can't believe I'm inside one of these," I said.

"Where is it?" Lali said.

She ducked under a steelcrete shelf. Then she hissed in delight. She pushed against a blank space in the floor and found a hidey hole. Four pyramids was in there. They glowed purple, orange, black, and milk-white.

"Yes!" She scooped 'em up, then hugged me.

"'Kay, let's get out of here," I said.

My UI was blinking red: sixteen minutes. One minute over. In my worry, I forgot to get in front of Lali. She was heading for the doors. My first mistake that night, and by Grey Tusk did I pay for it.

"Hold it!" Rhinos busted in and opened fire.

I ducked. Red lasers exploded into Lali. Hurled her backwards. She crashed into the wall.

Her little exoskeleton was completely crumpled. A green smear ran from her cheeks to her stomach. The metal on her stomach had ripped apart, showing pale brown skin hadn't never seen sun. Her hands opened, and them four pyramids fell out.

The world turned red. I stood and charged. Them rhinos sidestepped, but I flicked gel-grenades on 'em. Rhinos have a tough skin. We don't notice so much when small things touch it. They reached out to get my neck, but I slipped their grip.

They exploded in red mist.

I picked Lali up. Shoved the yoctobots into one of her Velcroed pockets. Her exoskeleton was one cheap knock-off job. She seemed to wince when I did it. I figured any sign from her was a good thing.

#

Drizzle coated everything outside. A shadow moved, and I raised the gauss-cannon. I aimed and almost pressed the trigger. But it wasn't nothing. I told myself to calm the fuck down.

Lali mumbled. I took her down and cradled her. Underneath a slit in her chassis was a little screen, displayed her heart rate. It said 25 beats per minute. If I didn't get help, she would flatline.

I lifted her up and ran to the pier. I ripped off the camo-tarp, jumped into our boat. I got out my knife. Was about to slice the rope when I heard a noise. I strained my ears. Then I thought, *Amalric, stop kidding yourself.* I went to slice the rope--

"Crack!"

I staggered, crunched to my knees, and stared at the three holes through my chest. They looked like glowy ends of cigars.

"What's a brickface like you runnin' and gunnin' with a human?" A rhino stood on the pier. The triple-muzzle of his bolt-rifle glowed. Rhino killers, that's what we call a triple-muzzle bolt-rifle. You can hit both them hearts in one shot.

I couldn't speak shit. My mouth tasted of iron. The world was goin' dark.

"Rhinos ain't no never run with humans. Especially one like that. She a biocrack whore?" The rhino neared the boat. I couldn't see him, but I heard his footsteps closer.

All I seen was the synth-wood planks that formed the hull. The red gushing onto the planks was my blood. There was a lot of it.

"Quickly!" Lali's voice hissed behind me. She sounded far away. Something prodded me in the back--the barrel of my gauss-cannon.

A massive boom and the boat rocked. The rhino was right in front of me.

"Gosh, you a tough one to kill, looks like I need to shoot yer again. You won't survive this one, brickface," he said.

The air moved.

I was quicker. My shot scored right above the knee, slicing him at the quads. He screamed. I got up and pushed--weakest push I ever done--but he went overboard. Somehow, I managed to slam the throttle to full.

The boat sped into the night.

It was so damn dark. Couldn't see shit. It was a miracle I found the cove we marked. Lali and me both needed serious doses of medibots.

"Lali?" I tapped her cheek. She stopped breathing and dizzied out. Her life force was on a sure fade.

I searched for the medipack. Things was starting to get weird. I saw two boats and two Lalis, and then two of everything. I grabbed the medipack and sucked in gushes of air. The pack had been shot to shit, and there was only two slim-packs left. That wasn't enough medibots for both of us.

"Shit, fuck, fuck!"

My body screamed for medibots. Now I knew how a biocrack whore felt.

I brought the medipack to the socket on my thigh, almost about to lock the pack in and save myself. I'd killed for medipacks before. No way I could give them up now.

My eyes shifted to Lali. She looked like one squished aluminum doll.

My medibot-starved brain worked clear just a few ticks. I thought of the first night I met Lali, how she looked at me so kind when I said I had no purpose. And I thought, *I've lived so far, and them war's gone. Maybe Lali's my new purpose.* She was like me in a ways, and that was why we got along so fine. There was no guarantees in life. Rhinos knew it best. You had to give things a go.

Gakit! I reached for her.

Her chest was cut and bleeding. She looked dead. I injected the medibots into her stomach. Her eyes rolled back, and all I seen was whites.

I'd only used one slim-pack when she made this "huuuh" sound, like her lungs got shot, then said, "The yoc…" and dizzied out again.

The world was dipped in biochems. Everything blurry and slow. I looked at the big empty bag I never got a chance to fill with our haul, then to Lali's pockets.

The yoctobots! I understood what she was trying to say. Them yoctos could heal as well. I undid the Velcro straps around Lali's thigh. The yoctobot-synthetics came tumbling out: purple, orange, black, and milk-white. All glittering.

I put one on her abdomen, removed the medipack's needle injector, connected it to the little pyramid, and pressed the needle in. The purple pyramid lost its color as the fluid went inside Lali. I done the same for the other three.

My body convulsed. Threw me back. I shoved the last slim-pack to my thigh socket, but it clattered against the armor. I tried again, but my hoofhand wasn't working right. For a sec I thought I'd die. But on the third try, there was a click, and them medibots surged in my veins like ice. I shuddered. Ecstasy. There wasn't much left, but the stack was enough to restore my left heart.

When I opened my eyes, Lali was glowing. Her body flickered purple, orange, black, and white. Damn yeah, the yoctos was working! Where her exo had been--the arms and legs was gone. Heat radiated from Lali like she was a piece of graphene being cooked in a superfab. I shaded my eyes and only looked when her body cooled down.

My Lali was brand new, from the crinkles on her knees to the fine hairs on her forearms. Her limbs was dotted with sweat. Her skin was soft, smooth, and very, very warm. Her nipples reacted to the cold. She curled up and shivered. I laid the camo-tarp over her. Then I got down next to her, put an arm across that tarp, and rested my snout on her head.

∞∞∞∞∞∞∞∞∞∞∞∞
∞∞∞∞∞∞∞∞∞∞∞∞

This anthology collection is ©Short-Story.Me! Genre Fiction.

All stories are ©Copyright their individual Authors.

Be sure to read the first Anthology:

Short-Story.Me - Best Genre Short Stories #1

Edited by Larry Crain & Dixon Palmer

www.Short-Story.Me

Made in the USA
Lexington, KY
24 November 2010